THE LOST SCOUT

❖

Also by John R. Riggs

Snow on the Roses

Killing Frost

Cold Hearts and Gentle People

Dead Letter

A Dragon Lives Forever

The Glory Hound

Haunt of the Nightingale

He Who Waits

The Last Laugh

Let Sleeping Dogs Lie

One Man's Poison

Wolf in Sheep's Clothing

THE LOST SCOUT

John R. Riggs

A GARTH RYLAND MYSTERY

BARRICADE BOOKS, INC.

NEW YORK

Published by Barricade Books, Inc.
150 Fifth Avenue
New York, NY 10011

Printed in the United States of America.

Book design and page layout by CompuDesign

Library of Congress Cataloging-in-Publication Data

Riggs, John R., 1945– .
    The lost scout / John R. Riggs.
        p.   cm. — (A Garth Ryland mystery)
    ISBN 1-56980-121-5
    I. Title. II. Series: Riggs, John R., 1945–   . Garth Ryland
    mystery.
    PS3568.I372L6   1998
    813'.54—dc21   97-32233
                                                                  CIP

First Printing

For Aunt Helen and Uncle Ray
and always to Carole

Special thanks to Kenny Barger, Mike's Guns,
Robert Woods, James (Cy) Young,
and Brian Zimmerman for your expert advice.

**The past is never dead.
It is not even past.**

William Faulkner

The Lost 1600 was not my favorite place to be at night. But there I was—and against Ruth's best advice.

Once described by my predecessor as "woods with a savage heart, where the sun never shines and the owls hunt at noon," the Lost 1600 lies about five miles southeast of Oakalla (my home) and is the largest roadless area in Adams County, Wisconsin. Also named Camp Collier for the Army training camp that was there in the 1940s and the Boy Scout camp that was there in the 1950s and 1960s, it had been without tenants for the past twenty-five years. Some still hunted it for coon, coyote, and deer. A few, like me, still fished it for brook trout and smallmouth bass. But most of the people in Adams County just left it alone.

I am Garth Ryland, owner and editor of the *Oakalla Reporter*, a small weekly newspaper in south-central Wisconsin, and the author of a syndicated column that has grown in circulation over the years throughout Wisconsin and spread into its neighboring states. A town of about 2,500, Oakalla is self-contained and self-satisfied as are most small towns in Wisconsin. It has a Jackson Street, a Corner Bar and Grill, Oakalla Community School, and an annual Homecoming parade. It also has a hardware store, a cheese plant, a five-and-dime with a soft broad-plank pine floor and black ceiling fans that turn lazily all summer long, and a reputation for being closed-ranked and close-mouthed.

My predecessor, then the editor of *Freedom's Voice*, which was the forerunner of the *Oakalla Reporter*, in describing the Lost 1600 as "woods with a savage heart" was lamenting the death of his nephew, a boy scout, who had fallen and broken his neck while climbing on one of its bluffs. That was twenty-eight years ago, and he was the last to die there.

But he wasn't the first. By my count there had been seven or eight who had died there in my lifetime. Eight, if you believed the Legend of the Lost Scout. Seven, if you did not.

And while you might question whether these woods, or any woods for that matter, could have a "savage heart," you couldn't deny the fact that the Lost 1600 did have canyons so sheer and deep that the sun rarely reached their bottoms, or that on more than one occasion I had seen and heard great horned owls hunting by day there, or that once the sun set and night came on you began to feel a little tug of doubt about being there, as if its true colors were about to show.

Squatted beside the coals of my campfire, I glanced up at the darkening sky to make sure that those few ragtag clouds in the west hadn't gathered on me. It was a typically cool mid-May evening and I was camped on a narrow ledge along the south bank of Owl Creek, which bisected the Lost 1600 on a northeast to southwest axis on its way to the Wisconsin River. Normally it's a quiet, if sullen stream with narrow big-rock riffles and deep blackwater pools. Owl Creek could turn into a terror following a cloud burst, as all the canyon creeks dumped into it, seemingly all at once. But though the forecast called for rain by morning, I saw nothing in the western sky that made me want to move my camp to higher ground. Besides, I had a belly full of bass and fried potatoes and no great inclination to do much of anything. What I really didn't want to do was think.

"Where did you say you were going again?" Ruth said that morning at breakfast.

Ruth is Ruth Krammes, my housekeeper, a tall, big-boned, no nonsense Swede, who in her prime, according to her, could turn a man's head or throw a hundred pound sack of feed over her shoulder with equal ease. I believe the part about turning a man's head, for though she is now in her seventies, she is still a handsome woman, with only a petal or three missing from the full flowered beauty that she once was. And while maybe she has lost a half step over the years, and that hundred pound sack of feed is now only a fifty, she is still a force to be reckoned with. Particularly when she thinks she's right, which is 100 percent of the time.

"The Lost 1600. Why? What's wrong with that?"

"Nothing, I guess."

We were on our third cup of coffee, following a leisurely breakfast of orange juice, eggs, sausage, and hashbrowns.

Ruth and I were usually never in too much of a hurry on Saturday mornings. It was our one morning of the

week to catch each other up on all the days that had gone
before.

"Come on, Ruth. Give."

Ruth was sometimes psychic—uncannily so. If I was
headed for trouble, which her somber voice and demeanor
seemed to indicate, I wanted to know about it.

"You'll go ahead and do what you want, so why
bother?" she said.

"True, but at least I'll be forewarned. And to be forewarned is to be forearmed."

"Not where you're concerned." She rose to clear
the table. "You're the fool that rushes in where angels
won't go."

"Don't I usually have a good reason?"

She ignored me, as she set our dirty dishes on the
counter and sat down across from me again. "So what's
your reason for going to the Lost 1600?"

"To catch some smallmouth bass."

"Besides that?"

Ruth was like a dog with a bone. She'd keep gnawing
away until she got to the marrow of things. So to save us
both time, I told her the truth.

"I need time not to think."

"About what?"

"You know what."

"Abby?"

"Yes."

"What's not to think about? I thought you two were
getting along."

"We are, and we aren't."

"You care to explain that?"

"If I could." I rose from the table and picked up my
tackle box and my rod-and-reel. My Duluth pack, along
with the utensils and supplies I'd need, was already sitting
on Jessie's back seat. "You sure you won't tell me what's

bothering you about the Lost 1600?" I said.

Whatever it was, it wasn't a sudden thing. She hadn't been quite herself for several weeks now, though there could be another explanation for that—something that involved us both and put us on opposite sides of the fence.

Ruth's look was evasive, which wasn't like her, since she usually met everything head on. "Just be careful, that's all."

"Aren't I always?"

She went on drinking her coffee, pretending she hadn't heard.

That was this morning at breakfast. Now, as night closed in, and the coals of my fire began to whiten, then crumble to ashes, I wished that I had pressed Ruth harder on the subject. From my arrival at Camp Collier, from the moment that I had parked Jessie in the shadow of the old mess hall and started down the long steep hill toward Owl Creek, I had felt uneasy. It was a general unease, nothing that I could put my finger on—unlike the tingle on my nape that told me without fail when someone unseen was watching me. It was almost like the unease that I'd felt in Vietnam during my brief stay as a student correspondent there—long before the Tet offensive came to TV, and all the body bags started arriving at our front doors.

You knew that trouble was about. You couldn't see, smell, hear, or taste it, but you and the grunts knew that it was about, despite all the assurances, all the official bright-eyed smiles to the contrary. Had I been a better journalist, I would have sniffed the trouble out and written the story of my life, though no one would have believed it at the time. Had I been a better man, I would have stayed and fought with those who later bled and died there. As it was, I went home, kept my student deferment,

and told my nose for trouble that surely it had been wrong
—or else, someone would have told me otherwise.

Night was upon me. I had retreated to the notch in
the canyon wall where my sleeping bag lay on a bed of
sandstone. What wind there was, was from the east. The
sprinkle of clouds in the west, now overhead, had a hollow, skeletal look to them, and a few early stars were fading in and out, like the first fireflies of June.

There was no moon. It had gone down shortly after
the sun had set behind the canyon wall. Strange to see it
there in the west, ablaze with the light of the absent sun,
then to see it darken from orange to red to purple to
black, then to see it no more. Wasn't the moon supposed
to hide by day, then come out at night. If for no other reason than to keep me company.

Abby, where are you now? I lay there half in and half
out of my sleeping bag, watching the stars now that the
clouds had moved on, trying not to think about her. I was
wishing that she was here with me, or that I was there in
Detroit with her. Anywhere together would be fine—from
now until doomsday.

Which, of course, was a lie, one of those that we allow
ourselves to keep our sanity. I could no more live in
Detroit than she could return to Oakalla now that she had
set her sights on a residency in pathology at Henry Ford
Hospital. Even if she had wanted to return to Oakalla, she
would have no place to live, since, with Ruth's help, she
was in the process of converting her house (Dr. William T.
Airhart's old house) into a shelter for abused women.
Unless she lived with me, which was about as likely to
happen as Ruth taking up knitting in her old age.

Two weeks before I had flown to Detroit and Abby
and I had spent most of that cold rainy weekend inside
her ninth floor apartment, not worrying a whole lot about
the weather, or the fact that we didn't get to do all the

things we'd planned. The few times that I did look out, through the rain and across the roof tops into the nearby projects, I felt at peace. This was her world, after all, not mine. I was merely passing through.

"What do you see out there?" she asked after one particularly long stint at the window. She was wearing an extra-large University of Michigan sweatshirt, and nothing else. The maize-and-blue sweatshirt went well with her periwinkle eyes and yellow hair.

"Nothing much," I said in answer to her question.

"I thought maybe you were missing Oakalla."

"Not when I'm with you."

I left the window to sit beside her on the bed, which, when folded, doubled as her couch. As I sat there in my boxer shorts, legs straight out in front of me, I noticed how white I had become over the winter. Over the years, really. But living in Wisconsin can do that to you.

"If only that were true," she said.

"It is true. I feel at home wherever you are."

"But for how long?"

"Long enough not to worry about it today."

She rested her head on my shoulder. I gently untangled her hair, which had become tousled in the course of our lovemaking. Around her, I never felt nearly as old as I sometimes did alone.

"You know what I mean," she said. "Could you be happy living here in Detroit?"

"I'm not sure how happy I am living in Oakalla."

"Fulfilled then?"

"That's a very large word. Let's just say that what I do best, I do in Oakalla. I can't imagine doing it anywhere else."

"What about Diana?" She pulled away to look at me.

"What about her?"

"Weren't you once in love with her?"

"Very much so."

"What if she came back to Oakalla to live? Would you be happy then?"

"No. Because she's not you."

"I see."

I thought my answer would please her because it was the truth. But for some reason, it didn't.

"What did I say wrong?" I said.

"Nothing. It's just hard, that's all, with me here and you there."

"Nobody said it wouldn't be." Then I started reading between the lines. "Are you having second thoughts about us?"

Her eyes—for her, who rarely let life get her down—seemed unusually sad, and her 500-watt smile, which would make even Scrooge jump up and click his heels, seemed buried under a bushel of woe.

"Not about us. Never about us," she said. "Just about me."

"I know the feeling."

She rested her head on my shoulder again. "So what are we going to do?"

"Keep on keeping on."

"You don't worry about cracking?"

"Every day. But somehow it doesn't do me any good. Particularly not when Ruth trudges off to work at your shelter. She's not great company, but she'll do in a pinch."

She punched me gently in the ribs. "Wait until I tell her you said that."

"Why did you do it?"

"What? Turn Doc's house into a shelter? I wasn't using it. I figured someone should. And despite a few grumbles, I'm sure Doc would approve. If not, I'm equally sure that he'll somehow find a way to let me know."

"Haunt you, you mean."

"What else."

I had to smile. l was sure he would too, if it was in his power. How I missed him, and that one bright fading speck of time, when he, Abby, and I rode life's carousel together.

"So that means you're not ever coming back to Oakalla?" It was one of those heart-in-the-mouth questions that you have to ask despite yourself.

"Not and live there in Doc's old house."

"Where would you live?"

Her hand was flat against my stomach, working its way down. "That remains to be seen."

The next weekend, which was last weekend, I spent missing her, wanting to fly back to Detroit, knowing that she was on duty and would be unable to spend any time with me. Whether she came to Oakalla or I went to Detroit, it was always hell for me our next weekend apart—until I got busy with other things and the sharp pang became a dull ache that didn't get worse as long as I didn't think about it. That was why I was there in the Lost 1600 on a moonless night in May—so I wouldn't think about it. Which only goes to show the lengths that we will go to fool ourselves.

CHAPTER

A shout in the night awakened me. An answering shout made me sit up in my sleeping bag. Whoever they were, they weren't far away and were making their way west to east along Owl Creek toward me.

"Outrigger one?" someone said.

"Here."

"Outrigger two?"

"Here."

"Point?"

No answer.

"Point?" Louder this time, with concern.

Still no answer. Point appeared to be out of hearing.

From their last exchange I determined that they were on the opposite bank of Owl Creek and not likely to cross over to my side. The water was deep, the current swift there along the canyon wall, and all there was behind me were canyons and more canyons, until you finally came to the old growth forest beyond. No one in his right mind went into those canyons at night. Not since the Lost Scout disappeared in there.

Minutes passed. It could have been five, as many as ten. I wasn't counting. The squad of men (which was what they sounded like—a military squad on maneuvers) had gone by when I heard the scream. It raised every hair on my head. It was followed by several more screams in succession. Screams of pain, they sounded like. Death screams, as things turned out.

They were coming from the woods somewhere to the northeast, so I grabbed my shoes and socks and jumped into Owl Creek, hoping that I didn't hit a boulder on my way down. The water, colder and swifter than I ever imagined, wrapped itself around my chest and squeezed my breath away. I didn't try to fight it, but let it wash me downstream toward the nearest riffle and the sandy beach that I knew was on the opposite shore. It was where I had crossed Owl Creek to get to my camp site. But with the sun out and the water only thigh deep, it hadn't felt nearly as cold that afternoon as it did now.

After catching hold of a boulder on my way through the riffle, I went ashore, stopping only long enough to put on white cotton crew socks and blue Adidas tennis shoes. Not my best pair, however. Those I saved for weddings and funerals.

I'd left my jeans and flannel shirt beside my sleeping bag in the sandstone hollow. I didn't miss them while in Owl Creek, or during those first few numb seconds after I climbed out. But when I stood and faced the cold east wind now whistling down the canyon, I surely did.

Silence. The man had stopped screaming. So either

help had arrived or . . . The feeling in my gut said that he was probably already beyond help.

My progress was slow up Owl Creek Canyon. Along the sand beach I could see well enough to make my way, but once I reached the high bank and had to go into the woods, I had to feel my way from tree to tree. At least it was warmer there in the woods away from the wind. It made the forest seem friendlier than I knew it to be.

I heard voices again. They seemed panicked and confused, with no one stepping forward to take charge. *Where was their squad leader*, I wondered, *while all this was going on?*

"Jesus Christ!" someone said. "I've never seen anything like that before."

"Shut up and give me a hand here, will you."

"Do you think we should move him?"

"We don't have a choice."

I saw the flicker of a flashlight. A small thin light, it sliced up the dark like a surgeon's knife, but did nothing to help me see what was going on.

That was the last thing that I remembered. I took one more step and the lights went out.

I was cold—as cold as I had ever been in my life. I lay on the sand beach at the edge of Owl Creek, shivering so hard that my teeth sounded like castanets. I had to move, find warmth somewhere. Either that or lie there and shake myself to pieces.

The problem was that the nearest hope of warmth lay across Owl Creek in the form of my sleeping bag. I hated the thought of going into the water again. It almost seemed better to make my way the half mile up the hill to Jessie. Almost. But without my keys I couldn't start her, or get to the Army blanket that I always kept in her trunk. Even with my keys, I sometimes couldn't start her. And

knowing her cold, cold heart, she'd never start for me
now.

I took a deep breath and waded into the water, shiv-
ers and all. When I reached the other side of the riffle and
crawled up onto the sandstone ledge that ran along the
base of the bluff, my hands, feet, arms, and legs had gone
numb. And my mind seemed to belong to someone else,
some impersonal being standing just outside of me who
really didn't give a rat's ass what my condition was.

"Run!" he seemed to throw down the gauntlet. "If
you can."

Run, I did. On legs of matchsticks and feet of straw.
It was a slippery perilous run right along the edge of the
creek that normally I would not have attempted in full
daylight under the best of circumstances. So I shouldn't
have been surprised when I fell and went down hard,
slamming into the wall of the bluff rather than risk falling
into the creek.

As I lay there dazed and trembling, blood running
down my nose from the cut above my right eye, I could
see that same being standing over me, shaking his head in
disgust, as if to say, "What's the use?"

Rising to my knees, I held my middle finger up high
where he would be sure to see it, then got up and ran on.

The way I was shaking, I knew I could never pull on
my jeans over my wet legs, but I hoped at least to slip on
my flannel shirt before I dove into my sleeping bag. While
I fumbled with it, losing the battle, I smelled smoke coming from upstream. The fire itself, partially hidden by the
woods, was little more than a red glow in the night, as distant and cold as a taillight, dimming even as I watched.

I gave up on the shirt and burrowed all the way into
the sleeping bag until even my head was covered. The
shakes continued to rack me. I went into a violent seizure
every time I moved the least little bit. When the convul-

sive shivering finally slowed, when I could at least uncurl my legs and my breaths were no longer gasps, I began to sweat.

The air had a damp dour feel to it, and the morning sky had the low grey look of rain. I had awakened a few minutes before and eased my head out of the sleeping bag to see if I could without setting off the shakes again. Afraid to expose any more of myself, I lay there stiff and unmoving, wondering how I could get into my clothes without getting out of my sleeping bag. Even the thought of reaching my hand out for them chilled me. But the thought of staying there in a soaking rain chilled me even more.

Once out of the sleeping bag, I set a personal record for getting my shirt, then my jeans on. I dug into my Duluth pack for my hooded sweatshirt and after putting it on and the hood up, fished my shoes out of the bottom of the sleeping bag and put them on. I wasn't toasty, but neither was I cold.

Breaking camp was no problem. My fire was out, my dishes and cast iron skillet washed and put away in the Duluth pack. Since I didn't have a tent to take down, all that remained was to stuff my sleeping bag into my pack, grab my rod-and-reel and tackle box, and take off. Then it hit me. To get home, I'd have to cross Owl Creek.

"Shit," I said, for all the world to hear.

"What was that?"

I looked up to see a man in waders standing across the creek from me. He appeared to be carrying a fly rod. He also wore a tie, a long-sleeve khaki shirt that the DNR (Department of Natural Resources) types are so fond of, and a handgun and holster. He was about five-ten, a couple inches shorter than I am.

"Who the hell are you?" I yelled.

But he shook his head, as if he couldn't hear over the east wind still whistling through the canyon.

I started walking toward the downstream riffle where the sand beach was and where Owl Creek narrowed to a couple dozen yards. Keeping pace, the man across the creek followed me downstream.

"You need a ride?" he yelled, as I stood there eyeing the cold black water.

"If you don't mind."

He set his fly pole and wicker creel down, unstrapped his gun and holster and laid them down, then waded across Owl Creek toward me. I noticed that his forest green floppy hat on which he'd hung his flies matched his forest green tie and even at that early hour, he appeared to be well scrubbed and clean shaven. His hair, what I could see of it, was short, brown, and greying at the temples—as was mine, though I guessed him to be a few years older than I. He had a slight build, wiry yet strong. He carried me piggyback across Owl Creek without missing a step.

"You DNR?" I said when safe and dry on the other side.

"Why do you ask?"

"Your tie for one thing." His handgun for another, though it didn't look like standard police issue. Up close, it looked more like a howitzer.

"I always wear a tie," he said with an automatic smile without answering my question. "Habit, I guess."

His eyes were a flinty blue, and his face and hands had the rough brown look of someone who had spent a lot of his time outdoors. He picked up his gun and holster and put it back on. The gun had ivory grips, and its muzzle reached halfway to his knees.

"I'm Garth Ryland," I said, offering my hand. "I own and edit the *Oakalla Reporter*. Which, if you've never heard of it, is a small weekly newspaper here in Wisconsin."

His grip was lean and hard like the rest of him. "Preston Kurtz," I thought he said. "Up until yesterday, I taught political science at the University of Wisconsin–Whitewater."

"You decide to quit?"

"Retire. To follow my passion. Which is what we're supposed to do, isn't it, once we get to be my age."

"I wouldn't know. I've been following passion all along." Though lately, the *Oakalla Reporter* and I had felt more like an old married couple. No surprises, but no big disappointments either.

"Then you're one of the lucky ones," he said.

We were walking back upstream to where we'd first met, where the trail led up the hill to Jessie. With any luck, I'd not only beat the rain,but get home in time for breakfast.

"What is your passion?" I asked when we stopped again.

"This," he said, showing me his fly rod, which was a well-made split bamboo pole that likely cost more than my last mortgage payment.

"I've never had the patience," I said, "to learn to be any good at it."

The same of which could be said for riding a bicycle with no hands, dribbling a basketball behind my back, or playing jacks, marbles, or checkers. Or a lot of other things for which I had neither aptitude nor passion. But I noted with pride that I could still field a baseball or play a mean game of euchre if the situation demanded it.

"It requires more than patience," he said with another automatic smile that, had I known him better, would have seemed condescending. "It requires love."

Hard to argue with that, so I didn't.

"You plan to be here awhile?" I said.

"What do you mean by *here*, and what do you mean by a *while?*"

He had removed a mayfly from his hat and was tying it on his line. Though his tone was still cordial, his flinty blue eyes said that I was about to wear out my welcome.

"Here meaning the Lost 1600. A while meaning hours, days, weeks?"

"So that's what they call it now, the Lost 1600. In my day it was Camp Collier."

"You were a boy scout?"

His smile had a bitter edge to it that made me wonder about his past. "About a hundred years ago. In the age of innocence."

"So that explains how you know about Owl Creek," I said.

"That and the fact that I've been coming here off and on for the last forty years. As for how long I'll be here . . ." He began to feed out his line, gracefully lengthening his cast a little farther each time without ever hitting the water. "That depends on how good the fishing is."

I was amazed at his skill, his feather-light touch on the fly rod, as the mayfly landed exactly where he wanted it without even rippling the water. Whenever I had tried to fly fish, I felt like Lash Larue.

"You only arrived here this morning, right?" I said.

"Not over an hour ago. Why?" Absorbed in his fishing, he was slowly tuning me out.

"Just keep your eyes open, that's all. This place is not quite what it appears to be."

"Was it ever?"

"You know its history then?"

He gave his fly rod a twitch, sending the mayfly skipping across the surface in a lifelike imitation of a bug in water, then he reached down and patted his handgun. "Why do you think I'm packing this?"

"I wasn't aware that anyone had ever been assaulted here," I said. Besides me, I could have said, but I didn't want to give anything away.

He gave the fly rod another twitch, then set the hook as a brookie rose to the bait. "That shows you what you know."

CHAPTER 3

"Y ou about done in there?" Ruth yelled from outside the bathroom door. "I might need some hot water for the dishes."

"Done," I said, reluctantly turning off the shower. "How soon till breakfast?"

"It'll be ready when you are."

Ruth went back downstairs. I dried myself off, then waved a path through the steam to the mirror, where I began to shave. Normally I shaved before I took my shower because I hated to wash a hairy face, but that morning, once I finally arrived home, cold, wet, and starting to chill again, all I could think of was getting warm.

After I had left Preston Kurtz contentedly reeling in his brook trout, I had climbed the half-mile hill to find a shiny new black GMC pickup with a fat marshmallow-like camper shell on the back of it parked beside Jessie. Normally I would have tried to look inside the camper to see what I could see, but already it had started to spit rain and my skin felt more clammy than sweaty after my trek up the hill.

Then there was Jessie to consider. Jessie, Grandmother Ryland's ancient brown Chevy sedan, and the bane of my existence. Jessie, who had survived all of my attempts to kill her, as I had survived all of her attempts to return the favor. Grandmother had loved me enough to will me her small farm and the money to buy the *Oakalla Reporter*. She hadn't loved me enough to give Jezebel, as Grandmother called her, to somebody else.

True to form, Jessie balked at starting until I put her accelerator to the floorboard and held it there until she fired; then she refused to send me any heat the entire way home. Already out of sorts from the previous night, I arrived at the back door ready to do battle with Ruth in case she was of that frame of mind. Instead, she had hardly seemed to notice me as I passed through the kitchen on my way upstairs. Now I went downstairs, wearing jeans, red plaid wool shirt, wool socks, and deer-hide moccasins, and the grey hooded sweatshirt that I had worn into the house.

Ruth took one look at me and said, "You looked at the calendar lately?"

I smiled to myself. Same old Ruth. Whatever was bothering her had apparently passed for the moment.

"If you'd been as cold as I was last night, you'd be dressed like this, too," I said.

"And who's to say I wasn't?" She poured us each a cup of coffee.

I reached for the carton of half-and-half. She handed me the sugar bowl. "Come again?" I said.

She had a platter of bacon and scrambled eggs warm-

ing in the oven. She set it on the table in front of me.
"Eat. Before it gets cold."

"You want to pray first?"

"Why bother starting now?"

"We've prayed before."

"Not since the last election." She watched with disgust as I put catsup on top of my scrambled eggs. "Where
did that prayer business come from anyway? You think
you're in need of one?"

I shrugged, watching the rain through the kitchen
window. It fell nearly straight down and seemed to be setting in for the day. A bread-baking day was what Grandmother Ryland would have called it. The kind of day
when you hunkered in with a good book, or went up to
your attic in search of lost treasures.

"Where's Daisy?" I said, ignoring Ruth's question.

The truth was that I did feel vulnerable, and had ever
since I arrived home, though I didn't know why. Prayer
might not help the situation, but then it might not hurt it
either. When in doubt, use all your options.

"She's in heat," Ruth said in answer to my question.
"I'm afraid to let her out of the basement for fear she'll
sneak outside."

Daisy was Doc Airhart's, now Abby Airhart's English
setter, who was usually underfoot from the moment I
stepped in the door, now that Ruth let her spend most of
her time upstairs.

"Where can she go?" I said, since our back yard was
fenced in.

"It's not her I'm worried about. It's that miserable
excuse for a dog next door that I caught trying to tunnel
under the fence yesterday."

The miserable excuse for a dog next door was a low-
slung basset named Fred that Ruth had tried for years to
kill with a high cholesterol diet of our table scraps. "You

can't blame him for trying," I said.

"Maybe you can't." She helped herself to the rest of the scrambled eggs.

"Why don't we just get her fixed?"

"She's not our dog, remember?"

Good point. Especially with Abby's own biological clock ticking down. Though we hadn't spent a lot of time on the subject, I knew that one day Abby would want a child of her own. Our child, as a matter of fact.

"Does Abby know that you can't father children?" Ruth, who was good at reading my mind, said.

"Yes. She knows."

When I had gotten my vasectomy a few years ago, I had thought that I was past the age of wanting to have any more children. That was before Abby Airhart came into my life. Now, I didn't know. Abby alone was more than enough for me, but a child of our own . . . Well, that might be pretty special.

"It's good she knows," Ruth said.

I nodded, though I wasn't so sure. "She'd make a great mother," I said.

"As you'd make a great father. What's your point?"

I sighed, finding comfort in the rain, which seemed to reduce everything outside to the here and now, leaving no horizons to worry about. "My point is, why couldn't I have met her ten years ago?"

"Because you didn't. If you're going to start down that road, you might as well try to rewrite the whole script because that's where you're headed anyway." She picked up a piece of bacon and chomped it down like a stalk of celery.

"You have no regrets, Ruth?"

"Garth, I've lost my husband and both of my children. What do you think?"

"I vowed to live my life with no regrets."

"And how many years ago was that? That's a young man's dream, Garth. Something to get you started, but not something you can ever hold yourself to."

She was right, of course. Even old Blue Eyes himself admitted to a few regrets. And Frost's sighs were reserved not for the road less travelled, but the road not taken.

"So what's the answer, then?" I said.

She eyed the last piece of bacon on the platter hungrily, then ate that one, too. "To be honest, Garth, I'm not sure there is one."

"Hemingway would say it's a heroic, though predestined to be futile, struggle."

"Hemingway also blew his brains out."

A half hour later we still sat at the breakfast table, our dirty plates and silverware stacked at the end of the table nearest the sink. I was on my third cup of coffee. Ruth was still on her second. Each of us had questions that we wanted to ask the other, but neither wanted to be the first to start.

"Tell me what's been bothering you," I finally said to break the silence.

"After you tell me about last night."

"Just your typical night in the Lost 1600. I'm awakened by men shouting and what sounds like a military squad passing through the woods north of Owl Creek. A short while later I hear a man start to scream, for his life it seems, and when I go to investigate, I see a light and hear voices, none of which I recognize. Then someone cold-cocks me and carries me back to the sand beach, where I awaken cold as death and with the worst case of the shakes I've ever had. I recross Owl Creek, run the ledge there along the bluff, and reach my camp site. But while I'm there wrestling with my shirt, trying to get it on, I see a fire in the area where I had heard the man's scream come from. But I don't go to investigate because I'm too damn cold."

"Are you sure it was a fire?" Ruth said.

"I smelled smoke."

"Go on."

"I awaken this morning more than glad to be alive and break camp. But before I can cross Owl Creek, which I don't want to do because I'm afraid I'll get the shakes again, I encounter a fly fisherman named Preston Kurtz, who carries me across on his back."

"Who just happened to be there."

"That's what he said."

"And you believe him?"

"At this point I have no reason not to."

Ruth thought for a moment, then said, "Before that, what happened?"

"What do you mean?"

"Before last night, did anything out of the ordinary happen while you were in the Lost 1600?"

I heard church bells and looked above the sink at the red round clock with the yellow face. Ten-thirty A.M. Somehow I felt it should have been later.

"I wouldn't call it out of the ordinary," I said. "But I had a bad feeling about the place ever since I arrived there. Nothing specific, just an uneasiness that wouldn't go away."

Ruth only nodded and said nothing.

I continued, "What is it, by the way, Camp Collier, or the Lost 1600? What I mean is, which came first?"

"The Lost 1600. It didn't become Camp Collier until World War II, when it was a training base for the Army."

She rose, dumped her coffee in the sink, and poured herself a fresh cup. I waited until she sat back down before I said, "But there's way more than 1600 acres there. Why do they call it the Lost 1600?"

"For the men that got lost in there. Some say it was a Civil War regiment on its way South, others say it was a regiment of volunteers on their way to fight Black Hawk. Whichever it was, they wandered around in there for the better part of a week before they found their way out again. By then, the whole state was looking for them."

"Do you believe that really happened?"

"It could have happened. That's all that matters, isn't it?"

"When did people start dying there?"

"From the beginning, I suppose. But people didn't start keeping count until old Jefferson Crow put his curse on it."

"Who was Jefferson Crow?"

"A Fox Indian. A shaman, he claimed. He owned the land, or at least said he did up until the Army commandeered it for their base."

"So who were the first to die there?" I said, double-checking myself.

"A couple Army recruits. Their squad went off a cliff during night maneuvers. The others in the squad had broken bones and other injuries, but only two died."

I thought about the squad I'd heard in the night, and the subsequent screams of anguish. A ghost patrol such as those sighted in recent years at Gettysburg? Not likely. It wasn't a ghost who had put my lights out and carried me to the sand beach. Still, I shuddered despite myself.

"You having second thoughts about this?" Ruth said.

"No more than you are. Who was the next to die?"

"A couple of teenagers. 1950, I think, right before the Boy Scouts took it over. Their names were Bruce Daniels and Sharon Finley. They jumped hand in hand off the highest bluff along Owl Creek."

Which was the same bluff under which I'd slept last night. "They committed suicide, in other words," I said.

"As far as anyone knows. For a while some people around here started calling it Lovers Leap. But the name never really did catch on."

"And the fifth to die?"

"The fifth was a coon hunter, the sixth a squirrel hunter, or vice versa. Danny Hitchcock and Manfred Woodruff were their names. One in the 1950s, the other in the early 1960s. And to save you from asking, the last to die there was the boy scout in 1969."

"You missed one," I said. "What about the Lost Scout? Or don't you believe that story? . . . Ruth?" I said when she didn't answer.

"I didn't use to believe it. Now, I'm not so sure."

"What changed your mind?"

She set her coffee down and folded her arms tightly against her chest, as if she were cold. "Some dreams I've had lately."

At last, we were finally getting to it. "What kind of dreams?" I said.

"Bad dreams, the kind you would never wish upon yourself. In them I see bones and a skull, and a pair of something. Duffel bags, I think, but I'm not sure. They're in a cave and that cave is near a stream that flows through a canyon."

"That could be about anywhere, Ruth. What makes you think it's the Lost 1600?"

"Who said I do?"

"You did. Or you might as well have. You warned me about going there and then when I mentioned the Lost Scout, who, as we both know, is supposed to have disappeared there, you mentioned your dreams. Do you think it's his bones that you're seeing?"

When she didn't answer right away, I was sure I'd guessed right.

"Garth, I don't know whose bones they are. What I

do know is that I'm drawn there . . . To the Lost 1600. It's almost overpowering at times, and I feel I'll get no peace until I go there and set the record straight."

I felt goose bumps the size of marbles all up and down my arms. Hadn't Preston Kurtz hinted at something along the same line? What was going on?

"What record is there to set straight?" I said.

"I have no idea, Garth. But somewhere in the Lost 1600 is some unfinished business."

"I don't want you going there, Ruth."

"And who's to stop me?"

"Me. If it comes to that."

"You should talk."

"That's why I am."

The sky had lowered with the rain. Midmorning looked like dusk. I had expected more of an argument from Ruth, and when I didn't get one, I wasn't sure how to proceed—whether to press the issue, or just let it ride, hoping that I had made my point. Ruth wasn't afraid of me, I was sure of that, but maybe the Lost 1600 itself was enough to keep her away.

"How long ago did these dreams start?" I said.

"A few months ago."

"That long? Why didn't you say something to me about them?"

"Because I hoped they'd go away on their own."

"And obviously they haven't."

She shook her head no. "But they've gotten more frequent lately. I had another last night. About the time that you were shaking in your shoes, so was I."

"Misery loves company."

"So I've heard."

Church bells again. These for someone's eleven o'clock service. Odd, that I could love the Messenger, but not necessarily the message.

"Ruth, what do you make of what happened to me last night? Do you think it could have anything to do with those dreams that you've been having?"

"I don't see how, Garth."

"Someone got hurt badly. Maybe even died."

"So what do you plan to do about it?"

"I don't know what to do about it. If we had a sheriff, I'd turn it over to him."

Our last two sheriffs had resigned, and the one before them had committed suicide. So rather than appoint someone else to the job, which hadn't worked well in the past, the County Council was passing the buck until November's election when the people of Adams County would elect their own sheriff.

In the meantime the state police were covering the county for us, and Cecil Hardwick had been appointed town marshal by the Town Board. Cecil Hardwick was a retired dairy farmer now selling real estate on the side. His brother, Grover Hardwick, just happened to be president of the Town Board. Cecil's first cousin, Wilmer Wiemer, just happened to own Oakalla Savings and Loan and the Best Deal Real Estate Company (for whom Cecil moonlighted), and held the mortgage to Cecil's old dairy farm.

I still had my tarnished special deputy badge that Sheriff Rupert Roberts, now retired, had given me one bitter cold winter's night near the end of a fifth of Wild Turkey. But I in no way wanted to think of myself as the law in Oakalla. The law required a better representative than I had proved to be—someone like Rupert Roberts, who could go by the book and still get the job done. Someone who *was* sheriff, not in the process of trying to be.

"We have a town marshal," Ruth said.

"Whose jurisdiction stops at the city limits. Besides,

how much faith do you put in Cecil Hardwick?"

"That remains to be seen, Garth. The man did run a good dairy farm. And like Rupert, he was an MP in the service."

"You think he'll run for sheriff when the time comes?"

"I wouldn't bet against it, so I wouldn't tweak his tail if I didn't have to. You saw how far that got you last time."

A day in jail, if I remembered correctly. "I'll call him first thing in the morning," I said.

"Why not now?"

The phone rang. Since she was the closest to it, Ruth answered it. "For you," she said with an accusing look on her face.

"Abby?" I said, wondering what I'd done now.

"No. Diana."

CHAPTER 4

"I see that I remain Ruth's favorite person," was the first thing that Diana said to me.

To say that Ruth and Diana Baldwin had always been at odds would not be true. Diana had never been one of Ruth's favorites, but their feud didn't start in earnest until I got involved with Diana. And it wouldn't have started then if, in Ruth's opinion, Diana had done right by me. I hadn't seen Diana for years, but the last time that I had seen her, then in her early forties, she was still one of the most beautiful women that I had never known. Pale grey eyes, long light-brown hair that she often wore in a ponytail while painting, a walk level and still, like that of a gunfighter, and a fire that started in her eyes and burned all the way through to her soul. I had never loved anyone in quite the same way that I had loved her—head over heels, with no reservations. Not even Abby, whom I loved completely. Which was why it had taken me so long to get over her—if one ever really does get over his first true love.

"How are things in New Mexico?" I said. Diana now lived in Santa Fe, where she freelanced as a landscape and portrait painter and taught art on the side.

"Going surprisingly well. I have two exhibitions scheduled this summer, and there's a new man in my life. But you probably don't want to hear about that."

She was right as rain. But I said, "A cowboy, I hope."

"How did you know?"

"What else is there in New Mexico besides cowboys and artists?"

"The same men as there are in Wisconsin. Technically, though, he's not a cowboy any longer, since he owns the ranch."

"Big spread?" I couldn't see her on a small one—not as mistress of the bunkhouse.

"Big enough," she said, not wanting to talk about it. "His late wife commissioned me to do a portrait of him, but I really think that she was looking for someone to take her place. Though I didn't know it until later, she was dying of breast cancer at the time."

"How old a man is he?"

"Sixty. But he looks younger. And . . . Well, let's just say that he has the stamina of a younger man. You'd like him, I think. He wants me to marry him."

I pulled out a chair from the dining room table and sat down. The news, though a long way from devastating, was still a shock. Here I thought she'd been pining over me all these years.

"Are you going to marry him?"

"I'm thinking seriously about it. I've been single for ten years now. That's long enough."

How long had I been single? Forever it seemed. "It

does get lonely being alone."

"How would you know? You've always had Ruth."

"A mixed blessing, I'd say."

"You know better. You'd be lost without her. At least once upon a time you would have been." At first awash in tranquility, her voice now had an edge to it.

"Nothing's changed, Diana."

"That's not what I hear. I wish I could say I was happy for you."

"Abby's in Detroit for at least the next two years. She might never come back to Oakalla."

"I don't think Gerald will wait that long for my answer."

"Gerald?"

"The man who wants to marry me."

"If he loves you, he'll wait. Till his cows come home . . . If you'll pardon the expression."

"They don't, you know. Come home. Gerald says that once they get out, they're gone, until you go after them and bring them back."

Somehow, I didn't think we were talking about cows any longer. "I would have once, Diana. Would you have come?"

"In a heartbeat."

In the silence that followed, I sat watching the rain, which was a model of consistency. Somewhere between sprinkle and downpour, its drops seemed to fall upon themselves one right after the other until the grass began to bend and the ground began to seep.

"Water over the dam," I said at last.

"Just thought you'd like to know."

I looked to Ruth for help, but she was elbow deep in soap suds. Feigning disinterest, but with both ears wide open.

"Is that why you called? To add insult to injury?" I said.

"No. Actually I need a favor from you. As you know, your friend, Abby, is starting a shelter for abused women there in Oakalla. I'd like to make a donation. But before I can, I'll need you to sell some things for me."

"What things?" As far as I knew, Diana had moved all of her belongings out of Oakalla after she'd sold her house, the Old Baldwin Place, there in the heart of town.

"The things I have in storage in the back of the building where Fran used to have his office. I've never been able to sell the building, but Mr. Phillips, who now rents the front part of it, was gracious enough to offer to help you sort through my things if you wanted. He seems to be in the business."

"He is."

Dale Phillips, the last of a long line of renters, had a secondhand shop in the front of the building, which he kept open through the week. On Friday evenings he would pack up his pickup and head for the nearest festival and/or flea market. He seemed to enjoy the life, though I didn't see how he could make much money at it.

I said, "What am I supposed to do with the stuff when it's sorted?" So far I didn't like any of this, particularly in sorting through old memories of Fran, Diana, and me.

"I've arranged to have a garage sale in two weeks at Connie Miller's house with the proceeds going to the shelter. Mr. Phillips said that he might be interested in some of the things himself. The rest you can pitch . . . or keep, if you're of the mind."

"Two weeks doesn't give me much time."

"There's not a whole lot of stuff there, if I remember right. And most of it is Fran's."

As if that made it any easier. "Why me? Why not Connie Miller?" Connie was Diana's best remaining friend in Oakalla.

"Don't you *want* to do it?" She sounded hurt.

"I'll see what I can do," I said.

"I hoped you would." She hung up before I could change my mind.

I sat there watching the rain until Ruth said, "Well?"

I told her what Diana wanted.

"And you're going to do it?"

"I don't see the harm, do you?"

"No. Besides it's for a good cause. Though I have to wonder how long her stuff would have sat there if Abby hadn't started her shelter. Until it rotted would be my guess."

"Don't be too hard on her, Ruth. That wasn't her only reason for calling. Someone has asked her to marry him. She wanted my blessing."

Ruth had momentarily forgotten her dishes. She stood there with her mouth open, dripping suds on the floor.

"You gave it to her, I hope."

"Yes."

"Then why the long face?"

"It's the rain, I guess." Though I knew it was more than that.

"Garth, you gave her every chance in the world and she didn't take it. So thank your lucky stars and get on with your life."

"I am getting on with it!" I yelled without meaning to. "But how much better off am I with Abby in Detroit, for God's sake?"

"You asking God or me?"

"You, at the moment."

She had her favorite black cast iron skillet by the handle and was using a copper scrubber to clean the scrambled egg off of it. "Are you better off with Abby in your life or without Abby in your life? That seems to me the only question. If you're better off with her, then quit asking life for favors it's not prepared to give. And quit hoping for answers to questions that haven't even been asked yet." She rinsed the skillet, then made a place for it on the drain board. "Garth, you've been loved, really loved, as much as they are able, by at least two beautiful women, faults though I may find in both of them. A lot of men can't say that. And those who can probably aren't any more grateful than you are."

"Make that three," I said. "My wife was no slouch either. It's just . . ." I threw up my hands. "Hell, I don't know what it is."

"Is it that you didn't think life would be this hard once you reached fifty?"

"That's it in a nutshell, Ruth. I thought I'd have it all together by now. Instead, I'm using all the hands I have, just trying to hang on, and still I can feel it slipping away." I stared at her, really wanting an answer. "Tell me the truth. Does it get any easier from here on?"

Out of respect for my fragile state of mind, she refused to answer.

CHAPTER 5

The rain continued on into the afternoon. Lighter now, it fell more like mist than rain, and it gave the water soaked yards along Home Street a welcome pause.

Ruth had gone to work in the shelter for reasons of her own, though the chances of anyone else being there to help on a Sunday afternoon were slim. I felt guilty about letting her go by herself, but not guilty enough to accompany her. I couldn't yet bring myself to tear out the wall in the bedroom where Abby and I had first made love, or remodel the kitchen where Doc and I used to sit and talk for hours on end. Change came hard for me anyway, and these changes seemed too much like "homicide."

I was on my way to see Dale Phillips, harboring the fervent hope that he wouldn't be there, so that I could turn around and go back home and take a nap. But his battered green Ford F150 pickup with the rust-stained white camper shell on the back sat in the vacant lot behind the post office where Dale always parked it.

As I walked up the alley between the post office and Fran Baldwin's old office building, I couldn't shake the feeling that I was being followed. There were no pin prickles running up and down my nape, as there usually were in such instances, but more of the same general feeling of unease and vulnerability that I had brought home from the Lost 1600 with me. Twice, I turned around to look, and twice no one was there. I didn't try a third time.

I knocked on the front door of Dale Phillips' second-hand store that he had appropriately named The Last Dance. Every time I went in there, which was about once a week to pick up his ad since he didn't have a phone, I left vowing that I would never go in there again. Whatever treasures that might have been in there were so obscured by junk that even I, who loved a bargain, didn't have the patience to dig through it.

As I waited for Dale Phillips to answer my knock, I glanced up at the face of the two story frame building and decided that it had been a rental too long. Its white paint had started to flake and peel and deep cracks had begun to appear in its windowsills that, along with the cracks, had begun to show rot. I tried to picture it fifteen years ago, when Fran was still alive, and he and I were new friends. Before I fell in love with his wife and he committed suicide.

The door opened with a jolt, startling me. Dale Phillips was in his stocking feet, which was why I hadn't heard him coming. He carried a can of Budweiser in his right hand and looked about as content as a man could, who had just been interrupted on a sleepy Sunday afternoon.

"Garth Ryland, it really is you," he said, throwing

open the door. "Come on in out of the rain."

"Thanks. I think I will."

Dale Phillips was a big man, though he didn't appear to be at first glance because he was stoop-shouldered and walked with a limp. His hair, white at the fringes, shading to a rich strawberry blond as it neared the center of his head, was long, thick, and unruly, as were the chest hairs that showed in the V of his dirty white T-shirt. His arms, long, lean, and muscular, had a ruddy glow, as did his face from his weekends in the sun. He had the tattoo of an eagle on one forearm and that of a panther on the other. The eagle clutching an American flag in its talons looked like it ate nails every morning for breakfast; the panther looked like it could eat the eagle, no sweat; neither looked like it could eat Dale Phillips, not even with his stoop-shoulders and his limp.

I followed him inside The Last Dance, where I immediately knew I had made a mistake. The rain made the store seem even more close and cluttered than usual and my claustrophobia began to kick in.

I stopped and waited for Dale to notice. When he didn't, I said, "Far as I go, Dale. It's getting a little crowded in here."

He turned with difficulty to face me. Today he didn't appear to have any flexibility at all in his right leg.

"Sorry, Garth," he said with a rueful smile. "It's the keys you're after, isn't it? Not my company."

"I could use your company later. After I have a chance to sort my thoughts."

"Mrs. Baldwin said to expect that. You'd need some time alone."

Damn her, I thought. Then she had to know what this was costing me. But maybe that was all part of the plan.

"She say anything else about me?" I hoped that I didn't sound as unbalanced as I felt in that shrinking room full of junk.

"That you loved hard and didn't give up easily. Not to make an enemy of you if I possibly could help it."

"Then you'd go a long way toward furthering your cause, if you'd throw me the key to the back door."

He spread his legs to balance himself, then reached into the pocket of his jeans and gave the key a soft underhand toss my way. I caught it easily. "Thanks, Dale. I'll be in back."

"Give me a holler when you need me. I'll be upstairs."

I glanced at my trusty Timex. "Why don't you come on down in about an hour. I should have made my peace with things by then."

"An hour it is."

"And Dale . . . I'm sorry if I seem a little weird. But the walls really do seem to be closing in."

The look in his eyes said that he understood perfectly. "Hey, I'm hip."

"You're claustrophobic, too?"

"No. I was in prison for ten years. See you in an hour."

He turned and limped up the stairs. I went outside and back into the alley, where, using the skeleton key that he had thrown me, I let myself into the back of the building.

An hour later, or whenever it was that Dale Phillips rejoined me, I hadn't made much progress. I was doing okay until I came to Fran's rod and reel and tackle box. The rod was fiberglass, an old medium-action five-and-a-half foot Shakespeare, with a white-handled level-wind Shakespeare reel still filled with blue Stren fishing line. Probably twelve-pound test, since Fran, believing every fish, no matter how large, deserved a sporting chance, never went any heavier than that.

His father had bought the rod and reel for Fran as a high school graduation present, and Fran had always kept

them immaculate and in perfect working order. Now caked
with dust, they would need a thorough cleaning before
they would even work—though I doubted that anyone but
Fran could ever make them sing with the same music again.

Inside his tackle box were an assortment of spoons,
spinners, flatfish, and Rapallas, along with the Pikey
Minnow and Lazy Ike that had once belonged to Grandmother Ryland and for which I had been searching for
years. Fran could outcast me, outrow me, outpaddle me,
and outswim me, but he couldn't outfish me, so he figured
it must be because of my lures, most of which had come
from Grandmother's tackle box. Even the gold Daredevil
spoon on which he'd caught his thirty-six pound muskey
that now hung on the wall in the back room of the Corner
Bar and Grill had come from my tackle box and still hung
from the muskey's mouth. That was on the Flambeau
fourteen years ago this spring. When I netted the muskey
for him, without tipping over our canoe, it had forever
sealed our friendship.

"How are things going?" Dale Phillips asked.

Again he startled me. I'd heard him come in, then
had forgotten about him.

"Very slowly," I said. "A lot of memories here."

"You want me to bug out?" It was all the same to him.

"No. I need your advice. I'm taking this rod and reel
and tackle box. What do you think they're worth?"

He sat down on the poplar floor beside me. It was
obvious that it took an effort to get his right leg where he
wanted it to go.

"What happened to your leg, if you don't mind my
asking?"

He used his hands to bend his right leg into place. "I
don't mind," he said with a grunt. "Just give me a minute
to catch my breath."

Up close, Dale Phillips looked about ten years older

than he did from a distance. The first time that I saw him, I had guessed him to be younger than I, but he was probably a few years older. Mid to late fifties. Maybe even sixty.

"Motorcycle accident," he said, while massaging his leg. "I had this old Indian that would flat-out fly. I was out in the desert at night. Hell, there was nobody out there but me, the lizards, and the sidewinders, so I let her all the way out just to see what she'd do. Went so fast, I scared even me, which was not an easy thing." As he spoke, his eyes widened and his hands tightened down on the grips. He wouldn't have been wearing a helmet either. I could see the stars in his tattoo-blue eyes, his blond ducktail flying in the wind. "So after I saw what she could do, I began to ease up on her because there was a curve ahead. Good thing I did because before I knew what was happening, she'd locked up on me, and I was headed into that curve straight on. I had to lay her down . . . It was my only chance. Wouldn't you know it. Out of a whole desert full of nothing, I had to hit a mesquite tree." Dale Phillips had begun to sweat. The memory was not a good one. "It was daylight before anybody came along. At that I had to drag myself to the highway and flag somebody down. Got lucky for the first time in my life. He was a cross country hauler on his way to Bakersfield."

"That your home, Bakersfield?" I said.

"Used to be. Way back when. Before I robbed a Sinclair service station to get out of there. Actually, it wasn't the only one I robbed. Frankie Swackhammer and me planned to rob our way clear across the country. But we only got as far as Texas."

"That's quite a ways, considering."

He smiled. "Me and Frankie thought so."

"Was this before or after you hurt your leg?"

"After. All along I'd planned to join the service when I was old enough, but the leg put the quietus on that. And it was hard to get any kind of good paying job with a bum leg and no education to speak of. If you've ever been to Bakersfield, you know it's not the garden spot of the world, particularly back in the 1950s before they air conditioned the place. So I figured I'd try to get out any way I could. Except it's also hard to make a fast getaway with a bum leg. That is, if you're robbing filling stations and need a running start."

"Why didn't you let Frankie do it, while you drove the car?"

He shook his head solemnly and in all seriousness said, "Frankie wasn't all that bright. I didn't think I could trust him with a gun in his hand."

I had to smile as I pictured Dale Phillips fast-limping his way past the Sinclair dinosaur on his way to his hotrod Lincoln. "How long did you say you were in prison?"

"Ten years, with five off for good behavior. It wasn't the first time I'd been in trouble, so the judge threw the book at me. Good thing, too, the direction I was headed. But the best thing about it was I taught myself to read there. Man, talk about an eye opener. Now, it's all I do when I get a spare moment."

"And after that?" I said.

"Carnivals mainly, until I got in the swap meet business, where I've been ever since. The thing is," he took pains to explain, "I was never meant to punch a time clock, no matter what. And being out of doors suits me a whole lot better than being inside. Except when it's raining outside, like it is today. Then I like to settle in with a six-pack and read me a good book."

"No women in your life?"

His grin was wide and innocent, like that of a ten-year-old boy. "No, sir. I figure they're more trouble than they're worth."

I studied him to see if he was bullshitting me or not.

He didn't seem to be. Rather, he appeared to be someone like Clarkie, our former sheriff, who just naturally felt more comfortable in the company of men. Not that he didn't like women, but some fundamental part of him didn't trust them.

I handed him Fran's tackle box and gave him a moment to study its contents. "So what do you think it's worth, it and the rod and reel both?"

"There are a lot of good old antique lures in here," he said, holding up a Heddon Spook still in its original box.

"Yeah, but at least half of them are mine."

"And the rod and reel are Shakespeare," he said after examining them. "That's the Cadillac of old rods and reels."

"So how much?" I said, knowing that I'd met my match.

"Two hundred dollars ought to cover it and that's a bargain."

"Then make a note of it. I'm going to take them with me."

I rose, offered him my hand, and pulled him to his feet. His hand had the strong hard calloused feel of a working man.

"You're not going to sort through the rest of this today?" He looked and sounded disappointed.

The rod and reel had been standing behind the door. Beyond them were several unopened cardboard boxes, an entire wall of books, and a cedar chest filled with Fran's Pendleton shirts. I knew what was in the cedar chest because I'd helped Diana pack and move it over here. Actually, I'd helped her pack and haul about everything here except the books. Fran, for whatever the reason, had always kept them here.

"I have a better idea," I said. "You go through and pick out what you want and we'll take the rest to the garage sale."

"Fair enough. But not today, not if you're not going to be here. When I'm home, Sunday's my day off."

"It usually is mine, too. I'll check back with you about Wednesday to see how you're doing. We probably should get this stuff to Connie Miller no later than next Monday so she can price it." I handed him the key.

"Garth?" Dale said on my way out. "You and Mrs. Baldwin, you were good friends at one time?"

"Very good friends."

"What happened to her husband?"

"He shot himself."

"I guess someone told me that. Was he sick, or something?"

"At heart, maybe. It's a long story, Dale, and I don't feel much like telling it."

I started on. His voice stopped me.

"Mrs. Baldwin, is she a looker?"

"Yes, Dale. She's a looker."

"I thought she might be by the sound of her voice. But nine times out of ten, I'm wrong about that."

I thought that he would be satisfied now, but I was wrong.

"What happened to the two of you?" he said.

"I really don't know, Dale. We just were never at the same place in the same time. It's sort of like the song, 'Send In The Clowns?'"

"I wouldn't know," he said sadly.

"The feeling or the song?"

"Either one."

"Wednesday, then?"

"Sure. Why not?"

CHAPTER 6

Normally, Ruth and I ate our Sunday dinner at home in the dining room. It was the one day of the week that we used the dining room and the one day of the week that we had more than soup and sandwiches for our midday meal. But today, since Ruth was working at the shelter, there would be no Sunday dinner, no pot roast, glazed carrots, and browned potatoes, or ham, scalloped potatoes, and creamed asparagus. There would only be me, and a horny English setter scratching at the basement door. So I didn't go home, but went to the Corner Bar and Grill instead.

Hiram, the bartender, and I had nearly the whole place to ourselves. The only other ones in there were Larry Sharp, Dennis Hall and Ned Cleaver, who sat in the booth farthest from the bar with empty glasses and a half pitcher of Leinenkugel's in front of them. Even Robby Rumaley, who was the most regular of all the regulars, had yet to put in an appearance. But then what did I expect at three-thirty on a Sunday afternoon?

"What'll it be, Garth?" Hiram said as I sat down at the bar.

"Bourbon and ginger ale."

"Ten High okay? I'm about to the end of a bottle."

"That will be fine."

As Hiram went to fix my drink, I looked longingly at the booth where Abby and I had spent so many happy hours. The first few weeks after she left, I used to sit there by myself, but no longer. It just wasn't the same without her there, and I felt a lot more comfortable and a whole lot less lonely at the bar.

My glance travelled from the booth to the Hamms clock above the mirror, where my all-time favorite bear was forever rolling a log, to the juke box, to the swinging doors between the barroom and the dining room, to the booth where Larry Sharp, Dennis Hall, and Ned Cleaver sat not drinking their beer. Usually it was a quartet wherever they went. I wondered where Albert Vice was.

Hiram set my Ten High and ginger ale down in front of me. "The boys don't seem to be taking their drinking seriously this afternoon," I said.

"No. They've been in here since one, and they're still on their first pitcher."

"Maybe they're waiting for Albert," I said.

"They're waiting for somebody, it looks like."

"Is there supposed to be a softball game at the park this afternoon?"

"Not that I know of. Otherwise, they'd all be in uniform."

"Maybe it was cancelled because of the rain."

"Might be. That might also explain that hangdog look

they're all wearing."

Larry Sharp, Dennis Hall, and Ned Cleaver all played for the Oakalla "Wheywackers," the local softball team that was sponsored by the cheese plant where they all worked. Larry Sharp, the tall lanky one, played first base. Ned Cleaver, the slow always steady one, pitched, and Dennis Hall, the squat fiery one, caught. Albert Vice, conspicuous by his absence, was the center fielder. Together they formed the nucleus of a team that had won the Adams County Cup five years running and were favored to win it again this year.

"What's on the menu today?" I turned to ask Hiram after noticing that Dennis Hall was staring at me.

"Bernice has already gone home for the day. Sandwiches and fries are about all that I can offer."

"How about a cheeseburger with fried onions and some macaroni salad?"

"I can do that."

Hiram went into the kitchen to fix my cheeseburger. I assumed that I was alone with my thoughts when Dennis Hall appeared at the bar beside me. "Something bothering you, Garth?" he said.

"A lot of things, but none at this particular moment."

Dennis Hall had green eyes, thick curly red hair, and was built like a fireplug. He wore jeans, black hightop tennis shoes, and a sleeveless grey sweatshirt turned inside out, and had freckles all up and down his face and arms. Aged in his early thirties, he hauled milk for the cheese plant. Early one morning while walking down the alley beside the cheese plant, I'd stopped to watch him unload ten-gallon cans of milk—one after the other, one in each hand. Dennis wasn't someone you wanted with his hands around your throat, if you could help it.

"You seemed to be taking a lot of interest in what was going on at our table," Dennis said.

"I just wondered where Albert was. You guys are usually a foursome."

Dennis Hall's thick red brows were knotted with concern.

"Yeah? Well, we were wondering the same thing, since he didn't show up for our poker game last night, and no one's seen him at all today."

"You talk to his wife?"

"His wife?" Dennis's thick red brows were now knitted in puzzlement. Dennis wasn't a quick study, it had been my observation.

"His wife. Last time I looked, Albert was happily married." Unlike Dennis, who had recently separated from his wife.

"We tried, but we can't get ahold of her either."

"Maybe they took a mini vacation," I suggested. "One of those spur of the moment jobs."

"Yeah," Dennis seemed to like that idea. "Maybe they did."

Hiram set my macaroni salad on the bar, then hung around to make sure that there wasn't any trouble between Dennis and me. In my opinion, Hiram was the perfect bartender; he knew when to talk, when to listen, when to serve one for the road, and when to say enough's enough. And he knew each of his regulars and their sticking points as well as they did themselves.

I said to Dennis, "But if you think you have reason to worry, then I might suggest you talk to Cecil Hardwick. He's our town marshal."

"I know who he is," Dennis said, edging away from the bar. "I just came over to find out what you were staring at."

"It was nothing personal, Dennis. Just idle curiosity."

"I wonder what that was all about?" I said to Hiram after Dennis had returned to his table.

"I don't know, but we might be about to find out."

Hiram went to check on my cheeseburger. I turned around to see what was going on.

Kristina Vice—who had just entered—was one of those tall leggy raven-eyed brunettes that turn heads wherever they go and have TROUBLE printed in invisible ink right across their backside. It wasn't her fault. She didn't go out of her way to draw attention to herself—hike her miniskirts crotch high or sunbathe in her white string bikini on the sidewalk out in front of the post office. And up close she wasn't all that pretty, not to me anyway. There seemed more sheen than substance, and a disheartening dullness to her eyes when you looked deep inside them.

But at first glance she was every man's dream, and no doubt Oakalla's fantasy queen now that Wendy Bodine and Amber Utley had both moved on. Which perhaps explained why her husband, Albert Vice, kept such a close watch on her, as if he were hearing footsteps.

After a moment's conversation with those in the booth, Kristina Vice slid into the booth beside Dennis Hall and poured herself a glass of the now warm beer. After she chugged that, she poured herself another. I turned around before Dennis Hall caught me staring again.

"The plot thickens," Hiram said, as he set my cheeseburger down in front of me.

I finished my drink and handed him my glass for a refill. "Does it ever. I wonder where Albert is?"

"And what's Kristina doing here in those shorts and heels when it's no more than sixty degrees out?"

Short black shorts, black spiked heels, black fishnet hose, and a see-through powder-blue blouse that told me that Kristina Vice was more than just legs. "Maybe they were on their way South when their car broke down," I said.

"Could be, I guess," he said, as he fixed my drink. "But that still doesn't explain where Albert is."

I heard the scuffle of feet behind me and turned around just in time to see Dennis Hall, Ned Cleaver, and Kristina Vice exit by the side door. Larry Sharp, however, was headed my way.

How tall was Larry Sharp? Six-five, I guessed, though he might have gone six-six. Tall enough to play forward for the University of Wisconsin–Green Bay, but not tall enough to play forward in the NBA, or quick enough to play guard. High-waisted and large-hipped and more graceful than his size should have allowed, he had put on a few pounds since his basketball playing days, but now in his early forties, he could still stroke a softball with ease over the right field fence, or make a silky smooth one-handed dig at first and in the same smooth motion gun the runner from third out at home. Today he wore brand new bib overalls, blue-and-white tennis shoes, and a white cotton sport shirt with purple baseball pinstripes. His black hair was thick and wavy and always parted on the right side. He had a dimple right in the middle of his chin.

"Good afternoon, Larry," I said, leaving it at that.

The plant manager of the cheese plant as well as its team manager, Larry Sharp had been after me for years to play for the "Wheywackers." My answer was always the same: What do you need me for? Finally, he must have taken my question to heart because two years ago he had quit asking.

"Good afternoon, Garth," he said without his usual warmth. "I just wanted to let you know that Albert Vice is missing."

"Are you sure?"

"I am now. Kristina came back from her sister's at Rockford to find the house empty. She thought Albert

might be with us, so she came up here. We're going looking for him now."

"You need any help?"

"If we do, you'll be the first to know."

"You might let Cecil Hardwick know about it," I said.
"Just in case something has happened to Albert."

Larry's sour look said he didn't think much of the
idea. "When we know for sure that's the case."

He left by the side door. I turned back to my cheeseburger, which was going begging.

The phone rang the next morning just as I was about to leave for my office at the *Oakalla Reporter*. I had finished my cheeseburger and macaroni salad in peace, and to celebrate, drank a third Ten High and ginger ale, polishing off the bottle for Hiram.

At home I had waited in vain for Ruth, who dragged in at ten just as I was climbing the stairs on my way to bed. Eight hours later, I was the first one down the stairs, so I had made the coffee, drunk a glass of orange juice, and eaten a bowl of Honey Nut Cheerios while again waiting in vain for Ruth to appear. I hoped they'd get that damn shelter up and going soon. Missing Abby was bad enough. I didn't need to be missing Ruth, too.

"Hello," I said, sounding as irritated as I felt. What else would they expect at six-thirty A.M.?

"Garth, it's Dale Phillips. I hope I didn't get you up."

"No. I was already up. What is it, Dale?"

"Something's happened. I think you should stop by here on your way to work." He sounded distraught, and for the first time since I had known him, angry.

"If you say so."

"I really think you should, Garth."

"By the way, where are you calling from?" If he now had a phone, that would save me from having to go into The Last Dance every week.

"The Marathon." He hung up with a bang.

"What was that all about?"

Ruth came down the stairs wearing her ratty pink flowered Martha Washington housecoat and the fur-lined moccasins that I had bought her years ago, during perhaps the most memorable Christmas of my life. I'd given up on the housecoat a decade ago, but while I kept waiting for her to ask for new moccasins, so far she hadn't. Perhaps that was just as well, since Big Charlie's Country Store, where I had bought them, along with the ivory-and-blue Indian bead necklace that Diana was still wearing the last time I saw her, was no longer in business. In its place was a bargain basement store that sold, among other things, Buffalo tools. The reprobate in me wondered if they were anything like donkey dicks.

"It was Dale Phillips. He wants me to stop by his place on my way to work. He sounds upset."

"Maybe somebody broke into his place. Though I can't for the life of me see why." She continued on into the kitchen and poured herself a cup of coffee.

"It might be strong," I warned. "I think I perked it a little too long."

"As Aunt Emma says, there's no such thing as too strong coffee, only too weak men."

"Grandmother Ryland said the same thing."

Ruth took a sip of her coffee and winced. "But then again," she said, as she reached for the half-and-half.

"How did you sleep?" I said, because her eyes still looked a little bleary.

She shook her head. She didn't want to talk about it.

"Well, I'm off. Don't look for me at noon because I probably won't be here," I said.

"That makes two of us. And don't count on me for supper either. The carpenters are coming today."

"They probably know how to read a blueprint."

"If there was one."

"How much longer does this go on, Ruth?"

She gave me one of my pat answers. "Until we're done."

I left by the front door. Two blocks later I walked up the alley between the post office and The Last Dance and knocked on Dale Phillips' front door. He must have been waiting right inside the door because the door flew open before I even finished knocking, nearly taking me with it.

"We're going to have to quit meeting like this," I said, willing my heart to slow down.

He stared at me as if he hadn't heard. "Come look at this," he said. "It just makes me sick."

I followed him inside the back door of the building, where someone had dumped all the cardboard boxes, emptied the cedar chest of all of Fran's shirts, and pulled down all of his books from their shelves.

"Well, at least you won't have to unpack all the boxes," I said.

"Doesn't it make you mad? It sure does me."

To prove his point, he buried his fist in the plaster wall. It was an impressive show of raw power and sheer stupidity, as evidenced by his bloody knuckles.

"You feel better?" I said.

"Not much," he said, while tenderly rubbing the

knuckles of his right hand. "What kind of person would do something like this?"

"I wouldn't know, Dale," I said, surveying the mess, which could have been a lot worse had there been malice behind it. But it seemed that whoever had trashed the place was simply looking for something that he may or may not have found. "But remember, you once knocked off filling stations for a living."

"I don't like to be reminded of that," he said, still rubbing his knuckles. Either he didn't know his own strength, or the plaster wall was a lot harder than he'd figured on.

"Well, it's a fact, nevertheless. The question as I see it is, what do we do now?"

"I'll clean up the mess, if that's what you're worried about," he said. "It's my fault that it happened, anyway."

Dale's color had visibly paled. The shock of busting all your knuckles could do that to you.

"How is it your fault?" I said.

"I knew I heard someone down there, but I thought it was you."

"What time was that?"

"After eleven. I was already in bed."

I put my hand on his shoulder to calm him. Hard as stone, it had no give to it. I might as well have been trying to soothe the panther on his arm.

"I'll be waiting for him next time," he said. "I've got a thirty-eight upstairs that I bought for just such an occasion."

I nodded, hoping for all our sakes that there wouldn't be a next time.

Sometime in the night, the rain had stopped and the skies had cleared. The sun was now out, trying mightily to make up for lost time as it warmed my face and burned away the last whiskers of fog hiding in the corners of the yards along Gas Line Road. The lawns were a deep dark green, the birds were singing their hearts out, and the air was rife with the scent of wet grass, and the memory of what it was once like to have the sun on your cheek, time in your pocket, and seemingly nothing but blue skies ahead. That was the best thing about May. It gave you, as long as you were willing and able, the chance to start over, to feel twenty-one again.

The first thing that I did when I got to my office was to sit down at my desk and think through the past thirty-six hours. The desk was solid oak, five feet wide and three feet deep, and my Rock of Gibraltar. It, along with my swivel oak captain's chair, had come from the boiler room of my father's dairy back in Godfrey, Indiana. Whenever I needed to thaw out as a kid, I went into the boiler room, propped my feet up on the desk, and leaned back in Pop's chair as far as the heat from the coal furnace would allow me. Now, whenever I had a problem to work out, I did much the same thing. The only difference was that there wasn't a phone on the desk in the boiler room, so if any-one wanted me, he had to come looking.

An hour or so later, after I'd talked to most of my sources, and two of my advertisers, who weren't happy with their ads, or at least with their results, I got back to my thoughts again. What did Albert Vice, who was now missing, have to do, if anything, with my getting hit over the head and with the break in at Fran's old office? What were Ned Cleaver, Dennis Hall, and Larry Sharp up to, and who was Preston Kurtz and what was he really doing in the Lost 1600 the very morning after someone had cold-cocked me? Then there was the ghost squad on maneuvers and the screams in the night. Where did they fit in the mix? As Stan Laurel would say, "It's a fine kettle of fish that you've gotten us into this time, Ollie."

I called the switchboard at the University of Wisconsin–

Whitewater and asked for Preston Kurtz.

A pause, then the operator said, "I'm sorry, sir, but I have no one listed here by that name."

I was disappointed, but not surprised. "Do you know if a Preston Kurtz has ever taught there?"

"I don't have that information. Was there anything else?"

I told her to transfer me to the political science department. But even though the woman who answered the phone had been a secretary there for the past thirty years, she had never heard of Preston Kurtz.

Score one for Preston Kurtz. He had lied to me and I believed him. Not an unheard of occurrence, but a rare one.

I thought about calling Clarkie, former Sheriff Harold Clark, at the Madison Police Department where he worked as a computer jockey, but I hated to bother him at work, unless it was an emergency. Preston Kurtz had not broken the law to my knowledge, and I didn't want to overuse Clarkie for fear that he would get tired of doing me favors that I couldn't reciprocate. He had no apparent vices, so I couldn't buy him sex, booze, or cigarettes, and I couldn't afford his taste in software. I could apologize to him for all of the times that I had made him miserable while he was still sheriff, but that was asking too much. Nothing. That's what I'd do for now. With any luck, and I was overdue, things would sort themselves out on their own.

Cecil Hardwick came into my office, stopped and took off his hat, then stood there stiffly with his hat in his hand, like an old-time preacher just entering the Lucky Lady Saloon. For a happy instant, until I saw who it really was, I thought that Cecil was Rupert Roberts, returned to uniform again. Cecil was built like Rupert—tall, thin, and angular, with Rupert's large big-knuckle hands. Like Rupert, his shirt was pulled in tight around his narrow waist in a military tuck, and since he had no hips to hold up his pants, his belt was drawn to its last notch. Unlike Rupert, however, he was nearly bald, except for a narrow rim of grey hair that ran from ear to ear behind his head, and unlike Rupert, he didn't carry a gun while in uniform. And as long as I was making comparisons, he also didn't wear his crown with ease the way Rupert always had. His face was drawn, his skin so tight that it seemed his veins would pop right out of the top of his head.

"Morning, Cecil," I said, as I stood to offer my hand.

His right hand extended, he quickly crossed my office and we shook hands. His grip was over-hard, his hand moist with sweat. And he held on just an instant too long for both of us not to notice.

"Sorry, Garth," he said. "I'm new at this."

"Have a seat," I said, retrieving one of the two chairs from the far wall where I usually kept them to discourage visitors. Straight backed and hard, they could only be matched for discomfort by those in Wilmer Wiemer's office.

He sat down in the chair. I sat down in my captain's chair behind my desk. With the desk between us, he seemed to relax.

"What's on your mind, Cecil?"

"I got word that Albert Vice might be missing. I wondered if you'd heard anything to that effect?"

"Has his wife reported him missing?" I said, wanting to find out how much he knew.

"Not to me, she hasn't."

"What about the cheese plant?"

"Them either."

Strange, I thought. Or maybe not so strange, since Ned Cleaver, Dennis Hall, and Larry Sharp all worked there. Not only worked there, but essentially ran the place, since Ned was foreman, Larry plant manager, and Dennis shop steward.

"Then who told you Albert was missing?" I said.

"His sister called me from Eau Claire."

"Who told her?"

"Nobody. She's been trying to get ahold of him since yesterday, and when she couldn't get him at home, she tried the cheese plant. He wasn't there, so she called me to see what was going on."

"Is she worried about him?"

"No. She has some legal papers that she needs him to sign. Not something that can wait, she said."

"What kind of legal papers?"

Cecil looked sure of himself, as he offered his opinion. "Not the kind that would cause someone to turn up missing. They own a joint piece of property. She just wants to buy him out and build on it now that spring's here, that's all. She'd like to be under roof before winter."

"Did you check her story out?"

"Not yet. I didn't see the point."

I didn't either, but you never know. "To answer your question, Cecil, I don't know anything more about it than you do. From all indications Albert Vice is missing, but until someone files a missing person report, your hands are pretty much tied."

"His sister said that she'd be willing to do that, then fax it to me.

"Is that a problem?" His frown seemed to indicate that it was.

"Not if I had a fax machine, or knew how to use one."

I smiled. I was beginning to like Cecil Hardwick more and more. "Put your cousin, Wilmer, to work on it. Tell him that it's the least he can do to help you out."

"And you know what he'll say to that. 'What's in it for me?'"

He was right. Wilmer Weimer didn't grant many favors, unless he expected to profit from them.

"Tell him he can put it on my account. I'm already so

far behind I'll never catch up."

Cecil warmed to that idea. "He just might do it for you," he said. "Nobody else in town, though."

I nodded in agreement. I didn't know whether it spoke well or ill of me, but I was Wilmer's one exception to all of his rules.

"You can ask him. See what he says," I said.

Cecil nodded solemnly and looked down at his hat. When he looked back up at me again, it was almost apologetic. Then I learned why.

"Ruth called to say you might have some information for me," he said.

"About what?"

"The Lost 1600. Something you saw there."

I wanted to tell him that Ruth was mistaken, but I could tell by the set in his jaw that it was already too late for that. Whatever he was or wasn't, Cecil was nobody's fool.

"I didn't see much of anything. But what I heard might be of interest to you." Then I told him what had happened in the Lost 1600 Saturday night.

Cecil was back to staring at his hat again when I finished. He ran his fingers along its crown and said, "This is a bad bull."

Instantly I knew what he meant without ever asking because I felt the same way. But he went on to explain.

"A bad bull. We had only a couple of them in my nearly sixty years on the farm. No matter how interested he might seem in something else, and unconcerned about what you were up to, you knew better than to turn your back on him, or he'd take you right then and there. That's what all this reminds me of—a bad bull."

"You don't know that, Cecil."

"You don't think those were Albert Vice's screams you heard?"

"I don't know what they were. At this point, I don't even want to guess."

He slowly rose, even more slowly scooted the chair back against the east wall where I had found it, then stood with one hand on my office door. "Then I guess it's up to me to find out," he said.

"I guess it is," I said, thinking that we'd said all there was to say.

"Garth, I've never conducted an investigation before. If it comes to that, will you be willing to help me out?"

I thought long and hard before I answered, knowing what it must have cost him to ask. But my worst mistake with Clarkie, and to a lesser degree with Wayne Jacoby, was trying to do his job for him. I didn't want to repeat that mistake.

"No, Cecil. You're the law in town now. Anything that you do, you'll have to do on your own, or people will never take you seriously."

"Just thought I'd ask."

"A long way from the dairy farm, huh, Cecil?" I said, as he prepared to leave.

He put on his hat and opened the door. "A long long way."

CHAPTER 8

It never pays to congratulate yourself prematurely. I had gotten through the day right up until the closing bell without incident and was locking the door on my way out when Ben Bryan pulled up outside in his brand new "harvest gold" Oldsmobile 88 with the Operation Lifeline ambulance right behind him.

A small serious self-made man who loved gardening and antique cars, Ben Bryan always looked dressed for the part, whether it was driving around town in his 1948 purple Mercury convertible, thinning his lettuce, or giving the lay sermon at the United Methodist Church. Ben was a retired mortician, who had received the county coroner's job by default when Doc Airhart retired and nobody else would take it. He had been grooming Abby for the job until she moved back to Detroit. He had yet to forgive me for that move.

"You got a minute?" Ben said. "There's something I'd like to show you."

"Animal, vegetable, or mineral?" I finished locking the door and joined him on the sidewalk.

"You'll see soon enough."

He took me by the arm and led me to the back of the ambulance. Too late I saw the looks of shock on the young EMTs' faces.

Albert Vice's body was inside. He was dressed in Army boots, camouflage pants, and a dark green T-shirt. With his face night-blackened and his short blond hair and widow's peak, he reminded me of the first casualty of war that I ever saw. My reaction then was the same as my reaction now, one of anger, sadness, and stunned disbelief.

"What a waste," I said to Ben.

"Multiply that by a thousand," said Ben, who had been a Marine medic in Korea.

I closed the back door of the ambulance. It was a relief to both of us not to have to look at Albert Vice any longer.

"Where was he?" I said, as I stepped away from the ambulance to warm myself in the afternoon sun.

"Hidden Quarry. The way he was weighted down with concrete blocks, he should've been at the bottom in about two hundred feet of water. But as luck would have it, he got hung up on a shelf no more than twenty feet down. Gerald Ruckle and Peachy White were out there crappie fishing this morning and hooked into him. Rather, their anchor did." Ben put a stick of Dentine gum in his mouth and the wrapper in his pocket. "You can imagine their surprise when they got close enough to see what they were hooked on. As it was, they had nearly tipped their boat over getting him that far."

I could see it all happening there in the back of

Peachy's fourteen-foot rowboat with Peachy and Gerald, neither a small nor a delicate man, each giving the other hell for not pulling his weight. It would have been funny under any other circumstances.

"How did he die?" I said.

"I'm working on that. But I can almost tell you for certain that he didn't drown."

Albert Vice was a tough, lean, handsome man, who had celebrated his thirtieth birthday at the Corner Bar and Grill less than a month ago. He had an abundance of nervous energy that always seemed to keep him on edge and one of the best throwing arms of anyone I'd ever seen outside of professional baseball. More than once I'd seen him throw out a runner from deep center field on the fly.

"What a waste," I repeated.

"All the way around," Ben said. "There'll be a lot of holes to fill with him gone. No kids, though. That's one good thing."

"Every cloud has a silver lining."

"There's no need to be that way, Garth. You know how I feel about Albert."

We all had our local heroes on the softball team. Ben's was Albert Vice because of his great arm and his speed on the bases, the lack of both of which had kept Ben out of the game. My hero was Ned Cleaver for his rock-steady performance game in and game out.

"Have you told Cecil Hardwick about this?" I said.

"He was there when we fished Albert out of Hidden Quarry. Along with half the volunteer fire department."

"Was Dennis Hall there?" Dennis Hall and Albert Vice were both volunteer firemen, and also best friends.

"Yeah. He took one look at Albert and spent the rest of his time tossing up his cookies. But he wasn't alone in that. It hit all the firemen pretty hard, having to haul up one of their own."

"How did Cecil Hardwick handle himself?"

"Surprisingly well for a man new to the job. He let you know he was there if you needed him, but he didn't get in the way."

Ben Bryan didn't hand out many compliments. I was encouraged by his report on Cecil.

"Does Cecil know that you were bringing Albert by here?"

"He sort of insisted that I did. He wanted you in on the ground floor in case something happened to him." Ben gave me a searching look. "You don't happen to know what he meant by that, do you?"

I knew, but there was no sense worrying Ben about it. Cecil had already called this case a bad bull, and that was before they found Albert Vice's body.

"No. But I'll ask him the first chance I get."

"The man shows promise, Garth." Ben said as he opened the door to his new Oldsmobile. "I'd hate to lose him this early in the game."

"How do you like your new car?" I said, changing the subject.

"Not as well as my old one. I wish now I'd never traded."

"What's the problem?" As far as looks went, the Oldsmobile was a beauty.

"Too many gadgets to suit me. That's why I like those old cars. They are what they appear to be."

"And this one isn't?"

Ben turned on the engine, then got out so that I could look inside. "Take a look at that instrument panel, which tells me everything but when I have to go to the bathroom. Hell, Garth, if I'd wanted an airplane, I'd have bought me one."

"Then trade it in on an older model."

"And buy someone else's junk? No. I'll just moan and

groan and make do, like the rest of the American sheepeople."

"Don't take any wooden nickels," I said as he put the Oldsmobile in gear.

"It's too late for that."

I watched Ben pull away, followed by the Operation Lifeline ambulance, then started the walk home. The sky, which had been all blue until about noon, now had several puffy white clouds floating around in it, and a couple of anvil-topped thunderheads, one to the south and one to the east, growing ever taller and darker as the day went along. The sun, though, was still warm and bright whenever it was out and felt good to me after having been inside all day. It wasn't until I reached home and saw Ruth's note on the table that I felt anything like a chill in the air.

Garth,

Am working at the shelter, so you are on your own for supper. There's meatloaf in the refrigerator if you want to warm it up and mashed potatoes, if you want potato cakes. Daisy is fed and in the basement, but could probably use some fresh air and a chance to stretch her legs. Watch out for that flea bag next door. I caught him sniffing around our back gate earlier today. See you when I get there.

Ruth

I crumbled up the note and threw it in the waste basket. Normally, leftover meat loaf and fried potato cakes would have been fine with me. But I had never much cared to listen to myself eat.

"Daisy, you down there?" I said at the basement door.

"Woof!"

"That's what I was afraid of."

The instant that I opened the back door, Daisy shot outside and had made a round of the back yard before I'd gotten off the stoop. Sam, the nefarious basset, immediately came up to the fence wagging his tail, which was more activity than I had seen out of him in the previous eight years, except perhaps for those rare nights I'd be cooking T-bone steaks on the grill. And while I sympathized with him, I had no intention of raising a litter of basset-setter puppies. About the only thing they'd be good for, besides company, was pointing fire hydrants.

"Forget it," I said to Daisy, who'd developed a sudden interest in Sam and was wagging her tail coquettishly as they nuzzled through the boards of the fence. "It's not that kind of exercise you're out here for."

"Woof!"

"Yeah, yeah, I hear you. Where's Rin Tin Tin when you really need him?"

Daisy continued along the fence. Sam followed her every step of the way until he ran into the rose of Sharon tree and had to make a detour around it and then the garage where he met her on the other side. Sam had forgotten his swayback and his arthritis and was acting like a pup again. Love, I heard, could do that to you.

"Time to go in, Daisy," I said after her fifth trip around the yard.

She pranced on by as if she hadn't heard. Sam meanwhile was starting to step on his tongue. Another round or two and Ruth's fondest wish for him might come true.

I have never liked to chase dogs. With their four legs to my two, and their ability to stop and turn on a dime, I'm at a distinct disadvantage. It has never seemed particularly satisfying to me even when I am successful at catching one. What, after all, is the prize, except to look like an utter fool?

But chase Daisy I did until sweat ran into my eyes and words flew from my lips that would have scorched Popeye's ears. Finally I cornered her between the apple tree and the rose trellis. The whole neighborhood, I knew, was dialing up the ASPCA as I carried her inside and down the basement steps.

"See if I ever let you out again," I said as I set her down, just as the phone upstairs had started to ring.

Her answer was to bolt up the basement steps ahead of me, where she was stopped by the basement door. Seeing me coming up the steps toward her and thinking that I was after her instead of the phone, she beat a hasty retreat back down the steps, getting in my way and leaving me two strides short of reaching the phone on time.

The hell with it, I thought. If it's important they can call back.

Once I calmed down, I drank an Old Crow and ginger ale, then walked to the Corner Bar and Grill for supper. It was a cool, but otherwise beautiful spring evening—the pink flowered redbuds dark-trunked and still, the scent of pine and lilac in the air. Herman Good had what smelled like barbecue chicken cooking on his grill, and somewhere to the northwest was the thin blue smoke of last year's leaves. All in all, it was a good night to be alive. Too bad Albert Vice wasn't here to enjoy it.

Inside the barroom of the Corner Bar and Grill, Robby Rumaley sat at his usual place at the bar, two stools in front of the north wall, but the rest of the stools at the bar were vacant. I took a seat beside Robby and ordered the Monday special, which was a shrimp basket with either french fries or onion rings and cole slaw as the side.

"Fries or onion rings?" Hiram said.

"Onion rings. And a draft of Leinenkugel's."

"That stuff'll kill you," Robby Rumaley raised his

empty beer glass to show me just what to expect.

"So I've heard."

Hiram brought Robby a refill and me my Leinenkugel's, then went into the kitchen to cook. Bernice, the owner, was the cook every morning (except Sunday) and noon, and Thursday, Friday,and Saturday evenings. The rest of the time she let Hiram fend for himself, and he seemed to prefer it that way. They'd had other cooks and several waitresses over the years, but the hours were so irregular that none had lasted for long. So it was usually up to Hiram and Bernice to keep the place going, and they did a splendid job.

I glanced over at Robby Rumaley, who seemed a lot quieter than usual and not at all his impish self. A small-ish man in a family of giants, Robby was the only one of five brothers not to play either basketball or football for Oakalla High School, and the only one not to go on to col-lege. Sober, he was a crack plumber, and three-sheets-to-the-wind, he could still fix all of your leaks for you, though it might cost you an extra hour or two for him to do so. Now in his mid-fifties, with four failed marriages behind him, he lived alone on the west side of Fickle Road in the first house south of the railroad tracks. He walked home every night after leaving the Corner Bar and Grill, then walked back into town the next morning to pick up his white panel truck and start the day's business. So if you needed a plumber in the middle of the night, which some of us Oakallans did, you had better be prepared to go after him and to have some tools on hand. As inconve-nient as that was, it was better than watching your base-ment fill up with water from a busted pipe. The only problem then was having him remember to send you a bill.

"I suppose you heard about Albert Vice?" I said to Robby.

Robby took a long pull on his beer and said nothing.

"I take it that's a yes."

Robby turned to me. His eyes were red and glazed, and he didn't seem to know quite what to do with his hands. He was a lot drunker than I had seen him in quite a while.

"I told them the shit was going to hit the fan now. I told anybody that would listen," he said. "Now that Bobby was back in town."

"You mean Robby, don't you?" I said, thinking that he was talking about himself and had slurred his name.

He glared at me for a moment, then said, "I know my own name, Garth. I'm not that far gone."

"Then who is Bobby?"

He glanced around the barroom to see where Hiram was. "Guy I used to know."

"And you say he's back in town?"

"I thought I said that."

"Where did you see him?"

He hesitated before answering, as if not sure whether to tell me. "My place. A few weeks back. He came in and stood beside my bed, not saying a word, just standing there. Scared the shit out of me." He reached for his glass, but whether it was bad aim, or because of the subject of our conversation, he knocked it over; it rolled across the bar, fell, and broke on the floor.

Hiram appeared with broom and dustpan, but Robby waved him away. "I'm talking to my friend, Garth here. You can take care of that later." Robby reached into his pocket and slapped a five dollar bill on the bar. "Here, that should cover the damage."

"How did you know it was Bobby?" I said.

Hiram left the broom leaning against the bar and the dustpan on a stool and went back into the kitchen.

"He told me it was. I said Bobby, is that you? He said yes."

"Then what happened?"

"I got the hell out of there. Walked all the way up here and spent the rest of the night in my truck."

"Leaving Bobby inside? Was he there when you got back?"

Robby reached over and helped himself to my Leinenkugel's. "No. I went back the next morning, but the place was empty."

"Have you seen him again?"

His look was evasive. "Not that I can say for sure."

"Then you *have* seen him?"

He hesitated, as he weighed his words. "Not in broad daylight, if that's what you mean."

"At night, then?"

"Maybe. I said I'm not sure."

"Robby, as much as it pains me to say this, were you drunk the first time you saw him?"

"Drunk as a skunk, but I know what I saw."

"Describe Bobby to me."

Robby had assumed The Thinker's pose and appeared to be doing his best to recall Bobby when the north door of the barroom opened and Ned Cleaver and Larry Sharp came in, closely followed by Dennis Hall and Kristina Vice. The steely somber look on all their faces said that this was the beginning of a long wake.

Seeing them, Robby quickly drained the rest of my beer, then slammed the glass down on the bar. "There's the asshole chief himself." Robby said loudly to Ned Cleaver, "I told you, you'd better watch out."

Ned Cleaver just stared at him with those flat calm eyes of his, then took a seat in the same booth where he and the others had been sitting yesterday and which was always reserved for them following a softball game. Larry Sharp, however, took exception to Robby's remark and came over to the bar where we sat.

"You'd better watch your mouth, little man," Larry said, poking a finger in Robby's chest. "We're not in any mood to listen to your shit."

Robby lifted my glass off the bar and dropped it at Larry's feet; glass splattered everywhere. "And you, big man, had better watch your back," Robby said, as he slid from the stool onto the glass. "He'll be coming for you next. And you, and you," he pointed to Dennis Hall and Kristina Vice in turn. "He's here to welcome each and every one of us to hell."

Then, with as much dignity as he could muster, Robby Rumaley walked out of the barroom, leaving a deadly silence in his wake. Hiram picked up the broom and dustpan and began to sweep up the glass. Then some of the regulars began to filter in, and unaware of what had gone before, began to talk among themselves. But even they, whether out of respect for Kristina Vice and company, or their own feelings for Albert Vice, were a lot quieter than usual, giving the place the look and feel of a mortuary. All we needed now was the sweet smell of roses, and a quarter's worth of "Rock of Ages" on the juke box.

"Where are you headed, Garth?" Hiram asked, as I downed my last shrimp and slid from my stool. My refill of Leinenkugel's, compliments of the house, sat half drunk on the bar.

"Home. To try to cheer myself up."

"Things will pick up once Kristina and the others leave."

I glanced over at Kristina Vice and the three men at her booth. Out of all of them, Dennis Hall seemed to be taking Albert's death the hardest, as he sat there walleyed, neither drinking his beer nor joining in the conversation going on around him.

"I'm not sure I want to wait that long," I said.

"Can't blame you none, I suppose."

"Hiram, you have any idea what's got into Robby?"

When he didn't answer right away, I saw why. Larry Sharp was staring at us.

"Ask me some other time, Garth," Hiram said, moving on down the bar to the cash register.

I followed him there, then said, "What about someone named Bobby? Have you ever heard Robby mention him before?"

"A time or two. Why?" Hiram said, still keeping an eye on Larry Sharp, who was still keeping an eye on us.

"Robby seems afraid of him."

"He is."

"Do you know why?"

"No. But the way he keeps bringing it up, I figure there must be something to it. Robby only brings up the big stuff when he's on a tear."

"As he was tonight?"

"You saw and heard for yourself. What do you think?"

Even without ESP, I could still feel Larry Sharp's eyes in my back. "I think it's time I left."

"I think that might be wise—for both our sakes."

At home I expected to find the house dark and Daisy my only company. Instead, lights were on in both the kitchen and the living room, and Ruth sat at the kitchen table, drinking a bottle of Miller High Life and eating the last few kernels of what had been a bowl of popcorn. The latest issue of *National Geographic* was open on the table in front of her, but she didn't appear to be reading it.

"It's about time you got home," she said.

"Good evening to you, too." I sat down across from her.

She closed the magazine, set it to one side, then set the now empty popcorn bowl on top of it. "Why didn't you tell me Albert Vice was missing?" she said.

"I would have, if you'd been here when I was. Except,

as I recall, you were working at the shelter."

"It's for a good cause, Garth."

"I won't deny that."

"Then what do you have against it?"

"Nothing. If it didn't take up all of your time, or take Abby's house."

"So that's it. You're jealous."

"I hadn't thought of it in those terms, but you might be right."

"Well, you'd better get used to it. That's all I can say."

She got up and rinsed out her beer bottle under the faucet and set it upside down on the drain board. She rinsed out everything, dog food cans included, saying that it helped keep cockroaches away. It must have worked because I never saw any cockroaches around.

"Ruth, does the name Bobby mean anything to you?"

"In regard to what?"

"Robby Rumaley."

"No. I can't say it does."

"Then can you tell me anything that Robby might have against Ned Cleaver, Dennis Hall, and Larry Sharp? Ned Cleaver and Larry Sharp in particular."

She thought it over. "Larry Sharp, I have no idea. Ned Cleaver, either, though I do know they were in the Boy Scouts together."

"How do you know that?"

"I was their den mother."

Ruth, a den mother? I supposed stranger things had happened. "Was there any friction between them then?"

"None that I could see. Ned was a natural leader and Robby was a natural follower. Whatever Ned said, Robby did, no questions asked." She sat back down at the table.

She was right about Ned Cleaver being a natural leader. Even though I'd never heard him raise his voice—in anger or anything else, he seemed to command respect, even obedience, by his presence alone. Once, while we were all working a fish fry together, Albert Vice and Dennis Hall were fooling around and accidentally dropped a case of Cokes on Ned's foot, breaking his big toe. All Ned said was, "God damn it, boys, why don't you watch what you're doing," then went back to frying fish. But judging by the look of chagrin on Albert's and Dennis's faces, you'd have thought that they had committed a capital crime.

"Ned was in Vietnam, right?"

"As was Robby. They each served two tours of duty there. Why?"

"What rank? Ned, I mean?"

"I think he was a staff sergeant like Robert. I repeat, why?"

Ruth's son, Staff Sergeant Robert Krammes, had been killed in Vietnam.

"No reason, I guess." Except for the ghost squad that I heard patrolling the Lost 1600 Saturday night. But that squad seemed lost and leaderless.

"What are you thinking, Garth?"

"I'm wondering how Cecil Hardwick is going to handle all of this."

"You don't plan on helping him?"

"Not if I can help it."

Her reaction was not what I expected. "You plan to hang him out to dry? I thought I knew you better than that."

Blame it on the evening I'd had, but that pissed me off. "While you're thinking, think about this, Ruth. Did all the interference that I ran for Clarkie help him any? Did you ever once say to me that it did?"

"Cecil Hardwick is not Harold Clark."

"No, but he's now the law in Oakalla whether he likes it or not. And until he proves otherwise, I'm going to give him every benefit of the doubt. Just like I didn't do with Wayne Jacoby."

"With good reason, it turned out."

"But that wasn't the tune you sang at the time. You can't have it both ways, Ruth. Neither of us can."

She rose slowly from the table. She looked as weary as I felt. "Suit yourself," she said with a shrug. "I'm going to bed."

"Does Daisy need to go out again?"

"No. I took care of that earlier."

"I'm tired, Ruth," I said, wanting her to understand. "I'm tired of carrying the ball where Oakalla is concerned. If Cecil Hardwick can do his job half as well as Rupert did, it'll make my life a whole lot easier."

Ruth stopped at the stairway to rest against the newel post. "We both keep saying that, but have you ever thought, Garth, that maybe life's not supposed to be easy, no matter how much we think it ought to be. I've never heard a single person who had to make a long journey to get where he wanted to go say that it was a cakewalk. It might be simple to some people, who have a plan all along and stick to it come hell or high water. Or those who wear blinders, or those who are either too dumb or too rich to be affected by it all. But easy? Even people who have more money than they can count have children who could care less about them or their money, and people with all the time in the world on their hands seem to search their whole lives for ways to spend it. So maybe we're the lucky ones, Garth. Maybe by being hard, life makes us feel it more, appreciate what we have when we get it and mourn extra hard when we lose it, and keeps us from passing judgment on somebody else's bad luck."

"And maybe life's a crock, too. Have you ever thought of that, Ruth?"

"More times than you have."

She continued on up the stairs to bed. Two hours later, after I had exorcised all the arguments for my getting involved in Albert Vice's death, I did the same.

CHAPTER

The next morning Ruth and I ate breakfast in silence. She seemed disturbed, deep in thought, and that whatever was bothering her had little to do with our discussion the night before. I wondered if she'd had another bad dream?

The phone rang. Since Ruth made no move in its direction, I answered it.

"Garth, this is Ben Bryan. You mind stopping by here on your way to work." It wasn't a question.

"If it has to do with Albert Vice, I'm not interested."

"Just stop by here. You can decide then if you're interested."

"Who was that?" Ruth said, not really caring.

"Ben Bryan. He wants me to stop by on my way to work."

She picked at her French toast, then angrily shoved it aside. "Are you going to?"

"I might, just to keep him happy. Are you okay, Ruth?"

Though she seemed to look at me, her eyes were still turned inward. "I think you might be right. I've been putting in too many hours at the shelter."

"I thought maybe you had another bad dream."

She didn't deny it, which meant that she probably had. "You'd better get going. You know how your days run."

I got the message. She needed some time alone to work things out.

"Will you be here for supper?" I said.

"Don't count on it."

"Rome wasn't built in a day."

"If they had the crew they sent us, they'd still be building it."

"Slow are they?"

"Grandma Moses looks like Jesse Owens compared to them."

"Hang in there."

"You do the same."

I should have worn a jacket. That became obvious my first few steps out the door when the cold reached out and slapped my bare arms, raising goose bumps. Though I had failed to check our thermometer that morning, deceived as I was by the bright sunshine and blue sky, it had to be in the low-to-mid-forties. Brisk by some in Oakalla's standards. Cold by mine.

Though I loved Wisconsin and its weather, I'd never had quite the thickness of skin that its natives had. Ashland to me was the Arctic. I couldn't imagine a colder place, unless it was Duluth-Superior. That was why I had to laugh when those in northern Minnesota talked about

going South for the winter, meaning Duluth. In mid-May
the ice was sometimes still on some of the Boundary
Water lakes up there. Not for me thanks. I'd take a morning in the mid-forties any day, and bitch about being cold.

Ben Bryan lived on the east edge of Oakalla in a large
two-story white frame house that had been a farmhouse
not all that long ago—before its barn burned down and
the town crept up around it. Ben's garden was on the east
side of the house between his well and Merle Perkins'
alfalfa field-soon-to-be-subdivision, if Wilmer Wiemer got
his way about it. A large sugar maple grew on the northwest side of the house and shaded Ben's front porch
throughout most of the spring and all of the summer. A
few yards east of the sugar maple grew an equally large
beech tree, whose top had intertwined with that of the
maple, giving them the appearance of lovers, leaning
against each other for support. Ben's new gold Oldsmobile
Eighty-Eight sat in his garage along Park Street at the end
of a row of silver maples. His 1948 purple Mercury convertible was safely hidden away in Merle Perkins' barn.

I climbed the steps to Ben's front porch and
knocked on his door. While I waited for him to answer, I
heard a wren giving Ben's grey tomcat what for, as it
hopped about on the lower limbs of a crabapple tree
next to the garden. The cat, oblivious to all of the
racket, sat there licking himself, until he finally finished
his business and trotted off.

Ben opened the front door just wide enough to say,
"Come around back. Faye's still asleep." Faye was Ben's
wife of forty years.

I went around back where Ben was already waiting
for me at his basement door. "Come on in. This won't
take long."

I knew where we were headed and I didn't want to go
there. Even Abby and Doc, for all of their charm, had a

hard time getting me inside a morgue. Part of my problem was my claustrophobia. The rest of it was I didn't like basements, let alone small, smelly, thick-walled rooms within them. Especially not those that contained a corpse, and/or various body parts.

"I'll pass," I said, stopping at the door of the morgue.

"Like hell you will." He dragged me inside. "This is important."

Albert Vice lay on his back atop a stainless steel table. His blond hair looked lighter than it had in life, his skin whiter. He was bloated from his stay in Hidden Quarry, but not so badly that I didn't recognize him. *What an arm*, I thought. *What a waste.*

"You see those puncture marks?" Ben said. "I thought at first they were bullet holes."

Albert was naked. The puncture marks that Ben was referring to were several evenly spaced ugly black welts on Albert's body. They ran from his biceps down his chest into his groin, and were about the size of a quarter in diameter.

"I see them. You mind if we go outside now." My head had started to spin. The walls of the morgue were closing in around me, making it hard to breathe.

"I thought Clarkie was the only one around here with a weak stomach."

"You thought wrong."

We went outside. I walked around for a while in Ben's yard, trying to keep my breakfast down. It would have been easier in the short run to have vomited and gotten it over with, but that was too much like giving up.

"You going to be okay, Garth?" Ben said.

"Just give me another minute or so."

What I didn't tell Ben was that the instant that I looked down at Albert Vice and saw the puncture marks, I began to hear his screams in the night. They had to be

Albert's. There was no other explanation for them. But what was he doing, running around in the Lost 1600 in the dark?

I sat down in the grass underneath one of Ben's silver maples. He joined me there. Overhead a robin, who had been busy feathering her nest, gave us a scolding, then flew off in the direction of the garden.

"You want to hazard a guess about what I found inside those puncture wounds?" Ben said.

"Wood fragments," I said without hesitation.

At a loss for words, he just stared at me.

"I was in Vietnam for a while as a correspondent. I saw a couple guys step on punji sticks, and another guy fall and run one through his hand. But I never saw anything like what happened to Albert. They were supposed to injure you and take you out of commission. Not kill you."

"That was going to be my next question." Ben said, as he pulled up a weed and tossed it out into Park Street. "If you had any idea what caused those wounds."

"Now you know." I rose and brushed my jeans off. It was cold sitting there in the shadow of the house.

"You mind if I send Cecil Hardwick over to talk to you later?" Ben said.

"What can I tell him that I haven't told you?"

Ben rose to face me. His look said not to take him for a fool. "Why it upsets you so. We've looked at bodies before, Garth, some in worse shape than this. None of them had quite this effect on you."

"Send him over, then," I said. "I'll try to get some of my own work done in the meantime."

"Life's a thankless business, Garth. Any parent or teacher can tell you that."

"That's not it, Ben."

"Then what is the problem?"

"It's Cecil's bad bull. I think he's about to take us all for a ride." I got as far as Park Street where I stopped and said, "For the record, Ben, which of those punctures was it that killed Albert?"

"None, and all of them. He bled to death."

"Just thought I'd ask."

I went down Park Street as Ben headed slowly for the house. The robin, I assumed, returned to her nest.

Cecil Hardwick was already there waiting for me when I got to the *Oakalla Reporter*. Standing solemn and erect, with his hat, boots, uniform, and tinted sunglasses there beside his brown Chevy Impala squad car—now on loan from the county—he almost looked the part of a lawman. But it's hard to be a real lawman without a gun. Otherwise, real criminals don't seem to take you seriously.

"You didn't waste any time," I said to Cecil.

"When I called Ben Bryan, he said to stop by here before I went anywhere else."

Cecil took off his sunglasses. His eyes were the feckless blue of a milk-water sky. He looked better with his sunglasses on.

"Ben tell you about Albert Vice?" I said.

"He said something about punji sticks, whatever they are."

"They are a sharpened bamboo stick, hidden in the ground and designed to go right through your Army issue boots, if you have the misfortune to step on one. They were made popular by the Viet Cong."

"They wouldn't have worked in Korea," Cecil said. "The ground was too damn hard to waste your time on something like that."

"Ruth said you were over there. When was that?"

Cecil lit a cigarette. We watched its smoke drift slowly to the southeast. "Right after the war. I was one of the peace keepers."

"As you are now."

"So they tell me."

The sun had finally topped the trees along Berry Street. Its rays were warm, and somehow reassuring.

"Now you think that those screams you heard came from Albert Vice?" Cecil said.

"Yes."

Cecil put his sunglasses back on. It was a relief to both of us. "You have any idea what Albert might have been doing there in the Lost 1600 on a Saturday night?" Cecil said.

"Not a clue. What about you?"

"Not so far. Nobody seems too anxious to talk about it."

"You tried the cheese plant?"

"I thought I'd head there next."

I nodded my approval. At least he had good instincts. "Where after that?" I said.

"That depends on what happens at the cheese plant."

"You talk to Kristina Vice yet?"

"I tried. She said that she was out of town all week-end, so she has no idea what Albert was up to. She's a tough nut, Garth." Cecil took a drag on his cigarette. "I don't know quite what to make of her."

"That makes two of us. What about Dennis Hall?"

Cecil and I watched Larry Sharp drive by in his new extended cab silver-and-maroon Chevy pickup on his way to the cheese plant. "I haven't had the chance to talk to him alone," Cecil said, keeping a close eye on Larry Sharp's pickup all the way up Gas Line Road. "His bud-dies always seem to be around."

"I'd work on him, if I were you. He's their weak link, if there is one."

"Weak link to what, Garth? I thought you said you had no idea what Albert was doing in the Lost 1600."

"I don't. But somebody who was with him surely does. Albert wasn't the kind of guy to go off on his own."

Cecil nodded as if that made sense to him. "Any other words of advice before I go?" he said, as he took a last drag on his cigarette and dropped it in the gravel at his feet.

"Do you own a gun?"

"A rifle and a couple shotguns. No handguns."

"Then I'd invest in one if I were you."

Cecil shook his head no. "Then I might have to use it."

"It was just a suggestion."

"Why? You don't carry a gun."

"I'm not the law in Oakalla either."

"Some might argue otherwise."

"To no avail," I said, starting for the long low concrete block building that housed the *Oakalla Reporter*.

"Garth?" Cecil said. "Thanks."

I stopped and turned back to him. "I haven't done you any favors, Cecil. You're heading into unknown territory, so watch your step."

"If you'll watch my back?"

I went inside without answering him. In my humble opinion, he'd do a whole lot better with a gun at his side than with me at his back.

CHAPTER 10

It was a Tuesday morning well spent. I spent the most of it laying out that week's edition of the *Oakalla Reporter* and doing my usual juggling act as to where everything should go. My biggest problem was the lead story—Albert Vice's death. I didn't know how many columns to allow for it, because I had no idea how much I would know about it come Thursday midnight. So I gave it a half column on the premise that nothing would be resolved by then. I was betting against Cecil Hardwick and, to a lesser extent, myself, but knowing Oakalla and its people as I did, I figured it was a pretty safe bet.

The rest of my time was spent calling my sources, to soothe any ruffled feelings for giving them short shrift yesterday. Sadie Jenkins had already threatened to take her business elsewhere if I didn't start printing her "news" in more detail. I had told her I'd try, but made no promises. I mean, how many of us, even in Oakalla, really cared who cleaned up what after the Community Club dinner at Saint Luke's Lutheran Church, or who took the potato peels home and fed them to her redworms without asking anyone's permission. After all, Sadie, it couldn't have been the baked steak.

After lunch at the Corner Bar and Grill, I went home to an empty house. I had hoped to see Ruth's unsmiling face there, but apparently she was at the shelter. Nor had I seen Robby Rumaley at the Corner Bar and Grill, which figured because I wanted to talk to him about yesterday. Robby was almost always in there when I was. I wondered if Ruth's tireless efforts on behalf of the shelter might have a little something to do with her bad dreams. Was working hard her way of taking her mind off them? I wondered if Robby Rumaley's absence from the Corner Bar and Grill was just a coincidence, or if he was avoiding me, or someone else. As I climbed into Jessie, I wondered if she would start.

The drive to Camp Collier took me out Madison Road, then left on County Road B two miles southeast of town, then right on County Road M, which began to dip and wind, as the woods thickened and the hills got taller and longer. The day, pleasantly warm in the sunlight, grew noticeably cooler in the shadow of the woods. The surrounding trees were mostly hardwoods—oak, ash, and maple, whose new spring leaves ran from kelly green to a bright, almost fluorescent yellow. Within them were pine and spruce thickets, rusted at the edges after a hard winter, but whose dark green would become even darker as the year wore on.

Red headed and pileated woodpeckers, jays, crows, grouse, finches, hawks, and titmice lived in those woods, or their adjacent meadows—songbirds, game birds, and birds of prey, along with coon, squirrel, fox, deer, mink, otter, badger, beaver, and if one were to believe Lonny Priest and Darrell Schoolcraft, a bobcat or two. Yet, just driving past the woods, eighty-acres deep on either side of the road, you wouldn't have any idea at all what was in there—any more than you would a stream by paddling a canoe across its surface. To really get to know a woods you had to become one with it. Some hunters, birdwatchers, biologists, and photographers had the knack. The rest of us had to depend on Walt Disney; or writers like John Muir, Aldo Leopold, and Sigurd Olson; or if we were really lucky, our own childhood memories.

Preston Kurtz's shiny black GMC pickup with its marshmallow white camper shell was still parked in the vicinity of where I'd last seen it, but he was nowhere in sight. I parked Jessie beside the pickup and got out just in time to see a wild turkey sail off into the woods. That made me feel a measure of reassurance. He wouldn't be about with human company.

The mess hall of what had been Camp Collier was a low concrete building much on the order of the one that housed the *Oakalla Reporter*, except that it was not nearly as long, and to my knowledge had never been whitewashed, so that its blocks had gone from grey to brown over the years, making it seem more a part of a woods than a campground. Its flat asphalt roof had never been designed to withstand the snows of a Wisconsin winter, so it wasn't surprising to see that it sagged in most places, and had broken completely through in others. Its painted red door gave grudgingly, and once inside, I could feel the breeze, still in the northwest, coming through a broken window and making it seem cooler inside than out.

Once the Boy Scouts left for good, the mess hall had been gutted of everything but its cabinets and used for everything from coon hunts to high school pot parties. A couple enterprising souls had even dragged a mattress inside for whatever their reasons, but it had gotten ruined when the roof gave way above it and was now a stinking soggy mess of stuffing. No help here, I discovered, and went outside again. Even if it had remained as I remembered it, those memories were too dim to depend on for any answers.

The two story pine sheds that had once served as army barracks and then as cabins when the Boy Scouts took over were staggered up the hill behind the mess hall. Ten of them in all, most of them had gone the way of the mess hall and the second smaller concrete building that we euphemistically called the bathhouse—even though its toilets and urinals stunk to high heaven and its showers ran cold, so we were never in there long enough to take a bath.

Cabin 10, however, the smallest of all of the cabins and the highest on the hill, had survived intact. Sheltered by a magnificent stand of Norway pines that had kept the rest of the surrounding woods away from it, Cabin 10 still had its roof, both windows, and its front, and only, door.

Dick Davis and I had stayed in Cabin 10, when as Cub Scouts we attended a week-long rendezvous at Camp Collier. We had slept in bunks on the second floor along with the rest of our troop. We spent most of our days hiding from our leaders in the nearby woods and most of our nights raiding the nearby cabins. At least that's how I remembered it. We also did some canoeing on Owl Creek, sat around the campfire telling ghost stories and scaring the bejeebers out of ourselves, and whiled away more than a few hours wishing there were some Brownies about.

I remembered that I wasn't quite ready to go home when the time came, but glad to get home once I got there.

The thing that I had missed most, besides Grandmother Ryland and the farm themselves, was privacy. Not that I required great drafts of it then, as I seemed to now, but it was still nice to be alone sometimes, or to have that choice.

The front door to Cabin 10 swung open without a sound, as if it had been oiled recently. Also, there was a smokey smell inside that none of the others had. It was welcome, yet unsettling, since legend had it, even before the Lost Scout spent his last night here, that Cabin 10 was haunted.

I went immediately to the small pot-bellied iron stove at the back of the cabin and learned that while it had no live coals, its ashes were white and powdery and seemed to be no older than that spring or late winter. But I found nothing else, not even a scrap of food, to indicate that someone had been staying there.

Upstairs, I stopped in amazement when I saw that all of the springs and mattresses were still on the beds, and except for some mouse droppings atop some of the mattresses they seemed none the worse for wear. Then something else caught my eye—a down Army sleeping bag, two of them in fact, rolled up under the eave in the near corner of the loft. After unrolling each and finding an Army mess kit inside, I rolled it back up and was preparing to leave when I felt a cold draft from somewhere that chilled me all over. Running my hand along the eave and then above the staircase, I couldn't find the source of the draft, but when I started down the stairs, it went away. Just as well, because my goosebumps from earlier that morning were back again.

Outside, I went through the stand of pines into the woods behind the cabin where I found an axe, its head buried in the stump of a small poplar, and a lot of wood chips and shavings. Scattered about the small clearing where I'd found the axe were also dozens of small branches that had been severed from larger limbs, which, I assumed, had been cut up and used for firewood. I also found a crude latrine hollowed out of a rotted stump, a garbage pit, and a shovel. Nothing ghostly about these discoveries, but nothing reassuring either.

I left everything as it was and started down the hill toward Owl Creek. I'd gone only a few feet when I hit what I soon determined was someone's trip wire that rattled a tin can hung from a bush behind Cabin 10. Examining the can, I found a couple small stones inside. I reset the trip wire, put the stones back inside the can, the can in the bush, and went on down the hill.

Owl Creek had changed since I last saw it. Sunday's rain had raised it at least a couple feet and made it seem a lot more rabid and muscular than before. The rapids that I had crossed now sprouted plumes, where on Saturday there had been only half submerged rocks baking in the sun. Its deceptively smooth murmur had become a roar. All of which only served to remind me how quickly things could change—and usually not for the better—in the Lost 1600.

The sand beach where I had lain had been swallowed up by the rise in Owl Creek, forcing me into the woods sooner than I would have liked. Being out in the open had its disadvantages if someone was either shooting or throwing hand grenades at you, but that aside, it was a lot easier on the nerves than walking through the woods, wondering if someone was going to step out from behind the next tree and conk you over the head. I found myself stopping and listening every few feet and was rewarded when at last I did catch a glimpse of someone in the woods ahead of me. But he wasn't waiting in ambush. Instead, he was kneeling down, examining something on the ground.

"You lose something?" I said to Preston Kurtz.

He moved a lot faster than I expected for a man pushing sixty. He rolled over and had his howitzer out, cocked, and pointed before I could react.

"You must be part Indian," he said, recognizing me. But I noticed that it was only after he saw that I was unarmed that he stood and holstered his gun.

"Nobody ever accused me of it," I said.

"Then why didn't I hear you coming?"

"Maybe it was the wet ground."

"Yeah. Maybe."

He didn't believe me, but so what? In his Army cap and camouflage greens, without his creel or fly rod in sight, he had his own explaining to do.

"What is it that you were looking at so closely?" I said, slowly starting his way.

As he backed up to give me room, his right hand went automatically to the butt of his revolver, which from the business end had looked even larger than I remembered it. "Take a look yourself," he said. "See if you can figure it out."

I took a look for myself and was sickened by what I saw. At first glance it looked like someone had had a wiener roast, then tried to burn their sticks in the fire. But I knew better. Only a few blackened ends of the punji sticks remained and they had been sharpened to a wicked point, then tempered by fire to nearly the hardness of iron. A couple of them had what appeared to be dried blood on them. I picked them up, planning on taking them back to Oakalla with me.

"I'll take those," Preston Kurtz said.

"I don't think so. They might be evidence."

His flinty blue eyes said he couldn't have cared less. "Evidence of what?"

"A fatality, perhaps a murder."

"On whose authority?" His right hand, I noticed, was

still resting on the butt of his revolver.

I took out my wallet and showed him my Special Deputy Badge. "The Adams County Sheriff's Department."

"You said you ran a newspaper," he said.

"And you said you were a retired political science professor from Wisconsin–Whitewater."

"And I'm not?"

"Not according to them."

"Next time you call, tell them I beg to differ," he said.

"If you insist."

"I insist."

"But that's not all you do, or have done," I said.

Which was exactly the wrong thing to say, as he pulled out his revolver and pointed it at me again. "Explain yourself," he said.

"I think I already have. But just for the record, what is that you're pointing at me? It looks a little big for killing snakes."

"It's a Colt .45," he said. "The one they called the Peacemaker. That's sort of what I do, have done. Now, give me those punji sticks."

"Why? What good are they to you?"

"Let's just say that the people I used to work for might be interested in them."

"There's no *might be* where I'm involved," I said, refusing to give them up. "The Adams County Sheriff's Department is definitely interested in them."

"Might makes right." He cocked the Colt .45. "Give."

I handed them to him. I didn't think I had a choice. The worst part about it was that he didn't even say thank you.

"What now?" I said, sure that I wasn't going to like the answer.

"You go back the way you came. I follow you."

"Then what?"

"That's up to you. You can either make it hard or easy on yourself."

"I'd like to make it easy if at all possible."

He smiled. I'd seen more warmth on the face of the puff adder that once had backed me out of a patch of horseweeds.

"Then do exactly as I say," he said.

On our way back up the hill, I had a lot of time to make a plan for when we got to the top. My problem was that I couldn't see how a plan would be of any help. If he intended to shoot me, he would have by now. Otherwise, why delay it and run the risk of being seen. If he had other designs on me, I'd learn them soon enough, and my perfectly good plan, if it misfired, might get me killed for no reason. So I concentrated on putting one foot in front of the other and tried not to think too hard about anything.

A waste of time, it turned out. Even with a Colt .45 pointed at my back, I couldn't keep the blinders on, or not notice that some of the trees deep in the woods had yet to leaf out. Late bloomers, they should, come fall, hold on to their leaves the longest, but that wasn't always the case. The black walnut tree, a notorious late bloomer, often dropped its leaves first, sometimes as early as August. If I needed reassurance about the ultimate fairness of life, I shouldn't look to nature; or take consolation in the fact that the black walnut wasn't prized for its leaves, or even its nuts, desired though they might be, but its heartwood, which was the most valuable wood in Wisconsin. No, I couldn't count among the blessed something with a price on its head; or anyone, me in particular, who had to take a long uphill walk through a May woods just coming into full flower, all the while wondering if his next step would be his last.

"That's as far as you go," he said when we got to Jessie. "Give me your keys."

"Why? She probably won't start anyway."

He didn't see the humor, but then he didn't know Jessie as I did. "Just give me the keys."

I gave them to him. He gave them a sidearm toss down the hill. I tried to mark them as I used to mark my slice when I still played golf by fastening on the most prominent thing in that direction.

"That wasn't necessary," I said, picking out a large white oak that stretched above the treeline. "I wasn't planning on following you."

That seemed to surprise him. "What were you planning on doing?"

"Going home. Maybe eating some supper."

"That doesn't sound like you."

He'd piqued my interest. "How do you know what I'm supposed to sound like?"

He nodded at his pickup. "I've got a computer on board."

"And I'm in your files?"

"Let's just say that someone out there has heard of you. Now, turn around and face me."

I reluctantly did so, knowing that I'd probably never find my mark again. Preston Kurtz, however, seemed to find the whole scenario amusing.

"Civilians," he said with a smirk. "It's just another word for amateur."

"He who laughs last . . ."

"I'm worried."

"You should be."

"Forget it, Ryland. If you do decide to come after me, I'll turn you every way but loose. Besides, by this time tomorrow I'll be five hundred miles away from here."

"Then you have nothing to worry about."

He pointed the Colt .45 at my chest. "Turn slowly around again, and this time do a full circle. I'll tell you when to stop."

So much for repartee when the other guy is holding a gun. I'd done about three full circles when I heard his pickup start. If I hadn't been so dizzy, I would've tried to have gotten his license number.

CHAPTER 11

I made it home by six, just in time to see Ruth leaving in her Volkswagen. She'd left me another note.

Garth,

There's a tuna casserole in the oven. All you have to do is warm it up. I took Daisy for a walk, so all you'll need to do is take her out again before bedtime. I don't know when I'll be home, but don't count on seeing me this evening.

Ruth

Good. That was exactly what I wanted to hear after crawling around on my hands and knees in the wet leaves for two hours before I found my keys. Ruth was gone for the night, and there was tuna casserole in the oven.

I called Clarkie at his apartment in Madison and was relieved to find him there. Otherwise, I might have gone out looking for Preston Kurtz myself.

"Clarkie, I need a favor," I said.

"Sure, Garth. What is it?"

Just once I wished he'd tell me to go to hell. Then I wouldn't have to feel so guilty about asking him for favors all of the time.

"There's a man named Preston Kurtz that I need some information on. He's about sixty years old, stands about five-ten or eleven, and weighs about one-sixty, with blue eyes and short brown hair graying at the temples. I'm guessing that he has a military background and maybe has done some government work—FBI or CIA, something like that.

I could hear Clarkie putting all of this information down on his computer. "Anything else I should know about him?"

"He claims he taught political science at the University of Wisconsin–Whitewater, but I called over there and they'd never heard of him."

"Might be a place to start," he said.

"Whatever you think best, Clarkie. You're the expert."

"I wish I could believe you meant that."

"Believe it. It's true."

There was an awkward pause. Clarkie and I had a lot of them whenever we talked. I sometimes felt like his too critical father, and he often acted like the son who could never quite measure up. Maybe one day we'd get back to where we were when Rupert Roberts was still sheriff and Clarkie was his deputy. And maybe those days, like Clarkie's time in Oakalla, were gone forever.

"You mind me asking why you're interested in this

Preston Kurtz?"

"He and I had a run-in today out at the Lost 1600. You might remember it as Camp Collier. I'd kind of like to know what angle he's playing."

"What sort of run-in?"

I debated on whether to tell him or not, since I didn't want the information to get out and involve other people before I knew what was going on. But since Clarkie might be putting himself in jeopardy, he had a right to know.

"He pulled a gun on me, Clarkie. A Colt .45 to be exact."

"He have a reason?"

"We both wanted the same punji sticks."

"What was that, Garth?"

"It's a long story, Clarkie. Just see what you can find out about him."

"I'll get right on it."

Damn, I wished he wouldn't say that so cheerfully. "Tomorrow will be soon enough."

"Tomorrow I'll be in Rochester, Minnesota, writing a new program for their police department. I'll probably be doing a lot of that in the next couple years."

"What's the occasion?"

"The year 2000 is coming up."

I had to think about that for a moment, then realized that all the computers in the world were supposed to go on the blink then. "When do you plan on being home again?" I said.

"Not before Sunday at the earliest. I'll probably be in Rochester through Friday. Then I'm going on up to Saint Paul to see my sister and her family."

Clarkie had a sister? I'd always thought of him as an only child, the way a lot of people thought of me. I guessed some of us didn't talk about our families much.

"Well, give me a call tonight when you learn something," I said.

"It might be late. I need to pack and get something to eat first."

"I'll be up. And Clarkie? Thanks."

"What are friends for," he said with a shrug in his voice.

After we'd hung up, I glanced at Ruth's note again. Tuna casserole. I hadn't misread it after all. The only thing worse would have been Spam salad. Or maybe liver and onions.

But I warmed it up and ate it anyway. I was tired of eating out and sitting on a bar stool. After my divorce, I'd done enough of that to last a lifetime.

I took a walk after supper, ending up at the Corner Bar and Grill. It was another cool evening, cooler once the sun dropped below the horizon. Yet the people of Oakalla didn't seem to mind as they pruned bushes and planted flowers and worked in their gardens right up until dark. I liked to see them hard at it, even though I didn't care a whit for gardening or yard work myself. It was reassuring for someone like me, who had grown up with back yards and gardens, alleys and neighborhoods, to know that while I was no longer part of the cycle, it still went on. And that small town America, for all of its problems, was still alive and well.

One glance around the barroom of the Corner Bar and Grill told me that Robby Rumaley wasn't there, and nearly all of the other regulars were. They were all clustered at the north end of the bar, but had left Robby's stool open in case he made an appearance. I took the stool at the far south end of the bar and ordered an Old Milwaukee. No sense in wasting a Leinenkugel's on someone who wasn't thirsty.

"Robby been in?" I said to Hiram, when he brought me my beer.

"I haven't seen him all evening."

"What time did you come in?"

"A little after four."

"Plenty of time for him to get here."

"That's what I thought," Hiram said.

We watched as Kristina Vice got up from the far booth and began pouring quarters into the juke box. She was wearing tight-as-they-come jeans, a long-sleeve light blue silk shirt that she hadn't bothered to tuck in, and shiny black cowboy boots that matched her shiny black hair that was styled in a French braid and hung to the middle of her back. She wore no makeup that I could see and had been sitting alone in the booth.

"Where are her buddies?" I said to Hiram.

"I don't know. I haven't seen them. She came in about six and has been drinking non-stop ever since."

I continued to watch Kristina Vice feed quarters into the juke box, as did every other male in the place. Her jeans, I noted, made a sharp bend where her shirttail ended and her butt began.

Thinking thoughts I knew I shouldn't, I made myself turn back to Hiram. "You said last night you might have some light to shed on the subject of Albert Vice and company," I said. "I wondered if I might steer Cecil Hardwick your way?"

Hiram didn't say anything. I wondered why until Kristina Vice put both hands on my shoulders. "Want to dance?" she said.

I listened to what was playing on the juke box. "Your Cheatin' Heart." How did she know?

"Why not," I said.

There was no dance floor at the Corner Bar and Grill, but there was some room between the bar and the booths where couples sometimes danced—usually very late on a Friday or a Saturday night. But then Kristina vice and I didn't need a whole lot of room. Stuck together like two postage stamps, we mainly swayed back and forth in time to the music. It didn't take me long to figure out that I was holding a whole lot of woman, who was a lot softer cheek to cheek than I expected. Sing it, Hank. A third and a fourth verse if you have one.

"Thank you," she said when the song ended.

"You're welcome."

We were still holding on to each other. "The Dance" by Garth Brooks was the next song up. It seemed a shame to waste it.

But halfway through it, Kristina Vice broke down and started to sob. It was all that I could do to hold her up until I could get her back to her booth.

"You going to be okay?" I said a couple minutes later after she had composed herself.

"Okay."

"Then I'll go finish my beer."

"Garth?" she said, as I started to turn away. "This doesn't mean anything."

"I know that."

Her eyes, shiny now with tears, were that deep purple-black at the base of a thunderhead. "No, you don't. We're enemies from now on."

"Until when?"

"Until I decide differently."

I shrugged, not understanding any of this. "If you say so."

"I do. And Garth?" She stopped me again. "I love your body. And it's not just the booze talking."

"Then we're even," I said, before finally making my way back to the bar again.

"You have a fan handy?" I said to Hiram, who was waiting for me.

"You look like you need one."

"Along with a cold shower. Where were we anyway?"

"You wanted to send Cecil Hardwick my way. But I'd rather talk to you."

"I'd rather you talk to Cecil. So that he doesn't get it second hand."

"Why? You out of the detective business now?" If so, it wasn't welcome news to him.

"I was never in the detective business, Hiram. For Oakalla's sake, I was just trying to help out where I could."

"And you aren't any longer?"

"Not officially. Not unless Cecil stubs his toe."

"How long do you figure he'll go before that happens?"

"A long time, I'm hoping."

"I'll give him a day."

"What do you know that I don't?"

Hiram raised his brows, then lowered them again. "I figure that's between Cecil Hardwick and me, seeing that you're out of it."

He drew a pitcher of beer and delivered it to the other end of the bar, where he stayed, deliberately keeping his distance from me. I finished my Old Milwaukee and waited in vain for Robby Rumaley to show up. When I left, Vince Gill was singing "Go Rest High on That Mountain," the song about his late brother, and Kristina Vice was slumped over the table, crying.

CHAPTER

The first thing I did when I got home was to put Daisy on her leash and walk her around the block. The stars were out in abundance, and the moon, now on the wax, was a bright white sliver in the western sky. I loved to look at the stars, loved to imagine what all was out there. The far side of the universe? If there was a life beyond this one and I was lucky enough to get my ticket punched, that was the first place I wanted to go.

Back inside the house, I put Daisy in the basement and made a phone call to New Mexico. Once, I could have dialed Diana in my sleep. Tonight, I had to look up her number and keep it in front of me as I dialed.

"Hello?" she said after the fourth ring.

"Diana, it's Garth. Do you have time for a couple quick

questions?"

"I guess so." Though she was a long way from sure.

"Do you have company?" Meaning old Gerald, or whatever his name was. The rancher.

"Yes." She sounded tentative. I could guess the rest.

"Am I interrupting something?"

"As a matter of fact."

It shouldn't have still hurt, but it did. "I can always call back later."

"I'm not sure that will be a good time either," she said.

"Ask him what his secret is."

"You don't need to ask anybody about anything," she said, sounding more like herself. "And what do you want to know? Gerald just went into the kitchen to fix himself a nightcap."

What *did* I want to know? With Gerald there, it was hard to keep my mind on business.

"For starters, was Fran ever in the Boy Scouts and did he ever spend any time at Camp Collier?"

"Yes, to answer both your questions. Our first summer together, he had to go off to camp for a week. It nearly broke my heart."

"And you were?"

"Twelve. Fran was fourteen, going on fifteen."

"July 8, right?"

"Right. That was his birthday."

I did some calculating in my head. If Fran was fourteen, that would have put him there in 1959. "Did Fran ever mention the Lost Scout to you?"

"No. But as you know, there were a lot of things that Fran never mentioned to me."

"Have you heard of him?"

She laughed. I'd always loved her laugh. It was evil itself. "Of course. There's hardly any of us baby boomers in Oakalla who haven't. It's our one claim to fame."

"Then there might be some truth to it?"

"None that I know of. But it still makes a great story, doesn't it?"

"Yeah, a great story."

"What got you interested in it?" she said.

"You did, as a matter of fact. Hours after I went to sort through Fran's stuff, somebody broke in there and made a mess of things. . . ."

"How big of a mess?" she interrupted. "I'm not sure I want to hear the rest of this."

"Nothing that couldn't be fixed."

"Is that really true or are you just saying that to make me feel better?"

"No, it's true."

She sighed in relief. "So what does that have to do with me?"

"I'm not sure what it has to do with you, if anything. But I'd been out to Camp Collier earlier that day; then that night somebody comes along and makes a mess of Fran's things; then the next morning Ruth tells me that she's been having bad dreams about the Lost Scout. I'm just covering all the bases, trying to make some sense out of it."

She laughed with the certainty of someone who knew me well. "Garth, what have you gotten yourself into now?"

"I'm not really sure. But it's Ruth, not me, that I'm worried about."

"Why? She's had psychic dreams before."

"And where did those lead me?"

There was a long pause before she said, "I don't think I've ever thanked her for saving my life. But it's probably too late now."

Way too late, though I didn't tell her that. "But you

can see where we're headed. Not only are the dreams weighing heavily on her, I think she's starting to lose sleep. She went to bed at eight the other night. I can't ever remember when she's done that."

"I'd help if I could, Garth, but I can't think of anything that Fran owned that had even the slightest thing to do with the Lost Scout. And as I said, Fran never mentioned him to me."

"And as you also said, we both know he left a lot of things unsaid."

"Don't we though." I could hear the wind go out of her sails. "Ten years and I'm still not over it. Or you either."

"But you still have Gerald."

"Don't be cruel, Garth. That's my style, not yours."

"If you feel that way, why are you planning on marrying him?"

"Because I don't want to be alone in my old age."

"There are worse things."

"I can't think of any."

"I don't have any answers for you. I never did."

"You had one. And I threw it away. Goodnight, Garth."

She hung up. I held on to the receiver for the longest time before I put it back in its cradle.

The instant I did, the phone rang. "Garth, it's Clarkie. I can't find a thing on Preston Kurtz, at least not the one you described to me. Are you sure that's his right name?"

"I think it is. He didn't hesitate when he told it to me."

"Then we're at the end of the line."

"Maybe his former 'employers', as he called them, have blocked access to his files."

"I don't think so, Garth. There's *nothing* on him. Zip.

I could find out something, even if the files were blocked."

"And if they were blocked, what could you find out then?"

"You might be surprised."

No brag, just fact. Clarkie truly was a computer genius. He was also a cop.

"Well, the next time that I see Preston Kurtz, I'll ask him what his real name is."

"What are the odds of that?"

"Pretty good, I'd say, despite his claims to the contrary."

"Give me a call Sunday if you do learn anything."

"Sure, Clarkie. Have a good trip."

Again, I held on to the receiver after I'd hung up, thinking that I should call him back. A thought had come and gone about Preston Kurtz, but for the life of me, I couldn't recall it.

I waited until eleven for Ruth to come home. When she didn't come home, I started making tracks for bed. I got as far as the stairs when the phone rang.

Clarkie, I hoped, with some information for me. Abby, it turned out.

"I'd about given up on you," she said.

"How so?"

"When I called at six, it was busy. At seven and eight no answer. At nine-thirty it was busy again. So I said I'd give it one more try and call it a day."

It was good to hear her voice, even when she was upset with me, as she was tonight.

"At six I was talking to Clarkie. At seven and eight I was taking a walk and at nine-thirty I was talking to Diana, or maybe Clarkie again."

"Diana, huh?" she said, trying and failing to keep it light. "Business or pleasure? And you'd better tell me it was business."

"It was business. I'm involved in a mess here and thought maybe she could help."

"What sort of mess?"

I told her to the best of my ability what was going on.

"And you're worried about Ruth?"

"Yes. It's after eleven and she's still not home yet."

"She's stayed out late before. You didn't worry about her then."

"That's different. She had a reason to stay out late."

"Fixing up a shelter for abused women is not a reason?" she said in a huff. "Maybe you should come to Detroit and work emergency at Henry Ford for a while."

"What I meant was that whatever work was done at the shelter today has long been over. When I went by there a little after seven, Ruth's Volkswagen was the only car in the drive. She might be there piddling, but she's not working."

"Why didn't you go inside to find out?"

"Because, damn it, Abby, you're not there. We've been over this before."

"So now it's my fault you're in a funk?"

"Yes. Part of it is your fault. I need you around to help keep me on track, and if not you, Ruth. Now, I don't have either one of you."

"Which is why you called Diana, to get on track again? I thought it was Ruth you were worried about."

I looked around for help. Seeing none, I banged myself over the head with the receiver a couple times."

"Garth, are you still there?"

"Still here. I told you why I called Diana, to see if there was any connection between her late husband, Fran, and the Lost Scout. And yes, my main worry is Ruth, but I'm also not at my best either. Getting hit over the head, nearly dying from hypothermia, and then having someone pull a gun on you and throw away your car keys will do that to a person. I don't need to go to Detroit to find abuse. There's plenty to go around here."

"I stand corrected." She could hardly keep from laughing.

"It's not funny, damn it." Though I too had started to smile.

"I know it isn't, and I'm sorry."

"No, you aren't. But I love you anyway."

"I know. It's one of my certainties. One of my very few." She suddenly sounded sad. I wondered why.

"Abby, is there something wrong?" I made the mistake of asking.

"One of the guys I work with asked me out tonight."

Immediately my heart started to thump. "And you said yes?"

"No. I said maybe. I'd have to think about it."

As I thought back to my dance with Kristina Vice earlier that evening, I remembered a line from an old Crosby, Stills, Nash, and Young song. "If you can't be with the one you love, love the one you're with."

"It's hard, isn't it?" I said.

"Damn hard at times. There are days when I'm ready to pack it all in and head back to Oakalla. Other days, I think I shouldn't see you any more because I feel so empty when you leave. That's why I have to think about going out with someone else. At least he'll be here in the morning."

"Yeah, I know the feeling."

"Aren't you ever tempted, too?"

If she only knew. "Yes. But the real temptation is not to try to find someone to take your place, which I'll never do. It's to say the hell with it and take whoever comes along. That's the low road, and I know where it leads."

"Tell me so we'll both know."

"Away from who I am. That's where it leads."

I thought I heard a car in the alley and looked hopefully out the south window to see if it was Ruth. When I didn't see headlights, and Daisy didn't give her welcoming bark, I knew I'd been mistaken.

"I'm not sure I know myself that well," she said. "I pretty much lead with my heart."

"Part of your charm."

"Part of my downfall, too. Leading with one's heart is not unlike leading with one's chin."

"What does your heart tell you about the guy who asked you out?"

"That while cute as hell, he'd be a poor substitute for you."

"Still . . . " I said.

"Still . . . " she said. "You're there and he's here."

At last I saw the lights from Ruth's Volkswagen at the same time that Daisy started barking. "Thank God," I said under my breath.

"What was that, Garth?"

"Nothing. I'm just relieved to see that Ruth's home."

"Well, I better let you go then. I know you're worried about her."

"I'm no less worried about you."

"Don't be. I'm a big girl."

"That's what worries me."

Needing reassurance, I got none when she said, "Whatever happens, happens." Then hung up before I could stop her.

CHAPTER 13

The next morning I lay in bed, listening to a robin singing right outside my window and wondering what the day would bring. Last night Ruth had hurried in the back door and without a word to me, gone straight upstairs to bed. Already this morning, with the sun barely up, she was downstairs, banging around the kitchen. I needed to talk to her, but I wasn't looking forward to it.

"How did you sleep last night?" I asked a half hour later when I finally made it down the stairs and poured myself some coffee. I'd slept about as I expected after my conversation with Abby—which was next to not at all.

"What business is that of yours?" she snapped.

I noticed that she was already dressed and wondered if she was still wearing the same clothes from yesterday. If so, it would be a first—not counting her recent all-night stay in a bowling alley when she had no other choice.

"You're the one who brought it up that you've been having bad dreams," I said.

"Yes, and I'm sorry now that I did." She banged her iron skillet down on the burner. "Sausage and eggs okay with you?"

"Sausage and eggs will be fine," I said.

"Why didn't you put the rest of the tuna casserole in the refrigerator?" she said. "I had to throw it out."

"I forgot about it." Which, in truth, I had.

"I'll bet."

"Scout's honor."

She gave me a look that would have withered a cactus.

"Sorry, Ruth. Slip of the tongue."

She took some sausage links out of the refrigerator and began putting them into the skillet. "What were you doing on the phone all night? I tried to call you several times to tell you not to wait up for me."

"That's the same thing Abby asked. I was talking to Clarkie, then Diana, then Clarkie again. I also walked Daisy and took a walk myself."

"And?" she said, throwing in more and more sausage until the whole package was gone. "Why did you call Clarkie and Diana?"

I told her. When I finished, the sausage was done.

"So what are you going to do about Preston Kurtz?" she said.

"There's not much I can do about him until I can get a line on him."

"And if he never comes back?"

"He'll be back, Ruth. The question is when and where."

"How many eggs do you want?"

"Two."

She broke four brown eggs and began to fry them in the sausage grease. She insisted that brown eggs tasted better than white ones, and while I couldn't taste the difference, I went along to keep peace in the family.

"You making any sense out of all of this yet?" she said.

"No. How about you?"

"No. But then I'm not trying either."

"And if I asked for your help?"

"Don't, Garth. I've got plenty to think about the way it is."

"The Lost Scout, you mean?"

She glared at me. "The shelter, I mean. That's where I was all last night."

"I know. I saw your car there."

That angered her, as she tried to empty the pepper shaker on the eggs. "I don't need a babysitter, Garth."

"I wasn't babysitting. I just happened to go by there on my walk. For old times' sake."

"Give it up, Garth. The way you feel about it, that place is off limits to you now, and probably always will be."

"The outside hasn't changed any. Neither have the smells coming from the yard. I need to touch those things that once mattered to me, Ruth. At least every once in a while."

"It's a waste of time, in my opinion. But suit yourself."

I got up and poured us each a glass of orange juice, then refilled my coffee cup. By then, the eggs were done.

"You going to the funeral this afternoon?" Ruth asked, as she mopped up the last of her egg yolk with a piece of bread. We'd eaten everything but the two pieces of sausage that would go to Daisy, who now was whining at the basement door.

"Whose funeral?"

"Who do you know that's died lately?"

"Albert Vice. But I can't believe that they're having his funeral already."

"Well, they are, though I wouldn't call it a funeral. It's a graveside service out at Fair Haven at two o'clock."

"What about visitation?"

"According to Kristina Vice's wishes, there is none."

"What about Albert's parents, or didn't they have a say in the matter?"

"Albert's parents are dead. They were killed in a car wreck three or four years back. Don't you read your obituaries?"

"Not every one," I admitted. Though, now that she mentioned it, I did recall something about their running into the back of a stalled semi on I-90. "What about Albert's sister, the one in Eau Claire?"

"The last I heard, they weren't on speaking terms."

"That's not what I heard. Cecil Hardwick said that Albert was about to sell half his share in some land to her."

"It's the first I heard about it," Ruth said. "Whatever the case, it can't amount to much. Rumor has it that Albert's father was in hock up to his ears when he died. There are some who even wonder how much of an accident it was."

"What did Albert's father do?"

Ruth's look was one of impatience. That morning she couldn't be bothered.

"He was a land developer, like his obituary said. He liked to brag that while he often played it deuces wild, he always kept an ace in the hole. But as far as I could ever tell, the only thing that he ever kept in the hole was himself."

"I still think somebody should call her," I said, referring to Albert's sister.

"Yes, but you're not calling the shots in this case," Ruth said.

"In many cases, it seems. Thanks for breakfast, Ruth." I got up from the table.

"You still didn't say whether you were going to the funeral or not."

"That depends on where I am with the *Oakalla Reporter*."

"Be a nice gesture on your part, seeing that you were dancing with his widow last night at the Corner Bar and Grill."

"She's the one who asked me." For whatever her reasons.

"Still, you know how things get started. You don't show up, people might wonder."

Let them, I thought. Out loud I said, "I'll see, Ruth. That's all I can do. In the meantime, where will you be?"

"At the shelter."

"All day and all night?"

"Unless you hear different."

"Just don't take it upon yourself to go out to the Lost 1600."

She didn't say anything, which told me that at least she had been considering it.

"You hear me, Ruth. Bad dreams or not, stay away from there."

"What did Abby want?" She conveniently changed the subject.

"What do you mean?" Now I was on the defensive.

"You said she called last night. What did she want?"

"The usual. To talk to me."

"Is that why you were tossing and turning all night?"

"How would you know anything about that, if you

were sound asleep?" The ball was back in her court.

She ignored me and began clearing the table. I took that as my cue and left for work.

A carbon copy of the past two mornings, today was cool, bright, and blue. But in spite of its radiance, the sun's white fire upon its dew-soaked leaves, in spite of its new-grass slippers and its bird song, the morning could not shake the feeling in me that Ruth and I were on the same fast track, headed for trouble.

Neither could the smile on Dale Phillips' face, as wide, it seemed, as all outdoors. "Morning, Garth," he said, as he stepped outside the door to The Last Dance. "I was afraid that maybe you wouldn't show up."

Dale Phillips' jeans had faded to the dull watery blue of Cecil Hardwick's eyes. He also wore a blue flannel shirt frayed at the cuffs, scuffed soft brown cowboy boots, a blue bandanna, and his hair in a ponytail. He looked like an old hippie, but one, I had to remind myself, who had done hard time for armed robbery.

"I said Wednesday. Wednesday it is. How are you coming along?"

We were walking north along the alley toward the back door. His bum leg seemed a little better today.

"I've about got everything back in the boxes again, sorting as I go. But I haven't sorted the books. There's some I think you should take a look at before I do."

He opened the back door to the building. We went inside where most of the boxes were stacked against the south wall, blocking the door that led into The Last Dance. True to his word, he had put almost everything back in place again.

"What about the books?" I said.

He shrugged. "Knowing you, I think there's some that you might like to have."

"For example?" I couldn't think of any of Fran's old

medical books that I would use for anything but a doorstop. And I'd never known him to read much of anything else.

Dale limped over to the pile of books, pulled one out, and handed it to me. It was the Grosset and Dunlop edition of *Big Red* with the dust jacket still on.

My hand seemed to have a mind of its own, as my fingers closed tightly around it and wouldn't let go. "There's more like this here?" I said.

"Several more from what I can see." He seemed pleased that I prized it so.

"You're right, Dale. I would like to look through them. But it might be the weekend before I can shake free again."

"No problem," he said. "I'll just hang the key inside the storm door."

"What if your late-night visitor comes back?"

He was philosophical. "He didn't need a key before."

As I glanced around the room, I noticed that not all of the boxes that he'd sorted were stacked against the south wall. A couple sat by themselves in the middle of the floor, and a few things seemed to have been shunted off to the corner like recalcitrant school children. "You find anything you want to keep?" I said.

He had, but seemed reluctant to admit it. "There's a whole box of *Sports Afield* from the 1950s I'd like to have, and another of *Outdoor Life*."

"Fran's?" I didn't know why that surprised me. His love of the out of doors more than matched my own.

"His name's on the mailing label."

"Anything else you'd like to have?"

Dale Phillips looked downcast for the first time that morning. "Yes. But I can't afford it."

He limped over to one of the boxes there in the middle of the floor and took out an old black leather satchel that had been worn almost smooth over the years. Inside were pill boxes, corked stopped medicine bottles, and medical instruments that I guessed were at least a hundred years old.

"Quite a find," I said, as I admired a bottle of what was labeled "Extract Of Smart-Weed" with the raised letters R. V. Pierce, M.D., Buffalo, N.Y. on the bottle. Then a squat squarish bottle of brownish gook from Dr. O. P. Brown, Jersey City.

"And look at this," Dale said, reaching over my shoulder to take out an old stethoscope and placing its cup over his heart. "It works, too. You want to try it?"

"No thanks, Dale." I had never found much fascination in listening to my own heart—perhaps because it reminded me too much of my mortality.

"Where do you suppose this came from?" he said, referring to the black satchel.

"It probably belonged to Fran's great-grandfather Baldwin. He came from a long line of doctors."

I rose and wiped my hands on my jeans. It was time to leave. Once I got started in here, I might not make it out before dark.

"It must be worth a fortune." Dale had picked up the satchel and was clinging to its leather handle as tightly as I was my copy of *Big Red*.

"To the right people, it probably is worth a fortune. But I doubt if any of them live in Oakalla."

"So what are you saying, Garth?"

What was I saying? Advertised and sold in the right way, that old doctor's bag could buy a lot of food for the shelter. On the other hand, did I really want to bother?

"I'm saying that I wish I could give it to you, but I can't. When the time comes, though, you can bid on it like everyone else."

In the moment that followed, I saw why Dale Phillips had done hard time. He didn't like to hear the word *no* any more than I did. His eyes had become as fierce as those of the eagle tattooed on his arm.

"It doesn't seem fair," he muttered to himself, as if I were no longer there. "A man does the right thing for once . . ."

"Chances are you'll end up with it anyway," I said.

"What's that, Garth?" He blinked hard a few times, as if trying to clear his eyes.

"I said, chances are you'll end up with it anyway. I'll advertise it and its contents in this week's *Oakalla Reporter* and ask for sealed bids. If you can beat the top bid, I'll sell it to you."

"How will I know what to bid?"

"I'll tell you."

It took him a moment to understand what I was saying. When he did, he was back to his old self again. "That's cheating, isn't it?"

My smile was conspiratorial. "Who's going to know?"

I went outside. Dale followed me, bringing the black bag with him. "I won't forget this. I really won't," he said, as he handed it over to me.

I said, "As far as those magazines go, they're yours. I figure you've earned them for all of the work you've done."

"Is it okay if I sell them?" he said. "I could probably move most of them this weekend."

"As I said, they're yours." Then I remembered the boxes in the corner and asked about them.

"Junk," he said. "Don't even waste your time with them."

"And the others?"

"I'll help you price them when the time comes."

"The time is coming next weekend."

"See me on Monday, then. Like you said, we'll take them to Connie Miller's and price them there. They'll move better there anyway."

As I thought about all the junk inside The Last Dance that had never moved, would never move, I had to agree. Guilt by association had more than one application.

"Where to this weekend?" I said as I put my copy of *Big Red* inside the satchel for safe keeping.

"LaCrosse. They're having a Mississippi Days festival right along the river. They're even having a canoe race and a fishing tournament. You ought to come and join in the fun."

"Some other time, Dale," I said. "It's not much fun going to those things alone."

"I'll be there," he said in all innocence.

I nodded, started walking away.

"Don't forget about those books."

I waved reassuringly. In truth, I already had.

CHAPTER

With the entire morning to myself without any major interruptions, I should have made better progress on the *Oakalla Reporter* than I did. But I couldn't stop thinking about Albert Vice. I didn't want to go to his graveside service that afternoon, despite what Ruth said. One dance does not a relationship make, so I didn't owe Kristina Vice anything; she as much as said so herself. I didn't owe Albert Vice anything either. I admired his skills at softball and appreciated his help as a volunteer fireman. That was all.

I couldn't stop thinking about the Lost Scout. Did he really have a hand in all of this, or were both Ruth and I reading too much into her dreams, and should I be looking harder elsewhere for answers?

Then there was my weekly syndicated column that I

had yet to write and for which I had no good ideas. Ever since I'd climbed down off my soapbox at Ruth's insistence, I'd been hard pressed for ideas. I'd written about everything from attics to basements, and was going to have to move outside soon, or I was going to run out of rooms in the house. No wonder most syndicated columnists chose political commentary. On that front at least, there was always something to gripe about.

It was a relief when the noon whistle blew, and I started my march on the Corner Bar and Grill for lunch. I hadn't gone a block up Gas Line Road when Cecil Hardwick pulled up beside me in his brown Chevy Impala with the big gold star on the side and blue-and-red bubble light on top.

"Give you a ride anywhere?" Cecil said.

"The Corner Bar and Grill, if you're headed that way."

I climbed in the passenger side and buckled up my seatbelt. For a sweet moment, until I realized that it wasn't Rupert Roberts sitting there beside me, it seemed like old times.

"What were you thinking just then, Garth?" Cecil said, as he put the Impala in gear and slowly motored on.

"I was thinking that I'm glad you're in the driver's seat, and not me."

"Is that a vote of confidence?"

"Yes. If you need one. Why?"

Cecil took his time in answering. We were stopped at Perrin Street when he did.

"I got my first death threat last night," he said. "I didn't get a whole lot of sleep after that."

When he took off his sunglasses to rub his eyes, I could see the red in them amidst the watery blue. The combination reminded me of a pale November sunset. I was thankful when he put his sunglasses back on.

"You have any idea who made the call?" I said.

"No. He or she disguised their voice."

"He or she?"

"I can't be sure it wasn't a woman."

"What exactly did he or she say?"

"They said to leave Albert Vice's death alone, or they couldn't be responsible for what might happen to me."

Not exactly a death threat, but close enough. "What time was the call made?"

"Late. Well after midnight. It liked to scared Helen to death. Just the telephone ringing, not the conversation itself. She thought there'd been a death in the family."

"She'll have to get used to late night phone calls . . . if you stay on the job," I said.

"That's what I told her."

"Then you plan to stay on the job?"

"Yes. I plan to stay on the job." He was looking right at me when he said it.

We crossed Perrin Street over into the alley that ran alongside the cheese plant. As we drove by, I noticed that we were getting a lot of hard looks from those workers on their lunch break. But the hardest look of all came from Dennis Hall and seemed directed at me.

"That's a friendly crowd," I said, feeling their eyes follow us all the way up the alley.

"You should have been inside the plant with them today. Even in Korea, I didn't get looks like that."

"You learn anything while you were there?" We had stopped at the end of the alley and were waiting for the traffic on Madison Road to clear.

"No. But I did learn that there was no poker game at Larry Sharp's house Saturday night, as he and the others claim."

"Who told you that?"

"One of his neighbors. She keeps a pretty close eye

on things in that end of town."

I thought I knew whom he meant. All of her life Opal Monroe had kept a close watch on things, particularly in her end of town. Now in her mid-eighties, she lived in the last farmhouse east within the city limits on Gas Line Road. She had sold the rest of her land to Wilmer Wiemer, who had developed part of it, and rented the rest of it to Merle Perkins as cropland up until the time that Wilmer needed it for further development.

Larry Sharp had bought one of Wilmer's lots and put a new Colonial style brick home on it. He and his wife, Becky, had lived there together until her death from cancer two years ago. Since then, Larry had lived there by himself.

"If they weren't playing poker, do you have any idea where they were?" I said to Cecil.

"No. But I'm working on that."

We pulled onto Madison Road and a few seconds later parked in front of the Corner Bar and Grill. "You might approach Hiram later this evening and ask him what he knows on the subject," I said. "You might be pleasantly surprised."

"He's told you?" With his sunglasses on, I couldn't tell if he was unhappy with me or not.

"No. I asked him to wait and tell you."

"Thank you for that. I guess."

"Don't let it get you down, Cecil," I said, as I opened the door to get out. "Rupert Roberts wasn't the most popular man in town either. It comes with the territory."

"I'm not worried about being popular, Garth. But I would like to stay alive long enough to enjoy my grandkids."

"Nothing's going to happen to you, Cecil. People threatened Rupert all of the time."

"And it didn't bother him?"

"Not enough to keep him off the job."

I left the rest of it unsaid, as I got out of the Impala and went into the lunch room of the Corner Bar and Grill. For the second straight day, Robby Rumaley failed to make his appearance there. On my way out, I asked Bernice, the owner, if he had been in at all that day. She said yes. He had stopped by earlier that morning to buy a twelve pack, than had taken off again.

"Was he drunk or sober?" I said.

"Sober. I'm almost sure of it."

"Did he give any reason at all why he hasn't been in to eat the last couple of days?"

"Not a peep. But you know Robby. He keeps his own counsel—except when he's been drinking."

Yes, I knew Robby—too well not to think that he was avoiding someone.

Ruth wasn't home when I stopped by there to pick up Jessie on my way to Fair Haven Cemetery for Albert Vice's graveside service. I still didn't want to go out there—I had helped bury too many of Oakalla's citizens lately—but could think of no good excuse to tell Ruth why I hadn't.

Daisy had heard me come in and began to whine plaintively at the basement door. She wanted out. What the hell, I thought. Why shouldn't she, on such a beautiful May day, be allowed outside to romp among the sundrops and the apple blossoms? Then I saw Fred, the basset, eagerly running the fence line between our yard and his.

"Later, Daisy, I promise," I said on my way out the back door.

I drove to Fair Haven. For once, Jessie was on her good behavior and I made it there on time for the service. As I glanced around, taking roll, I noted that the entire cheese plant seemed to be there, along with all of the members of Albert's softball team. Few of us had dressed up for the occasion. Most of us were there in jeans, tennis shoes, and flannels.

Larry Sharp wore the tan slacks, blue sportshirt, and brown penny loafers that he normally wore to work, and Ned Cleaver wore the jeans, navy blue T-shirt, and scuffed brown work boots that he wore practically everywhere. Only Dennis Hall wore a sportscoat. A green tweed with leather patches on the elbow, it went well with his dark green slacks and ivory turtleneck sweater. But Dennis Hall, who had no neck, was one of those people who don't look good in a turtleneck. And no matter what his ensemble, or perhaps because of it, he reminded me of a giant toad.

"What are you staring at?" he yelled to me from a few yards away.

As a matter of fact, I had been staring—at Kristina Vice, who wore a scarlet red suit, white ruffled blouse, and in her scarlet red heels stood about three inches taller than Dennis Hall. No one would ever have mistaken them for Barbie and Ken. Together, yet standing woodenly apart, they looked like a pair of mismatched Christmas ornaments.

The service was mercifully brief. The young minister in charge said a few platitudes designed to fit almost anyone short of a pedophile or a serial killer, then dismissed us with a prayer. I had intended to be gone after that first amen, but when I raised my head to pick my escape route, I saw Ned Cleaver standing in my way. He nodded for me to follow him, so follow him I did.

We went as far as the crest of the first hill to our west where we stood looking out over Fair Haven Cemetery. The sun was warm, and welcome after the shadow of the tent, and it felt good to stand on real grass again after mortuary crepe. I could see a swatch of yellow down in the hollow, either dandelions or buttercups, and from somewhere to the northwest came the sure clean scent of pine.

"I saw you looking at Kristina earlier," Ned Cleaver said. "You have any designs on her?"

"No. Do you?"

As he turned his gaze upon me, I could feel myself take notice. Ned Cleaver wasn't a particularly tall man; neither was he a very large one. At five-ten and one-fifty, he was considered skinny by Ruth, who liked to see men with some meat on their bones. His eyes were a robin egg blue, and not remarkable in either their color or intensity. His hair, which he wore in a closely cropped flattop, was by now nearly white, and his face, always clean shaven down to the last whisker, had nothing remarkable about it either. Even his job as foreman at the cheese plant was a dead-end one. He had passed up promotions so many times in the past that they had quit offering them.

Yet he commanded respect from everyone who knew him, and like E. F. Hutton, when he talked, you listened. Maybe that was the source of his power. Calm, flat, and slow, his voice seemed not only unhurried, but unhurriable, as if he could stand in the midst of a tempest and command the wind to lie down, and fully expect it to do so.

"No. I have no designs on Kristina Vice," he said.

I followed his gaze back to the tent and saw that most of the mourners had left for their cars. Only Kristina Vice, Larry Sharp, and Dennis Hall remained, along with a brown-haired woman in a yellow suit, who from the back looked like Diana, which was impossible, but enough of a resemblance to give me a start.

"Who's that," I said, "leaning on Dennis Hall?"

"His wife, Sandy."

Now, I recognized her. "I thought they were separated."

"They are. But they're still friends."

Kristina was kneeling at Albert's grave. Larry, Dennis, and Sandy all appeared to be watching her closely, but out of respect were keeping their distance.

"It didn't have to happen," I said, turning away.

Ned Cleaver watched a moment longer; then he too turned away— but reluctantly it seemed, as if his heart were down there with them. "I know that," he said. "What I want to know is what you're going to do about it?"

"Nothing. It's not my job."

"Cecil Hardwick seems to think it's his."

"A likely assumption, since he is now the law in Oakalla."

"Only until we elect a new sheriff."

"Which won't be until November. The trail might be pretty cold by then."

"What trail are you talking about?"

"The one that leads to Albert's killer."

Ned Cleaver glanced down the hill again, where only Dennis Hall remained at Albert's grave. The others were slowly walking in the direction of Larry Sharp's silver-and-maroon Chevy pickup. Dennis seemed to be having a hard time saying goodbye. He had fallen to his hands and knees and was tearing up clumps of grass by their roots.

"There is no trail that leads to Albert's killer," Ned Cleaver said as he turned back to me. "Albert's death was an accident."

"You're sure of that? Because I'm not."

His eyes showed their interest. "For what reason?"

Because I was there, I was tempted to answer, but that would be giving too much away. "Cecil Hardwick says so. That's good enough for me."

"You're taking your cues from Cecil Hardwick now? That's not like you, Garth." His voice was dead even, as if he knew that I was lying.

"We all get tired, Ned. Feel the need to lay some burdens down."

"Not you, Garth. Not me either. Though God knows we might have reason."

He took off down the hill. Moments later he was helping Dennis Hall to his feet. With nothing more to do there, I got in Jessie and started back to Oakalla. I had a lot on my mind and wasn't paying much attention to my driving until I saw Dennis Hall's black Dodge Ram pickup riding Jessie's back bumper. I slowed down and pulled over so that he could pass. When I did, he pulled alongside of me and began crowding me off the road.

I decided that I didn't want to go there. Fair Haven Road has a high berm and a deep ditch running along either side of it. Once you are off the road, it's too easy to lose control and end up upside down in the ditch.

I swerved at him and he swerved away, afraid that Jessie would ruin the new paint job on his truck. But then he was back at me again, seeing how far he could crowd me before I'd flinch. Already riding the berm, I swerved again at him, and that's when the left front tire blew.

Dennis Hall sped on past me just as I looked up to see a car coming at me from the other direction. Off the right side of the road I went, and stayed there, as the other car, apparently in a hurry, went on by and kept on going. With two wheels on the berm, and two wheels in the ditch, I bumped along until I came to a flat spot in the ditch, where I wheeled back onto the road and nearly off the other side before I got Jessie back under control, and stopped.

While I lay there in the middle of the road, looking at her undercarriage to see if Jessie still had her oil pan, Ned Cleaver slowly drove by in his red Jimmy. He neither waved nor offered to stop. The last I saw of him, he was turning right on Diamond Street, heading for home.

CHAPTER 15

J essie's spare tire was flat, so we limped on in to town where we stopped at the Marathon service station. From the noises coming out from under her, Jessie sounded terminal, but I knew that was too much to hope for. Danny Palmer, owner of the Marathon, Oakalla's volunteer fire chief, and all around good man, confirmed that diagnosis after he'd looked at her.

"Sorry, Garth, you just need a new exhaust system, that's all. Everything from the exhaust manifold to the tail pipe."

A crack mechanic, who could fix just about anything from cars to lawnmowers, Danny finally had been forced to admit that Jessie was his one failure. Even he couldn't keep her running right for more than a few months at a time, and that was the good news. The bad news was that we both agreed that while she had heart, she had no soul—nothing that, when tools failed, even prayer could reach.

"When can you have her fixed?" I said, feeling that I might need her again soon.

"By tonight, if I had the parts. But since I'll have to order them, Saturday morning at the earliest. What happened anyway?"

"Dennis Hall ran me off the road."

"On purpose?"

"Yes. I'd have to say that."

Danny gave me a knowing look. "You don't suppose dancing with his best friend's widow up at the Corner Bar and Grill last night had anything to do with it, do you?"

I heard a loud sniff behind me and knew immediately who had spoken. Sniffy Sniff, my longtime barber, who only cut hair on Fridays since he officially retired a few years ago, had his second home at the Marathon. A small, soft, opinionated man, who had earned his nickname from the loud sniffs he gave out whenever angered or excited, Sniffy seemed to prefer to live always on the edge of sadness, as if too much joy might shatter everything that he had come to believe about life.

"I was helping her through a hard time, that's all," I said to Sniffy.

"That's not the way I heard it." He was indignant, not hard for Sniffy. "The both of you were hanging on to each other like a flea to a dog's back." He then crossed his arms to make it official.

"Well, that's the way it was," I said, not wanting to talk about it.

Then Danny said, "Sniffy, why don't you run up to the Corner Bar and Grill and get me an iced tea. Get yourself one while you're at it."

Sniffy gave out another loud indignant sniff. "As if you have room to talk," he said to Danny. "What size iced tea?"

"Large. Plenty of ice."

"Anything for you, Garth?" Sniffy said, as Danny handed him a wad of one-dollar bills.

"No. I plan to be gone by the time you get back."

"I know why you're doing this." Sniffy was counting the bills to see how much money he had before he put in his own order. "You've got unfinished business here."

Since neither Danny nor I could deny it, we waved Sniffy on his way.

"Now that Sniffy mentioned it, how *are* things at home?" I asked after Sniffy was out of hearing.

"Better. Actually good most of the time." Though he didn't sound happy about it.

"A year from now, you'll probably be glad it worked out the way it did," I said.

"If I can survive that long."

We watched as Sniffy crossed Jackson Street between the post office and the hardware store. He seemed to defy an oncoming car to hit him as he walked out in front of it, but the car swerved, blew its horn, and went on around him.

"Ernie Hanson," Danny said. "It's a game he and Sniffy play."

"One of these days one of them is going to zig when he should zag."

"That's what I told Sniffy. He said there are worse ways to go."

Sniffy went in the north door of the Corner Bar and Grill. It was time to ask my question.

"In all of your years at the Marathon, have you ever heard anyone talk about the Lost Scout, Danny?"

"The subject's come up, but to my knowledge,

nothing's ever been made of it."

"Then do you think it's just a legend?"

"As far as I know. Why?"

I wasn't ready to tell him yet. "You ever hear Robby Rumaley talk about his friend, Bobby?"

Danny nodded. "When he's on a toot. He'll climb up there on that stool where Sniffy usually sits and tell us that we're all in for it when Bobby comes back to town. But nobody pays any attention to him."

"So nobody in town believes his story about Bobby?"

"Nobody that I ever talked to. Why? Do you?"

We both were watching the north door of the Corner Bar and Grill. When Sniffy made his reappearance, it would be our signal to wrap things up.

"I don't know, Danny. There might be something to it—if I could ever corner Robby long enough to talk to him about it."

Sniffy backed out of the Corner Bar and Grill carrying a large brown paper sack in both hands. It looked like there was a lot more than a large iced tea in there.

"There go all your profits," I said, as I started out across the drive for home.

"Garth, you didn't mention Dennis Hall once," Danny noted.

"Sure, I did. I said he ran me off the road. Sniffy gave me his opinion as to the reason why, and I tend to agree with him. Are you saying there's more to the story?"

Danny took a look to see how much progress Sniffy had made. "I'm saying that, yes."

"Should I send Cecil Hardwick by to hear it?"

"No. I'll tell you, no one else."

"It's that sensitive?"

"In my opinion."

He went back inside the Marathon. I went home.

No note from Ruth awaited me, so I took Daisy for a

walk, then went up to the Corner Bar and Grill for an early supper, thinking that if Robby Rumaley *was* avoiding me, I might beat him at his own game. Robby, however, failed to make an appearance, and I left an hour later no wiser than before. Once at my office, I took a quick inventory of the black doctor's bag that Dale Phillips had given me and made a list of what I thought were the most saleable items, which I'd advertise along with the bag in the *Oakalla Reporter*. In addition to the stethoscope, medicine bottles, and pill boxes were a bone-handled scalpel, bleeding tubes, suturing kit, and my favorite, a tiny brass balance for measuring out medicine. I didn't take the time to go through everything, but when I finished my inventory, I felt I had a fair representation of what was there.

What I hadn't told Dale Phillips, because I doubted that he would have taken the news well, was that it wasn't likely that he could beat the highest bidder once the black bag was advertised across five states. But that was his problem. Mine was to do the best I could by Abby, Ruth, and their shelter.

I had to edit what I already had written, then shuffle everything around to make room for the advertisements, since adding two more pages to the paper was out of the question. Once I'd done all that, I went back to the morgue to look for the Lost Scout.

Sometime that evening, without my noticing, it had gotten dark on me. I could have looked at my trusty Timex to find out how late it really was, but I preferred not to know. Anyway, my eyes would tell me when they'd had enough.

I'd searched the April–October issues of *Freedom's Voice* and found no mention of the Lost Scout. Thinking that I might have the year wrong, I also searched

April–October 1958 and 1960, but didn't find him there either. To add more cold water to my fast dwindling fire was the gnawing belief that despite Ruth's dreams to the contrary, there had never been a Lost Scout. He was likely the product of a campfire story, or someone's overwrought imagination.

So as I found my interest in the Lost Scout waning, I found myself being seduced by other stories that had their roots firmly in reality and that I could use for my monthly "It Happened When" column. In October 1959, the long-standing feud between the Beeseckers and the Burrises, both of rural Colburn, finally erupted into violence and death when Clem Beesecker, on the mistaken belief that Ancil Burris had poisoned his prize Holstein bull, ran Ancil through with a pitchfork, pinning Ancil to his own barn door.

An autopsy then revealed that the bull had eaten fermenting wild cherry leaves in its own pasture and died from cyanide poisoning. The result was that Clem Beesecker got twenty years to life for second degree murder, and both families decided to sell out and move somewhere else.

A happier story was that of four-year-old Charlie Swanson, who, unknown to his father, William, had followed William out to the woods where William was cutting locust fence posts. Shouldering a post to carry it to the pile, William, on hearing a noise behind him, swung around and hit Charlie in the head with the post. Charlie soon recovered consciousness, but was then unable to walk—not until a few weeks later, when, while sitting on the porch watching his mother, Sarah, shell peas, he got up to retrieve one that she had dropped. Charlie's family called it a miracle.

Charlie, who was more matter of fact about it, said, "I saw the pea and went after it."

Finally, there was the armed robbery and murder that occurred in June 1959 in the town of Linberg, a mill town about fifty miles east of Oakalla. The two armed robbers, who were later identified as Robert Anderson and Tony Jenkins, had entered the Linberg State Bank early on a Friday (the paper mill's pay day), robbed the bank of nearly $100,000, and killed Green Lake County Sheriff, Milton Frasier, who while acting on a phone tip, had interrupted the robbery in progress. The getaway car, a 1956 red Ford hardtop with Wisconsin license plates and registered to Tony Jenkins, age 19, of Linberg, was found wrecked and abandoned the next day on Marquette County Road E about forty miles west of Linberg. Two weeks later, thanks to the unrelenting pursuit of Green Lake County Deputy Sheriff, R. P. Curtis, Robert Anderson was arrested at his home in Barstow, California. Six months later he was sentenced to life imprisonment in the federal district court in Madison. However, Tony Jenkins and the stolen money had yet to be found.

There were photographs of the four principals involved. Sheriff Milton Frazier looked like the hard working, God fearing, family loving ex-Marine that he was made out to be. Deputy Sheriff R. P. Curtis looked like a young fresh-faced Ned Cleaver might have looked in a coat and tie. Robert Anderson, whose photo was snapped at the time of his arrest, had his hand over his face, so it was hard to tell anything about him, except that he appeared to be wearing jeans and a white T-shirt with a pack of cigarettes rolled up in his sleeve. Tony Jenkins, who by then had a $10,000 price tag on his head, had the thick porcine beetle-brow look of a playground bully. And while it seemed incongruous (if I were to judge on looks alone) that Tony Jenkins was the mastermind of the bank job, as Robert Anderson claimed, the fact remained that six months later he, the money, and the gun used in the

CHAPTER 16

"Concussion, three cracked ribs, multiple contusions, possible internal injuries . . ." Cecil's injuries, as they were being listed by the young male intern on call, were starting to sound like a litany.

"Will he live?" I said.

"I don't see any reason why not."

"Thank you, doctor."

He went on with his rounds. I stood there in the hallway of the emergency room, wondering where to go from here.

After finding Cecil, I had taken him to the Adams County Hospital there on Madison Road south of Oakalla, then called his wife, Helen, who was with him now. Cecil had awakened on the way to the hospital, but was too groggy to tell me what had happened to him. He was groggy still, but I needed some answers.

"Helen, may I talk to you a minute?" I said from the doorway of Cecil's room.

Helen sat at Cecil's bedside, holding his hand. If he was aware of her presence, he didn't show it.

"I hate to leave him, Garth."

"I promise I won't keep you long."

She rose, kissed Cecil on his forehead, then came to the door. A plump, pretty woman in her early fifties, Helen Hardwick had short, naturally curly brown hair, large doe-brown eyes, and the smooth white skin of a twenty-year-old. A capable woman, who as a farm wife had raised three very capable daughters: a lawyer, an accountant, and a pediatrician. She had always been content to let her husband and daughters shine, while she remained somewhere in the background. In return, she had a family who adored her.

"I told him not to go," Helen Hardwick said. Her eyes, brimming with tears, were still on Cecil. "I told him to call you first."

"Go where?"

"He wouldn't tell me. He was about to go on night patrol when he got a phone call that seemed to upset him. He said he had to leave that instant."

"And you have no idea who the caller was or what it was about?"

She couldn't take her eyes off Cecil for fear that, in her one moment of inattention, he might die on her. The power of love. I believed it saved more lives than it changed.

"No. I don't have any idea what the call was about. But Cecil did say that he might be gone for quite a while, so not to worry about him. 'Gone where?' I asked. When he didn't answer and I saw that he wasn't going to, that's when I said to at least call you and let you know what was up. He said no, that you were counting on him to handle the job himself."

Had there been the slightest crack in that smooth concrete floor, I would have tried to crawl through it. "I never dreamed he'd put himself in jeopardy like that," I said. "I'm sorry."

"You should be," she said, not letting me off the hook. "Now, may I go?"

"Did Cecil ever get the chance to talk to Hiram at the Corner Bar and Grill?"

"He never said. Why?"

I shook my head. "It doesn't matter now. Take care of Cecil. I'll be back in the morning."

"It didn't have to happen, Garth." She wanted to be angry with me, but couldn't. She was too worried about Cecil.

"It won't, the next time."

"How do you know there will be a next time?"

"I know Cecil." Or at least was starting to.

"Not well enough, it seems," she said, as she turned her back to me.

Since Cecil wouldn't be needing his patrol car the rest of the night, I drove it back to Oakalla and parked it in front of the Corner Bar and Grill. Ned Cleaver was leaving the Corner Bar and Grill just as I was going in. As he stood there white-faced, staring at Cecil's Impala, it was the closest that I had ever come to seeing him rattled. Even an opponent's home run, rare though it was when Ned was on the mound, earned from him no more than a shrug.

"Is something wrong, Ned?" I said.

"What are you doing in Cecil's patrol car?"

"I'm taking it for a late night spin. Now, if you'll excuse me . . ."

But as I started past him, he grabbed my arm. He had

a powerful grip, perhaps from pitching softball all those years, and it hurt where he held me.

"Did something happen to Cecil?" he said.

I jerked my arm away and went on inside the Corner Bar and Grill. Ned Cleaver didn't follow me in, as I had expected him to.

Hiram was about to wrap it up for the night. With the barroom empty, he was washing glasses and putting them away. He'd wipe the tables and fill all the shakers that needed filling before he started turning off the lights.

I took a seat at the bar. "Go ahead with what you're doing," I said, when Hiram stopped to wipe his hands on his apron. "I'm just here to talk."

"I'm glad somebody is," he said as he plunged his hands back into the soapy water.

"Ned wasn't long on conversation, huh?"

"I think maybe he said ten words to me the whole time he was in here."

"He drink much?"

"About as much as he talked. Nursed a beer, that's all."

"How long was he in here?"

Hiram stopped washing glasses. "Is there a point to these questions?"

"Somebody beat up Cecil Hardwick to within an inch of his life tonight. I'd sort of like to find out who."

"Ned was in here a couple hours or so."

"No longer than that?" It had been at least that long since I found Cecil Hardwick outside my door.

Hiram had to think about it. "No. I don't think so, Garth. But if it comes up in court, I can't swear to it."

"Did Cecil ever get in to talk to you?" I said.

Hiram had washed a sink full of glasses and was now rinsing them. "No. He never made it in. I don't think this is his favorite place to come, Garth." Hiram sounded apologetic. "Seeing how we serve liquor here."

"Cecil doesn't drink?"

"Not to my knowledge. It has something to do with a vow that he made to his mother at an early age. The way I understand it, she had a favorite brother who went the way of the bottle."

"Guess it doesn't matter," I said. "But I wish I'd known that sooner." Otherwise, I would have asked Hiram myself what he knew, then delivered that information to Cecil.

"I thought you did know, or I would have told you."

I watched Hiram dry and stack his glasses. In a way, I envied his life, and its routine. In a larger way, I didn't.

"So what light do you have to shed on the subject?" I said.

"I'm not sure I have any, seeing what happened to Cecil."

"I might have another source. You want me to check him out first?"

"That might be a good idea, Garth. In case anybody asks, I can tell him with a straight face that I didn't say anything."

I slid down off the bar stool, landing with a jolt on the hard wooden floor. The bar stools didn't used to be so high. Either that or I was shrinking in my old age.

"Take care of yourself," I said.

"You do the same. And, Garth? If your other source doesn't pan out, give me a call at home tomorrow."

"We'll see," I said, not wanting Hiram to suffer Cecil's fate if I could help it. "By the way, did Robby Rumaley ever make it in here for supper tonight?"

"No. I didn't see him."

"Thanks, Hiram."

"Watch your back, Garth," were his parting words of advice.

I drove Cecil's Impala home and parked it in Jessie's place in the garage. I could get used to this, I thought, driving a car that actually ran. Not only ran, but had a radio, fan, heat, and windshield wipers that worked more than half the time. So while I didn't wish Cecil any complications, I did hope that he was a slow healer.

Ruth sat at the kitchen table, drinking a cup of coffee. After pouring myself a cup of coffee, I sat down across from her. The coffee pot was nearly empty. Either she had made a short pot, or she had been there for quite some time.

"Where have you been?" Ruth said.

I told her.

"I hope you're satisfied," she said.

"Not particularly, but I'm not willing to shoulder all the blame either. Cecil's the one wearing the badge, not me. If he needed backup, he should have asked for it."

"How badly is he hurt?" She got up and poured the remaining coffee in her cup, then turned off the stove.

"Badly enough. But he'll live to fight another day."

"So you hope," she said, adding sugar and half-and-half to her coffee. "What are you going to do if he doesn't? More to the point, what are you going to do now?"

"That remains to be seen. Are you offering to help?" I was hopeful.

"No."

"You could take a break from the shelter for a while. If you were busy helping me out, you wouldn't have to think so much about the Lost Scout. Who, by the way, I'm convinced never existed."

When she didn't answer, I already knew that I'd lost the argument. But there was nothing to be gained by giving up.

"So what do you say, Ruth?"

"About what? Helping you? I already gave you my

answer. It's no. About the Lost Scout? You can believe what you want, I'll believe what I want."

I took a sip of my coffee. It was strong enough to float pennies. "As long as you don't act on it, you can believe whatever you want," I said.

"Meaning what?"

"What I mean is, I don't want you going out to the Lost 1600 under any circumstances. I hope I've made that clear."

"I thought you said there was no Lost Scout."

"There isn't. But there's something else going on out there and I don't want you walking into it."

"Better for you to walk into it, is that what you're saying?"

"At least I'll have both eyes open."

"Meaning?" She was spoiling for a fight.

"Meaning you haven't been getting much sleep lately. I'm starting to worry about you."

"Don't worry about me. I can take care of myself. I have been for quite a few years now. But thanks, Garth," she said before I could protest. "For your concern."

I got up from the table and poured my coffee into the sink. If I drank any more, I'd spend the rest of the night counting sheep.

"I mean it about the Lost 1600," I said. "Stay away from there."

"If you will. I'm in no less danger than you are."

"From the Lost Scout?" I said, just to see what she'd say.

"Yes. From the Lost Scout."

"Get some sleep, Ruth. You need it."

"Might I suggest you do the same."

CHAPTER

The next morning I was up before the first bird ever made a peep. It seemed I took off my clothes, climbed into bed, rolled over, and put my clothes back on again. I didn't even take time to shave and shower that morning. I had too many stops to make before work.

As quietly as possible, because I didn't want to awaken Ruth, I went downstairs and poured a glass of juice and a bowl of Honey Nut Cheerios. I thought I was alone down there until Ruth said from the living room, "Where to today?"

I jumped, spilling milk and Honey Nut Cheerios all over the table, "Jesus Christ, Ruth," I said as I went for the dish rag. "Don't you ever sleep anymore?"

After cleaning the table, I took my bowl of cereal into

the living room. Ruth sat in her favorite chair with her eyes closed and the lights off, but obviously not asleep. I turned on the table lamp at the end of the couch and sat down.

"I wasn't asking for company, just asking a question," she said, using her hand to shield her eyes from the light.

"It's Thursday, so most of my day will be spent on the *Oakalla Reporter*," I said. "But I've got a couple stops to make in the meantime and who knows where they will lead. What about you? Where will you be?"

"The shelter, once I leave here."

I noticed that she wore the same tan slacks and green-and-gold Green Bay football jersey that she had been wearing the night before. The slacks were this year's model, but the jersey went back to before Lombardi.

"Why don't you at least *try* to get some sleep?" I said.

"I have *tried* to get some sleep," she said, not wanting to talk about it. "You think I like sitting here at four A.M., listening to that lecher next door sniffing at our basement window? Either you're going to have to shoot him or I will."

I smiled. "Patience, Ruth. These things pass."

"Not soon enough for me."

I finished my cereal and drank the remaining milk from the bowl. Ruth raised one brow in disapproval, but didn't say anything. I turned off the light in the living room, then set my bowl in the kitchen sink on my way out the back door.

I drove to the Marathon, where Danny Palmer sat at his desk, counting out change and putting it in the cash register. It was quiet in there, and in the near dark, comfortable. I would have liked to have pulled up a chair and stayed awhile.

"Yes, Garth?" he said, noting my arrival. "It must be important for you to be here this early in the day."

"As a matter of fact, it is."

He quit counting change. "Fire away."

"Somebody put Cecil Hardwick in the hospital last night. I hoped maybe you could tell me why."

Without a word, Danny got up and shut off the light over his desk. Both the darkness and the quietness deepened. I could smell motor oil, see the headlights of someone's passing car.

"This is between you and me." Danny stood at the door watching the drive. "I can't afford for it to go any further."

"Then maybe you'd better not tell me," I said. "Until Cecil's back on the job, I'm the law in Oakalla."

"I see his car out there."

"I sort of hoped you wouldn't."

"Let's put it this way, Garth. There are a lot of people involved."

"Most of them at the cheese plant?"

"You said it, not me."

"Some of them volunteer firemen?"

He didn't answer.

"Well, I guess I'd better go and see what Cecil has to say. Thanks for that much, Danny."

I clasped his shoulder on my way out the door. The last I saw of him, he was still standing there, wondering if he had done the right thing.

The drive to the hospital was a lonely one. Only a couple other cars were on the road, and they were well ahead of me, leaving just me and my thoughts on the bill of goods that Danny and I both had bought into years ago.

Do the right thing. It sounded easy enough. You played by the rules, stood by your wife and raised your kids, paid your taxes and did your part to make your community a fit place to live—until the day you realized that some asshole somewhere, anywhere, including you, could take it all away in an instant; or as was most likely the case, through several small nicks to the soul, which insidiously bleed the deep well dry over time. What doing the right thing didn't allow for was all of the things that were beyond your power and all of the things that weren't—the deliberate conscious no-win choices that you had to make in your life. It didn't allow for giving up someone you loved in order to keep everything else you loved, or its corollary, giving up everything else you loved in order to keep someone you loved more.

Once, you thought it did—if you were wise enough to know your own heart, and strong enough to follow it to the end. But, slowly and with great reluctance, you gave up that certitude for the hope, however frail, that while life might fail you, you would not fail it, or yourself. That when it was all said and done, you could lift that faded, dog-eared photo of youth and look him straight in the eye; and if you were lucky, wink.

This morning was unlike the previous few mornings. I determined that as I stepped out onto the hospital parking lot. At the heart of it was the warmer temperature. I could almost see the flowers nodding to themselves, as if this is what they had been waiting for all spring.

Cecil Hardwick was awake when I entered his room. He pushed aside an untouched tray of food and tried to smile, but his swollen face wouldn't allow it. So he smiled with his eyes instead.

"Still here," he said.

"I see that. No sense asking how you're feeling."

"Have a seat," he said. He could move his eyes, but not his head because of his neck brace. "I think there's one here somewhere."

I moved the burgundy-padded aluminum chair from against the wall to near the foot of Cecil's bed, so that he wouldn't have to try to turn his head to talk to me.

"Do you feel like talking?" I said.

"As long as I'm awake. Those pain pills they're giving me sure do the job."

He spoke slowly through swollen black lips. It was almost as painful to watch him as it was for him to speak.

"We don't have to do this now," I said.

"I know. But we will."

"Then tell me where you were when it happened."

"The Dunes."

He started to explain, but I held up my hand to stop him. "I know where they are, Cecil."

The Dunes were a high sandy bank along Stony Creek about two miles southwest of town. High school kids liked to camp out there and have all night parties during the summer. Others in the county, since Creek Road gave them easy access, used it as a dump. Hardly anybody called it Bare Ass Beach anymore, or swam, fished, and lazed in the sun there, as Dick Davis and I did when we were kids.

Cecil said, "I got a phone call late last evening, saying for me to go out there, if I really wanted to find out what happened to Albert Vice . . ." Cecil stopped speaking, as his eyes went to the open door behind me. I turned to look but no one was there.

I got up, stood for a while at Cecil's window, where I saw a familiar truck hurriedly leaving the hospital parking lot, then closed the door. "Man or woman?" I said, sitting back down again.

"Woman."

"I mean the one who called you."

"That's what I mean, too."

"Did she identify herself?"

Cecil's eyes showed his frustration with me. I didn't know why I ever thought they were weak.

"Just let me tell the story," he said.

I nodded for him to continue.

"I'm not a complete fool, though it might seem like I am. I drove out to the Dunes, but I had no intention of getting out of my car until I thought it was safe. When Kristina Vice drove up and got out of her Blazer, I thought it was safe."

It was hard, but I waited for him to continue.

"Kristina said she didn't want to talk there along the road for fear someone might see us, so she got back in her Blazer, and I followed her on into the Dunes a ways. When I got out of my car, that's when they jumped me . . ."

Cecil's eyes began to fill with tears at the memory of it. If I read him right, he felt betrayed more than anything else—to think that someone in Oakalla would want to do him harm.

"Who were they, do you know?"

Cecil blinked some tears away. "No. It all happened too fast. But I do think they all wore some kind of uniform."

"What kind of uniforms?"

"Army uniforms, if I had to guess. But without any brass or insignias that I could see."

"How many of them were there?"

"Three or four. It all happened so fast, I . . ." He stopped to catch his breath. He was having a hard time breathing through his broken nose.

"What did Kristina Vice do?"

"Ran off, I guess. I never saw her again."

"Do you think she set you up?"

For the first time that morning Cecil wouldn't look at me. "I'll pass on that."

So would I, since I saw how much it cost him to deny it. "What did they hit you with?"

Cecil spoke in a whisper. His thoughts were still on Kristina Vice, as were mine. "Their fists was all."

"Then they weren't trying to kill you?"

"No. I think they were just trying to send a message." Cecil's voice was growing stronger. I took that as a good sign.

"Do you remember anything about your trip back to town?" I said.

"I remember waking up and seeing car lights coming at us, but they were so bright I couldn't stand to look at them."

"Us? Weren't you driving?"

"No. Somebody else was. The next thing I remember, somebody was strapping me on to something."

"That was here at the hospital."

"Helen said you were the one who brought me in."

"I did. Somebody must have dumped you off at my office, knowing that I'd be working late."

"Sending a message to both of us," he said.

"It sounds like it."

"So, are you scared off?"

"No."

"Me either."

I took a deliberately long look at him. His watery blue eyes were steadfast, resolute.

"Good," I said.

CHAPTER

From the hospital I drove to
the cheese plant where Dennis Hall was busy unloading
ten-gallon cans of milk onto the outside conveyor belt.
Most of the dairy farms around Oakalla were fully automated, and the milk went straight from the cow via automatic milkers through plastic pipes to a stainless steel
cooling tank where it was then pumped into a tanker and
hauled to either a nearby dairy or one of the many cheese
plants in the area. But a few of the farmers around had
refused to fully automate for whatever the reason and still
used milkers that required pails, cans, and milk houses.
Dennis Hall's first job of the day was to collect these cans
and bring them to the cheese plant. His second was to
haul the finished rounds and wheels of cheese to the local
distributors. A man who seemingly loved his work, he

could often be heard whistling as he off-loaded the ninety-pound cans of milk with the ease of an organ-grinder.

That morning, however, Dennis Hall was silent, as he literally threw the cans from his truck onto the conveyor belt. And it was only through the grace of God, or dumb luck, that they all landed upright.

"Morning, Dennis, a penny for your thoughts," I said.

He stiffened at the sound of my voice, wouldn't even turn around to look at me. "What the hell do you want, Ryland?"

Dennis wore jeans, work boots, white socks, and a white T-shirt. The jeans and T-shirt bulged with muscle and were stretched skin-tight. He looked a lot better than he did in yesterday's toad suit, and a lot more like himself.

"I just wanted to thank you for running me off the road yesterday," I said.

He turned to look at me, using the shoulder of his T-shirt to wipe the sweat from his eyes. "You learn how to drive that junk heap of yours, things like that wouldn't happen."

"It's still nice to know who your friends are."

Dennis went back to work again, but at a less frenzied pace. "Whoever said we were friends, Ryland?"

"We've fought a few fires, cooked some catfish, raised a few glasses together. Friends do things like that even if they don't go around beating up on people together."

Dennis's next can missed the conveyor belt altogether. It was a good thing that its lid was on tight, or there would have been spilled milk all over the alley. I retrieved it for him, then nearly threw my back out hoisting it up onto the conveyor belt.

"Jesus, Dennis," I said, as I straightened my back to make sure I still could. "How do you make it look so easy?"

"Practice," he muttered. "Just like softball." He stopped his unloading again. "How come you never joined the team? You too good for us or something?"

Was this softball we were talking about, or something else? "To be honest, Dennis, I never felt that I had the time to give it what I thought it deserved. Besides, pitcher is my best position, and with Ned on the mound, you didn't need me."

"Why is it then, that you have the time to stick your nose in everybody else's business? Dance with my best friend's wife before he's even in the ground?"

"That might have been a mistake, Dennis. I'm sorry if I made things any harder on you than they already are."

"Who says things are hard on me?" he said, taking issue.

"Think about the last twenty-four hours, Dennis. You've buried your best friend, run me off the road, beat up on Cecil Hardwick, and then come back to the hospital to finish the job. Or wasn't that your truck I saw leaving the hospital parking lot earlier this morning?"

"You don't have to answer that question, Dennis," Larry Sharp said from behind me. "Or anything else that he asks."

Meanwhile Dennis's face had turned a deep red. It was either the flush of anger, or guilt.

Then Larry Sharp said, "Garth, I'm going to have to insist that you quit bothering my employees while they're working. And Dennis, I'm going to have to insist that you get back to work."

"I'm not getting paid by the hour, Larry," Dennis let it be known.

"Still, you are getting paid. Think about that, Dennis."

Dennis went back to unloading milk cans. I followed Larry Sharp into the cheese plant and then up the steel stairs into his office.

"I don't believe I invited you in here," Larry said.

I closed his office door behind me. "No, I invited myself."

Larry Sharp's office was on an elevated concrete slab, along with the lunch room, directly above the restrooms and about ten feet above the main floor of the cheese plant. His office walls were concrete and painted a pea green that resembled my office walls at the *Oakalla Reporter*. Through his thick glass door, he could oversee the pasteurizer and the stainless steel vats where most of the cheese making was done. On his grey metal desk was a photograph of his late wife, Becky. She was wearing a black-and-white striped top, baggy white slacks, and was standing beside a palm tree on a white sand beach with the ocean as a backdrop. I loved her smile. Wide as a country mile and straight from the heart, it made you feel that you actually deserved it.

"What are you staring at?" Larry said.

"Becky. I was wondering what she would think of the mess that you've gotten yourself into."

He sat down hard in his chair. For an instant, we both thought that it was going to slide out from under him.

"What mess is that?" He put on his half-frame reading glasses and found some papers on his desk that seemed to require his immediate attention.

"I think you know."

He gave me his best example of plant manager's frown. "No. I don't think I do."

"You mind if I sit down?" I said.

He looked up at me over the top of his glasses. "You invited yourself in here. It's up to you whether you sit or not."

Since it was the only chair in his office, I chose the straight-back aluminum one with the thin orange plastic padding that was sitting against the wall just inside the door. I pulled it up close to his desk and said, "Let's start with Albert Vice. His death, while not yet officially a homicide, is at the very least suspicious. He didn't impale himself on punji sticks, then wrap himself in concrete blocks before plunging in Hidden Quarry."

"What the hell are punji sticks?"

"Weapons of war. You can ask your old friend, Ned Cleaver, about them. Or perhaps you already have."

He went back to shuffling papers. "I don't know what the hell you're talking about."

"I'm talking about the poker game that never was. The one that Albert Vice was supposedly attending at your house."

"Albert never showed up."

"Neither did anybody else from what I hear."

Larry threw the papers down on his desk. "That's because . . . And you can tell that old crow, Opal Monroe, this herself . . . We changed our minds at the last minute and moved the game to Ned's house."

"You have witnesses?"

He was looking past me, out at the workers assembling below us. "If I need them."

"That's the way it is, huh?"

"That's the way it is. Any more questions?"

"A couple. Where were you last night, say between nine and eleven P.M.?"

"Attending Albert's wake at Kristina's house. We all were. Ned, Dennis, and I, along with several others from here at the cheese plant."

"The whole time?"

"Except for when I went for more ice."

"What time was that?"

"Ten. Ten thirty, I don't remember. Maybe your buddy, Hiram, can tell you."

At the mention of Hiram's name, I felt myself tighten.

I didn't want to drag him into this.

"Leave Hiram out of it," I said. "He's kept your dirty little secret."

It was Larry's turn to feel some pressure. "What dirty little secret is that?"

"The one I'm working on." I stood, scooting my chair back against the wall where I'd found it. "The one that, if it doesn't put you behind bars, is at least going to leave you miserable."

"You don't know what you're getting into, Garth," he said. "So take my advice and leave it alone."

"Larry, you're full of shit," I said. "And that's a direct quote. So either call off your dogs or sic them on me. I don't care one way or the other."

I left his office door wide open and went down the steel stairs into what I had already determined was the enemy camp. Harsh, hateful looks followed me everywhere I went. If I didn't find Ned Cleaver soon, I was going to develop a complex.

"You looking for me, Garth?"

Ned Cleaver seemed to appear out of nowhere. But he wasn't the same Ned Cleaver that I had always known. Grizzle showed on his normally clean-shaven cheeks and his jeans and navy T-shirt looked like he'd slept in them. Something in his eyes, too, was different. Gone was the old serenity, the old assurance. In its place was a harried, haunted look. Maybe he and Ruth should get together and compare notes.

"I'd like to ask you a few questions. In private," I said.

"Sorry, Garth, no can do. Work has already started for the day."

As if to make his point, the men and women standing in an ever tightening circle around us found somewhere else to be. Some began stirring the vats of curing cheese, others disappeared into the cooler and the storeroom. If I had ever wanted to witness a display of pure power, I'd just had my chance. Their master's voice. Those at the cheese plant knew it well.

"Maybe we can talk at your break, then," I said.

"I don't take a break during the day."

"Lunch, then."

Ned's look went from neutral to deep in the icebox. "Garth, why don't you get out of here while you still can."

"If you'll answer one question. Who held the winning hand Saturday night?"

"Nobody did."

"Then you didn't play?"

His look seemed both sad and arrogant. "Of course we played. At my house."

CHAPTER

Three down and one to go. As I drove slowly east on Gas Line Road, I saw that I had been right about the day now unfolding. It *was* warmer than the previous days had been and more like the Mays of memory, which were always deep in soft green grass and steeped in the warm glow of an all-day sun. Even the rainy days came back lush and leisurely, never lasting into evening, or if they did, never spoiling the fun.

I left Cecil's Impala at the *Oakalla Reporter* and walked the rest of the way from there. Kristina Vice lived in the last house on the right as you went south down the drive into Centennial Park. Hers, the one that she had occupied with Albert Vice, was a single-story, red brick, ranch-style house built in the early 1960's after the park had become a reality. Once people became convinced that the park would be funded and maintained, and not revert back to the woods it had been, lots had been sold along the west side of the drive and a row of houses built. Then the houses looked like ducks out of water, since all the trees were in the park on the east side of the drive. Today, thirty-some years later, the houses had their own trees—spruce, cedar, and red-leaf maple, and looked like they belonged.

Kristina Vice's house had a large picture window that faced the park, white shutters on each side of it and on either side of all its other windows, an aluminum storm door, and a white wooden front door with a large brass knocker on it. The front door had been painted recently. I could see my shadow outline in its glare.

Kristina Vice came to the door wearing a white terry robe and nothing else that I could see. Her hair was wet and plastered to her robe, as if she'd just stepped out of the shower in time to light a cigarette before answering the door. I noticed wet footprints on the blue shag carpet as I followed her through the living room into the combination kitchen and family room. She opened the drapes on the large sliding door that led out to the patio so that we could look out at the softball field where Albert used to play. The summer softball league would be starting soon. I wondered who now would be playing center field for the Oakalla Wheywackers?

"Coffee?" Kristina Vice said.

"Sure."

She went to her Mr. Coffee and poured us each a cup. We sat on wooden stools at the counter in the kitchen. She crossed her legs, resting a bare foot on my shoe, and smoked her cigarette. I noticed that her toenails were painted red.

"So what brings you here so early in the morning, Mr. Newspaperman?" she said. I had always thought of her eyes as black, and somewhat shallow, like a prairie mud-wallow, but in this light they looked almost violet, and unfathomable.

"I was wondering why you set up Cecil Hardwick last night?"

"Cut right to the chase, don't we?" She blew a puff of smoke my way.

"I figured I'd save us both some time."

"I know you don't believe in fraternizing with the enemy. How about sleeping with the enemy? As long as we're saving time."

"Julia Roberts, right?"

"Right. It worked for her. She got her man in the end."

I added sugar and took a sip of my coffee. It was surprisingly good. But lots of things about Kristina Vice surprised me.

"What did you do before you married Albert?" I said.

"Why do you want to know?"

"I'm curious, that's all."

She stubbed her cigarette in her ashtray and swung off the stool, taking her coffee with her. "Follow me."

"Where are we going?"

"Wouldn't you like to know."

I swung down off my stool, knowing full well that the last man who had followed her somewhere had ended up in a hospital. We went into the living room where she pulled open the drape that covered the picture window and sat down at the upright piano that stood against the north wall of the room. Her and Albert's wedding picture was on top the piano. In his gold hair and powder blue tux, he looked like a young Robert Redford. In her white satin dress and long black curls, she looked like a fresher, happier version of herself.

"What are you staring at?" she said.

"I'd forgotten how handsome Albert was."

"And how innocent I used to be?"

"Somehow I never thought of you as innocent."

She patted the piano bench. "Sit down. You won't be in the way."

I sat down beside her, but left some space between us in case she needed the room. Then for the next ten minutes or so I listened to her play a medley of classical tunes without, to my untrained ear, ever missing a note. "That's what I studied at the University of Minnesota," she said when she finished. "Here's how I made my living." She began to play "Hound Dog," followed by "Soul Train," "Twist and Shout," and "Rock Around the Clock." She stood, just like Jerry Lee Lewis, when she played "Roll Over Beethoven," then sat back down again to play and sing "The Long and Winding Road." She had a deep rich mournful voice that reminded me of Bobbie Gentry, and which would have left even the hardhats crying in their beer. When she finished, I wasn't ready for her to be done.

"Say something," she said when the silence grew unbearable for both of us.

"You're very good."

"You have no idea."

She rose from the piano, taking me with her back into the kitchen, where we sat back down on our stools, and she put her bare foot back on top of my shoe.

"I could have taken you to bed just now," she said.

I didn't deny it.

"So I'm not a complete bitch."

"What are you, then?"

She lighted another cigarette. "You figure it out. You're the great solver of mysteries."

"Where did you meet Albert, at school?" I knew he'd gone to college for a couple years, then dropped out.

"At a bar in Hayward. The band I was singing with was about to break up. I was looking for other options."

"Why? You're a talent. I know that much about music."

"True. I had the talent, but I didn't have the drive anymore, if I ever did." She was looking out across the softball field as she spoke. "To be honest, Garth, I'm a pretty lazy person. At twenty-eight I was ready to settle in. Or settle." She turned her gaze back to me. "That's what we all do, isn't it? Eventually."

"And you're what now?"

"Thirty-three. Though today I feel much older."

"Beating up on people will do that to you."

"Tell me about it," she said without remorse. "But if it comes down to it, I was here all night. I have at least twenty witnesses who will testify to that."

"It pays to have friends, I guess."

"You might try it sometime." She gave me a look that said she could arrange it.

"You mind if I take a look at Albert's things?" Her foot was starting to wear a hole in my resolve.

"Why?"

"To see what I can learn about him."

"His death, you mean?"

"That too."

"They're in our bedroom. Do you think you're safe in there?"

"As long as you're not in there with me."

"Meaning?" She blew another puff of smoke my way.

I slid down off the stool. "You figure it out."

Albert's and Kristina's bedroom covered the entire north end of the house. It had a white carpeted floor, large walk-in closets, both his and hers, dried flower arrangements in gold frames on the walls, and a king-size waterbed with a royal blue spread that had been dragged up over the pillows, but not tucked in. I had never slept, let alone made love in a waterbed. Knowing me, I'd probably get seasick.

One glance around the room told me that Kristina was the reader in the family. Her side of the bed had a stack of books on the floor, most of them thick paperbacks; it was also where the night stand, table lamp, and ash tray were. Albert's side was bare, except for a copy of *The Turner Diaries* and a right-wing newsletter addressed to him and titled *Armageddon*.

Why had Kristina let me see these? My only conclusion was that she wanted me to see them.

In Albert's walk-in closet was a lot of military gear that included a camouflage outfit for every season, a couple pairs of boots, night goggles, a .30-.30 Remington with an infrared scope, an AK-47 assault rifle, and a German Luger in a black leather holster. There was enough fire power in there to hold off a whole company of muggers, if need be. Though I doubted that was what it was for.

"I see you found Albert's toys." Kristina stood at the door of the bedroom, towel drying her hair. "You can have them if you want."

"I have no need for them," I said.

"That makes us even. Neither do I. And for the record, I hated what happened to Cecil Hardwick."

"Then why did you do what you did?"

"I thought I had no other choice." She threw the towel at my feet and untied her robe. "The only way out of here is through me."

Kristina Vice had a nearly perfect body, and I was seeing most of it. Long legs, large round full breasts, eyes that held you, stroked you, even as they saw right through you. Then I glanced at the waterbed where Albert Vice had been sleeping not so long ago. Too easy to dive in there and never come up for air.

"I'll hate myself in the morning," I said as I approached her. "But I have work to do."

Grasping her by the arms, I swung her out of the

doorway and onto the bed. She grabbed me on her way down, but couldn't maintain her hold. Had she succeeded in pulling me down with her, that would have been all she wrote. I wasn't made of steel. I wasn't even made of high-grade aluminum.

I didn't dare look back at her once I got my feet in gear. That would have been tempting fate.

"Garth?"

I stopped in the hallway. "Yes, Kristina?"

"This isn't the end of it."

Why did I already know that?

CHAPTER 20

I went out Kristina Vice's patio door straight for my office at the *Oakalla Reporter*. The first thing I did when I got there was call Abby. I didn't care if I got her machine. I just needed to hear her voice.

"Hello." She sounded sleepy. She must have worked the night shift.

"Abby, it's Garth. I just needed to get in touch."

"Why? What's wrong?" Then she started reading between the lines. "It's Diana, isn't it? You're having second thoughts about her."

"No. It's not Diana."

"What is it, then?"

I sat back in my chair. How did I tell her the truth without telling her the truth? "You remember that guy you told me about, the one who asked you out. Well, I've run into something like that here."

"Another woman, you mean?" She didn't take the news well.

"Yes. But it's not like it seems. I'm not in love with her or anything."

"No, you just want to bonk her."

Bonk her? Yes, that about said it all.

Abby continued, "I'm afraid I can't help you on that one, Garth. I fell off the wagon last night."

It took me a moment to understand what she was saying to me. When I did, it was as if everything in and about me stopped all at once.

"Is he still there?" I said.

"No. We went to his place."

I rested my head on my desk. I wanted to cry, but was too numb to feel the tears.

"Just answer me one question," I said. "Was it worth it?"

"No." There was a long pause. "But that doesn't mean it won't ever happen again."

"In a way, it's a relief," I said. "I was worried it might happen sooner or later. Better sooner than later."

"How so?"

"It's already happened. Now, I don't have to worry about it anymore."

"And it sets you free?" She didn't want to ask, but did.

"As strange as it may sound, Abby, I don't want to be set free. Like Janis said, 'Freedom's just another word for nothing left to lose.'"

"I'm glad. I couldn't stand to lose you—or the thought of you making love to another woman."

"That cuts both ways," I said. "So I don't want a running account."

"It may never happen again. I don't honestly know. But if it does, you'll be the last to know."

"That's good," I said, even though I had a knot in my stomach the size of my heart.

"I am sorry, Garth. About your dilemma, I mean. I wish I could have been more help."

"Believe it or not, you did. I've forgotten all about her for now."

"Pain over pleasure, they always say."

I couldn't have agreed more.

Morning gave way to afternoon. I sat at my desk, doodling on my calendar pad, which was still stuck on January 1983. January had worn through to February in several places, but I hadn't yet had the heart to tear it off. Most of my life at the *Oakalla Reporter* was somewhere on that sheet, which to me seemed worth saving. But as I thought back on that life, all the days that had come and gone, I couldn't remember a tougher day than this one.

I didn't eat lunch. To begin with, I wasn't hungry and secondly, I had yet to write my column for that week's *Oakalla Reporter*. Writing the column was usually not that hard for me, especially when wounded, as I was now. Most writers, even hackers like me, fed off of their emotions, and if the fuel was there, so was the writing. It might not be good writing. I might throw it all away later. But still, I had no trouble putting words on paper.

My problem of late was finding the right subject. It had to be something that I cared about, or it would fall flat, but if I cared about it too much, I found myself on my soapbox with my fist in the air. So I approached my subject that day with a great deal of concern about where I was going to land, once I left the three-meter board. Did I really believe in the paranormal, ghosts in particular, and if so, how did I reconcile it with my very serious doubts on the subject?

Once I finally sat down with my old black Underwood and started typing, I didn't stop for five hours. Not all of that time was spent typing. Most of it was spent thinking about what I wanted to say and how to say it, and answering an occasional phone call. But the entire five hours was spent writing, or in the process of. Not once did I think about Abby, Diana, or Kristina Vice; Ned Cleaver, Dennis Hall, Larry Sharp, or the Lost Scout. And when I finished and read what I'd written, I wished I had a one-way ticket to the Virgin Islands. But it was too late then to make any changes. As the saying goes, I had other fish to fry.

CHAPTER 21

Supper at the Corner Bar and Grill included a perch sandwich with lots of tartar sauce, cole slaw, a Dr. Pepper, and cherry pie a la mode for dessert. The cherries in the pie tasted fresh. Maybe somebody far to the south was picking already.

"Has Robby been in at all this evening?" I said to Hiram.

Robby Rumaley's seat at the bar was still vacant. I was starting to worry about him.

"Nope. I haven't seen him." Hiram took a quick glance around the barroom to see if anyone was watching us. Seeing that they weren't, he said, "You have any luck today finding out what's going on?"

"I found out that Albert Vice was a closet revolutionary. Does that mean I'm on the right track?"

"Yes. But you didn't hear it from me." Hiram quickly put some distance between us.

From where I sat, that was a wise decision on his part. I had the whole south end of the bar to myself, and as people filtered in, in couples and groups of three to six, they either went to the tables, booths, or through the swinging doors into the dining room. Soon the place was packed, except for my little corner of the world. If I didn't know better, I might have felt like a marked man.

Among those who came in were Ned Cleaver, Dennis Hall, Larry Sharp, and Kristina Vice. They didn't have to worry about finding a booth. Theirs had been kept open for them.

"What's the occasion?" I asked Hiram on his way by.

"No occasion. Everybody just showed up tonight."

"Must be the weather."

"Must be." He hurried on.

Dennis, Larry, and Kristina were all wearing dark new jeans, cowboy boots, and colorful western shirts—in combinations of blues, yellows and reds. Ned wore the same jeans, work boots, and T-shirt that he'd been wearing earlier that day, along with the same grey stubble on his chin. I noticed one other person besides me taking an unusual interest in them—Sandy Hall, Dennis's estranged wife, who was sitting at the opposite end of the bar from me. She, too, had on boots, designer jeans, and a colorful pink-and-white western shirt. Maybe there was a line dance scheduled that neither Hiram nor I knew about.

Sandy Hall noticed me looking at her, but instead of turning away, she picked up her drink and came down to my end of the bar. "You look lonely down here," she said as she sat beside me.

Sandy Hall was about Diana's height and build and had Diana's light brown hair and pale gray eyes, but there the resemblance ended. She wore a lot more makeup

than Diana ever had, spent a lot more time in front of the
mirror teasing her hair, and a lot less time at home. Sandy
liked to be where the action was, and most of the action
in Oakalla took place in somebody's bedroom. In Sandy's
case, it often wasn't her own.

"Buy me a drink?" Sandy said, slurring her words a
little.

"Sure," I said, even though a drink seemed the last
thing she needed. "What are you drinking?"

"Jack Daniel's."

"Straight up?"

"That goes without saying."

With some difficulty, I finally got Hiram's attention,
and he went after Sandy's Jack Daniel's. Meanwhile I
noticed Ned, Dennis, Larry, and Kristina staring openly at
us.

"Why aren't you with your buddies over there?" I
said to Sandy.

"They didn't invite me. Too good for me, I guess. Isn't
that right?" she turned all the way around on her bar
stool to shout. "You're all too fucking good for me."

Embarrassed, they all looked away. Except for
Kristina, who only had eyes for me. But they weren't the
soft bedroom eyes of earlier that day—rather the baleful
eyes of a woman scorned.

It was time to make my exit. If I stayed there much
longer, something bad was bound to happen.

"Give me your keys," Hiram said to Sandy before he
would serve her.

"Fuck you, Hiram. Garth here is going to drive me
home."

"If you're leaving now," I said, sliding off my stool,
"I'd be glad to."

"It's your call," Hiram said to Sandy.

"Then put that sonofabitch in a plastic cup," she said

about her Jack Daniel's.

A couple minutes later Sandy Hall and I left a dead silent Corner Bar and Grill together. I decided to take her car and leave Cecil's patrol car parked there in front of the Corner Bar and Grill, since I didn't want anyone to know where I was going after I took her home. Her car turned out to be a black five-speed Chevy S-10 pickup. She gave me the keys, then scooted over to help me drive. Every time I shifted, I first had to nudge one or both of her legs out of the way.

"This is nice," she purred, both hands on my shoulder, as she dribbled Jack Daniel's down my shirt.

I'm dead, I thought, as I shifted once more.

Sandy Hall lived in the far west end house where she and Dennis Hall used to live before they separated, and he went to live in an apartment over the post office. Originally it was a one-story frame starter home, but during the ten years that they had lived there, Dennis had added a fireplace, deck, and second story, then bricked it. According to Ruth, that was one of the reasons why Dennis had stayed in his marriage so long and was still reluctant to get a divorce, even though Sandy was seeing other men, and had been when they were together. He had put so much of himself into his house, he hated to give it up. Sandy wouldn't agree to sell her half to Dennis, since that was the only hold she still had on him. So there it stood—a beautiful two-story brick home with a single occupant.

"You're coming in, of course," Sandy said, after we'd parked in her driveway.

"I'm sorry, Sandy, I can't. I have a newspaper to put out tonight."

I hadn't tried yet to untangle myself from her. I was counting on her to do that for me.

"Won't take us long," she said, blowing in my ear.

"I'm a fast starter."

Part of me said what the hell. I was going to do the time anyway, so why not do the crime. Better judgment said be that as it may, it would still be a mistake.

"Okay," I said. "Let's go."

"Right here in the truck?" She was willing if I was.

"I was thinking about inside."

With some difficulty we both squeezed out the driver's side door at the same time. I noticed, as we walked arm in arm toward her front door, that night was about to fall. Where had the day gone, I wondered, and what would the night bring?

"Ladies first," I said when we got to her front door.

She opened the screen door and went inside. I stayed where I was. It didn't take her long to size up the situation.

"You bastard," she said, as she threw the rest of her Jack Daniel's through the screen at me.

I shrugged.

"What has she got that I haven't got?"

She was pressed against the screen, peering out at me. She reminded me of a child, wanting, against her own better judgment, to go outside and play in the dark.

"Who?"

"Kristina. I hear you two have a thing going."

"You heard wrong."

"Yeah, yeah, that's what we all say. But for your information, you're not the only one she's screwing."

Did I want to hear this, even though it might shed some light on Albert Vice's death? I didn't think so. Not under these circumstances anyway.

"Goodnight, Sandy. Your keys will be somewhere out in your yard."

I gave her keys a toss and started walking. With any luck, she'd find them again in the morning.

"Why not me?" she shouted, as she opened the screen and stepped outside. "If I'm not your type, just say so."

She wasn't my type, but what would be the point in saying so? "Sandy, you can believe me or not, and I really don't care if you do, but I'm in love with someone else."

"That's nice," she said. "That's real fucking nice. Well, so am I." She slammed both doors on her way inside. To my relief, she never even tried to look for her keys.

Oakalla by day is not Oakalla at night. By day, when the sun is out, the birds are singing, and the gods are beaming with benevolence, Oakalla is a Norman Rockwell painting, casual and colorful, with, even on the sternest, hardest-bitten faces, the crinkled corner of a smile. But after dark, when the gods put on their sleeping caps and the ghosts and goblins come out to play, the scene changes.

The smiling face of noon becomes the leer of night. Every fear, every sound is magnified by the thickening wall of shadows, and every blackguard's heart seems to grow blacker. Imagination, given nowhere else to turn but inside, finds within itself all the horrors left over from childhood, and hears, following everywhere upon the dark deserted streets, the hobnail clatter of death.

Of course, nothing's really changed. You just can't see, that's all. But that didn't keep me from stopping every fifty yards or so to cast a worried glance over my shoulder. Somebody was out there somewhere. The hair on my nape never lied.

Robby Rumaley's small grey bungalow had been the one beneficiary of Robby's four failed marriages because each time he married, he did something to spruce up the house in order to please his new bride, and to show her, if nothing else, that he was a handy man to have around.

Each of the women that Robby had married was, according to Ruth, a "good" woman. Each had filed for divorce
only as a last resort, when Robby's drinking finally got the
better of her. Robby wasn't a mean drunk. He was just the
opposite—too willing to buy drinks all around, or to help
somebody down on his luck, until, at closing time at the
Corner Bar and Grill, he had very little to take home from
his day's work. It was hard to set a budget that way, or to
pay the bills when they came due. Also, Robby wasn't
home very much, once he got the place spruced up.

After each divorce, Robby had vowed to quit drinking
and had done so until he got married again—except for
his last divorce nearly a year ago when he said to hell
with it and kept right on drinking.

I had gotten to know Robby Rumaley when, in an
earlier, more innocent time, he had bartered a small
plumbing job at my house for a fishing trip to Grandmother Ryland's pond. It was the first of many fishing
trips that we made there together, and I knew of no one,
except Grandmother herself, who took more delight in
catching bluegill than Robby Rumaley. Sometimes his
stringer would almost drag to the ground as we walked up
the dusty lane to the house, where his truck was parked.
One other thing that I noticed, no matter how much beer
Robby brought along, whether a six-pack or a twelve-
pack, it was always gone at the end of the outing. I'd drink
my two and he'd drink the rest. He was married to his
second wife then and vowing that this time it would be
different. After that marriage failed, our trips to Grandmother's pond became less frequent. When his third marriage failed, we stopped going altogether.

Robby's white panel truck was parked in his drive,
but there weren't any lights on inside his house. This near
to town with only the railroad between us, I would have
expected to hear more town noises there. Yet, as I sat on

his front porch wondering what to do, all that I could hear were the peepers singing in the small lowland meadow behind his house and the faintest rustle of wind in the giant sugar maple that shaded most of Robby's front yard.

"Is that you, Garth?" Robby's voice came from inside the house.

"It's me. How did you know?"

Robby opened the front screen door and stepped out onto the porch carrying a can of Old Style. "I figured it either had to be you or Bobby. I was hoping it was you."

He sat down beside me on the top porch step and set the can of Old Style between us. "I'd offer you one," he said. "But this is my last."

"That's okay. I've got work to do when I leave here."

"It's my first beer of the day." It was important to Robby that I know that.

"You been rationing yourself?"

"Trying. But it doesn't work very well."

"How come you've been staying away from the Corner Bar and Grill? Are you avoiding me?"

"You and Bobby."

Bobby again. "Just who the hell *is* Bobby?"

"I thought you knew, Garth. He's the Lost Scout."

In the moments that followed, the peepers picked up their chant to a fever pitch, then suddenly stopped as if something was prowling the meadow below. Although it was a warm evening compared to evenings past, I had to brush my arms to take the chill away.

"You mind explaining yourself?" I said.

"If you've got time."

I didn't even look at my watch to see how far behind schedule I already was. "I'll make time."

Robby took a drink of his beer and set the can down between us again. He seemed to be nursing it, trying to make it last as long as possible.

"This goes back to the summer of 1959. June, I think," he said. "It was early in the summer, whenever it was, because school hadn't been out for very long and I was on my way to Scout camp. Camp Collier, if you know where that is."

"I know" was all I said.

"I'd already been to a couple summer camps there and couldn't say I cared for it much. There wasn't much to do there except to climb up and down rocks and maybe take a canoe trip, if you could ever get a canoe. Of course, there was the usual Boy Scout stuff, and everybody except me was always buck-eager to earn all the merit badges they could. Survival stuff, mostly. Stuff I was never much good at—unlike my older brothers, who, to hear my old man tell it, were God's gift to the Boy Scouts."

Robby picked up his beer, but set it down again without taking a drink of it. He said, "Then there was Ned Cleaver, the splendid splinter himself, who, just by looking at you, could make you feel lower than whale shit on the bottom of the ocean. So our troop wasn't much on playing pranks and bending the rules, the way some of the other troops were. And stuck as we were way up in Cabin 10, with only the ghost for company, it seemed we were completely out of the swim of things. Hell, a camping trip out to Bare Ass Beach would have beaten Camp Collier hands down, as far as I was concerned. At least we could have brought some girls along."

I listened as the peepers started up again. Whatever was out there had moved on.

"So, like I said, I wasn't too excited about going back to Camp Collier, but my old man said go, so I went. It was either that or listen to his shit for a week." Robby eased his right hand into his lap and away from the beer. "Things started out pretty much the way that I expected them to. Once we unpacked, I knew the first thing that

Ned would want to do would be to head for Owl Creek.
That's where the steepest bluffs were, and he took no end
of delight in seeing how high and fast he could climb,
leaving all of us eating his dust. We were already there on
the other side of the creek where all the bluffs are, with
me tagging along behind as always, when I just happened
to look up and see this kid flattened out against the rock
above us. He wasn't moving a muscle, just standing there
stiff as a wedding prick, as if waiting to pounce on one of
us. But the minute he saw that I had seen him, he jumped
down from the rock and fell in beside me.

"'What's your name?' I said.

"'Bobby. What's yours?'

"'Robby.'

"'We rhyme,' he said, putting his arm around my
shoulder. 'That must make us buddies.'

"'Are you from around here?' I said.

"'Yeah, but my squad's a bunch of sissies, so I'm
deserting. Can I join up with you guys?'

"'Sure. Why not.'"

It was there that I interrupted Robby. "Are you sure
that he said *squad*, instead of troop?"

"Yeah. That wasn't the only thing he got wrong either.
He always referred to the dining hall as the mess hall and
the cabins as the barracks. And when I told him that
Cabin 10 was haunted, he said that was no big deal since
he was a ghost himself. If you want to know the truth,
Garth, I don't think Bobby was really a Boy Scout."

I rubbed my arms again to get the blood going. "If
you're asking my opinion, Robby, I don't think he was
either."

"It didn't matter, though," Robby said, "whether he
was or not, because he was the best buddy I could ever
ask for. We won the canoe race and nearly every other
two-man contest they had that week; and every troop

contest they had, we won that too, since there was no way we could lose with Bobby and Ned Cleaver pulling on the same rope. Bobby was a natural. There was no way of getting around it. And the things he didn't think of to pull on the other cabins . . . Well, they just weren't worth doing, that's all."

Robby's smile went from ear to ear. He seemed to have forgotten that I was even there—immersed as he was in the past.

"What did Ned Cleaver think about Bobby?"

Robby's smile began to fade, then went away altogether. "It's funny you should ask that, Garth, since I don't think Ned took to Bobby at all, seeing the way Bobby took some of the shine out of Ned's star. On the other hand, Bobby couldn't have cared less who got the glory. You could tell he was doing everything just for the fun of it. It was like . . . I don't quite have the words for it. It was like 'damn the torpedoes and full speed ahead.' Like he was living on borrowed time and wanted to take a good big bite out of life while he still could. Like that guy in a book I read once, who dies in the end because his buddy pushes him from a tree, or like those people who die, then get a second chance to come back to earth for a while. He'd walk right along the edge of the highest bluff, just daring one of us to nudge him and push him off." Robby paused, his face suddenly sad. "Which I believe is what happened to him."

I waited for Robby to finish his beer. It didn't take him long once he started.

"Another dead soldier." Robby set the beer can down, then gave it a nudge, which sent it rolling down the steps. "How many of those have I killed in my lifetime?"

We both listened as the beer can rolled along the sidewalk, then out into the yard. I noted the peepers were silent again.

Robby said, "That last night we were there at Camp Collier we had our traditional snipe hunt for all the Tenderfeet. We'd been talking it up to them all week, filling their heads with all kinds of stories, Bobby in particular, so we had them all primed for a good time, or so we thought. Bobby was in the lead and Ned was next in line, the rest of us falling out behind, when Bobby just disappeared, like the night had opened up its jaws and swallowed him whole. Ned, who was then leading, wouldn't let any of the rest of us look for Bobby. He said it was too dangerous out there off the beaten path, too easy to fall off a bluff, or step right off into a blind canyon. So we went ahead with our snipe hunt, but for me the fun had already gone out of it.

"We were on our way back to camp later on that night when, somewhere out there, I heard someone screaming for help. Bobby, I was sure of it, but when I tried to get Ned to stop and go look for him, he wouldn't. He claimed that it was just a wildcat, that there was not now, and never had been, a Bobby. And if I knew what was best for me, I wouldn't say anything more about it."

"What do you think, Robby? Was there really a Bobby?" Because for all of his talk, he no longer seemed sure.

Robby wouldn't look at me. He looked at the steps of the porch instead. "I think Ned Cleaver is, and was then, a bald-face liar. But after all these years even I started to believe him. Until I saw Bobby again."

"You were drunk at the time, Robby," I said.

"True, but I wasn't drunk that week at Camp Collier. Maybe everything didn't happen exactly the way I said it did. I'm a little fuzzy on the details sometimes. Maybe Bobby was gone from sight more often than not, but he *was* there. I'd swear that on my mother's grave."

I wanted to believe him, but wasn't sure I did. If

necessity is the mother of invention, loneliness is the father of deception.

"What did Bobby look like?" I said.

Robby was staring at something terrifying that I couldn't see—perhaps, if I were lucky, would never see. "You know, Garth, I've been trying to picture him all these years, but I can't. He was a presence more than anything else, more spirit than body."

"A large or small presence?"

"A giant presence to somebody like me—short, small, never been anywhere and going nowhere. Bobby was all of the things that I wanted to be, would have been, if I'd just had the guts."

"It's not too late, Robby."

"It was too late then, Garth. It's way too late now."

We watched Robby's beer can blink on and off in the lights of a passing car. "What does Larry Sharp have to do with all of this?" I said.

"Larry's got nothing to do with it. I'm on his case for another reason."

"Which is?"

"He's a baby killer, Garth. Or wants to be."

"I don't think I understand, Robby."

Robby got up, walked out into the yard, and brought his beer can back to the porch with him. He seemed less afraid with it there beside him.

Robby said, "Larry and some of his buddies there at the cheese plant have got themselves a little militia started. He asked me to join, but I told him what he could do with it."

"In all fairness to Larry," I said, "I don't think the purpose of his militia, or any militia, is to kill babies."

"That's what happened in Oklahoma City, isn't it, and Waco? Babies got killed, Garth. Never mind who started it. I mean, that's the way some of these people think. They'll use any excuse, and all the firepower they've got to go out and blow somebody away."

I watched another car drive by, this one headed south on Fickle Road. As it topped the next rise in the road and disappeared, I felt the night settle in again.

"I still don't think it's that simple, Robby. I don't trust the government to always do right by me. Do you?"

"No, but I don't trust a bunch of yahoos running around the countryside carrying AK-47's either. That's what we have elections for, to throw the bums out if we don't like what they're doing."

"And if we don't like our choices, or feel we have one?"

"Then beat the bushes until somebody crawls out. Mark my words, Garth. Larry Sharp needs to be stopped. That whole outfit there at the cheese plant does."

"Do you think they mean you any harm?"

"No. I'm no threat to them. They don't even know I'm here. But I couldn't swear about you. With Albert Vice dead and all, they've gotten their necks stretched out way too far."

I got up from the porch and took a couple steps to get my legs back in working order. Gone were the days when I didn't have to think about such things.

"Garth, if for some reason I don't see you again, it's been nice knowing you," Robby said. "Those days fishing out there on your grandmother's pond—well, they were something to remember. It was like being a kid all over again."

"Then why did you quit going with me?"

"Why did you quit asking?"

"I'll see you again, Robby," I said, trying, and failing, to sound upbeat.

He shook his head. "I'm not so sure, Garth. I think Bobby might be coming for me tonight. If he does, I'll have to go."

The peepers fell silent once again as I walked down Robby's drive on my way to Fickle Road. Though I saw no sign of Bobby and doubted that he even existed, I could feel his presence as surely as I could my own heartbeat. He *was* watching and waiting somewhere out in the shadows, and if he didn't come for Robby tonight, he would someday soon.

CHAPTER 22

The next few hours I was too busy to think about much of anything. For good or ill, the *Oakalla Reporter* had to go to press that night, and I had to make sure that it did. Help would have been welcome anywhere along the line, but permanent employees, even temporary ones, opened the door to a lot of government red tape that I could do without. So I agreed wholeheartedly with those who thought that less government was the way to go. But no government at all appealed to me about as much as a crushed glass sundae. So while I respected the right of Larry Sharp, Ned Cleaver, Dennis Hall, and their cohorts at the cheese plant to form their own militia, I thought that they were playing a dangerous game. In case I had any doubts, I need only think about Albert Vice and Cecil Hardwick.

"What do you think?" I asked my printer about that week's first off the press *Oakalla Reporter*.

I never tired of holding that very first paper, still warm and fragrant with the smell of printer's ink. I hoped I never would.

"I think we got everything where it should be," he said.

"I mean my column." I knew he'd been reading it because he always did.

He handed the paper back to me and went to check those now coming off the press. "I think we got everything where it should be."

Suspicions confirmed. I'd laid an egg, my first in a while. The phone rang.

"*Oakalla Reporter*," I said, thinking it might be Ruth calling to find out how far along I was.

"Garth, this is Hiram at the Corner Bar and Grill. I think there might be trouble headed your way."

I wasn't at my best at that hour of the morning. It took me a while to figure out what he meant.

"How many of them are there?" I said.

"Four, by my count, when they left here."

"Is Kristina Vice with them?"

"I might be wrong, but I think she's leading the pack."

Shakespeare was right. Hell hath no fury like a woman scorned.

"They're all three sheets to the wind," Hiram went on to say. "Except for maybe Ned Cleaver. But he's as far gone as I've ever seen him."

"Walking or driving?"

"Walking. I took their keys away a long time ago."

Which meant that they were probably in no shape to listen to reason. "Thanks, Hiram, I owe you one."

"Just remember, mum's the word."

"Who was that?" my printer said, as he carried in a bundle of papers, all of which needed mailing labels.

"A friend. How about we address these at your place?"

To his credit, he didn't even ask me why, as he turned around, bundle in hand, and started back the other way. "How much time do we have?"

"Not much, I don't think."

"Then you might pick up those mailing labels on your way out."

My printer owned an old green Pontiac station wagon that looked like a tank and drove like one. We loaded it in record time, and as soon as I turned off the lights and locked the door, we took off. We met Ned Cleaver, Dennis Hall, Larry Sharp, and Kristina Vice on their way down Gas Line Road. As they ducked away from the Pontiac's bright lights, Kristina flipping us the bird as they did, I thought I saw something long-handled resting on Dennis Hall's right shoulder that gave rise to a sickening thought. What if they weren't after me, but the *Oakalla Reporter*?

"There's been a change of plans," I said to my printer. "Take me to the Corner Bar and Grill."

Thank God. Cecil's squad car was still parked out front when we arrived, and all four tires appeared to be up. Maybe they didn't think it was any danger to them there, or maybe they weren't thinking period.

"This is as far as I go," I said to my printer. "Thanks. Can you get the labels on yourself?"

"If I can't, Mary Ann can help me. You sure *you* don't need any help?"

"I think I'm beyond that," I said as I got out of the Pontiac.

Once I saw that Cecil's Impala was going to start, and run once it started, I put my plan into immediate action, with a silent thanks to Rupert Roberts who, since I was riding along anyway, insisted that I learn how to operate a squad car. Lights whirling, siren whooping, the Impala and I headed for the east end of town. I also called the state police for backup in case I needed them. This had gone far enough. It was time to start treating those involved like the thugs they were.

I arrived at the *Oakalla Reporter* to find the back door standing open, and no one inside. They must have left in a hurry. They'd even left their sledgehammer there beside my press. Where had it come from, since I doubted that they had brought it to the Corner Bar and Grill with them? The cheese plant, I guessed, since it was on their way.

A few minutes later a state police car pulled up and parked beside the Impala. When the young cop inside got out, I knew everything was going to be okay. He and I had done business in the past.

"I might have known it was you," he said with a smile. "How are you?"

He offered his hand. I shook it. His was a large hand. He was a large man with remarkably clear blue eyes and a smooth ruddy face that never seemed to need a shave.

"I'm fine now that you're here. Thanks," I said.

"What do we have besides a breaking and entering?" he said, examining my back door, which had been forced open.

"I've got a list that will fill your notebook, but I don't think I'll bother you with it just yet."

We went inside the *Oakalla Reporter* where we could survey the damage. But the only thing that had been broken was the back door.

"It looks like they planned to do some serious damage," he said, picking up the sledgehammer.

"One might assume that." Just looking at the sledgehammer left me with a sick feeling inside.

"You have any names for me?"

"Yes, but I'd like first crack at them."

He was still smiling, but beneath the smile, he was all cop. "Then why don't you give me the names in case something happens to you."

"Nothing's going to happen to me."

"I imagine that's what Marshal Hardwick thought." He took out his notebook. "Names, please."

I gave them to him.

"This have anything to do with that fellow they found in the quarry?" he said as he put his notebook away.

"It might. I don't know yet."

"Are you in charge now that Marshal Hardwick is laid up?"

"Who else?"

"It must be hard wearing so many hats."

"That's not the half of it."

We went outside, where there appeared to be a million stars in a moonless sky. I still planned to visit every one of them.

"You get in a bind, you let me know," the young cop said.

"You'll be the first."

He smiled. He had large, even white teeth. With his blond hair and boyish good looks, he could have done cop commercials, if there were such a thing.

"I wish I could believe that," he said.

What I had left out of his resume was that he was exceptionally perceptive for someone so young.

"I like to keep these things in house if I can," I said.

"I know. But that might be the death of you some day. I'd hate that." He opened the door to the squad car to get in, then had a second thought. "I hear you found that revolver you were looking for," he said, referring to our last case together. "You mind telling me how, the way

212 John R. Riggs

the snow was drifted?"

I tapped my temples. "Kidneys."

"Truthfully."

"Truthfully, I waited until the next day and got a search warrant."

"It was in the house all along?"

"Much to my surprise. Some people, it seems, never throw anything away."

"I'll have to remember that."

He got in his patrol car and drove away. I closed the back door to the *Oakalla Reporter* as best I could and drove home, parking the Impala in front of the house because I was too tired to put it away. I wasn't surprised to find a light on and Ruth sitting in her living room chair when I walked in the front door. If she had been asleep, she was awake now.

"You're home early," she said.

"You couldn't prove it by me."

I felt instead like I had just put in a thirty-six-hour day. I handed Ruth a copy of the *Oakalla Reporter* and sat down on the couch.

"Am I supposed to read this?" she said.

"Only my column."

While she read, I took note of her haggard appearance, the vivid dark blotches under her eyes. I had never seen her look any worse. To the uninformed, it would appear that she was seriously ill. A few more days of lost sleep, and she might be.

"Well?" I said when she finished.

"You don't want to hear it."

"Yes, I do."

"Okay, I think it's about the worst thing you've ever done. I'm trying to remember if it *is* the worst, but memory fails me at this point. Whatever possessed you, Garth, to straddle the fence? You know you can't write that way."

I took the paper back from her and dropped it on the coffee table, where it could stay until it rotted, as far as I was concerned. "I thought you were the one who told me to get off my soapbox," I said.

"I did. But I didn't tell you to go stick your head in the sand. Do you believe in ghosts or not, Garth? I can't tell after reading your column. Neither, I bet, will anyone else."

I picked up the *Oakalla Reporter* and started to read my column, then threw it back on the coffee table. I already knew what I'd written. In brief, what I had said was that every claim to the supernatural, including religion, was subjective. Just because God had never spoken to me personally didn't mean that He didn't talk to someone else more in His favor; or just because I couldn't say for certain that I had ever seen a ghost, or felt its presence, didn't mean that they didn't exist, or couldn't exist. Some people believed in God but didn't believe in ghosts; others believed in ghosts but didn't believe in God. Still others laid everything at the feet of extraterrestrials and had the stitches to prove it.

So what did I know? What I knew, or strongly felt anyway, was that if you were in for a penny, you were in for a pound. If God existed, so did ghosts, goblins, Darth Vader, ET, and so did Satan, as much as I disliked that fact. To think less would be to diminish God—for Whom all things were possible. Unless, of course, He chose otherwise. So then we were back to splitting hairs about what He chose to reveal and to whom He chose to reveal it. To say that there was some disagreement over that brought to mind the phrase "countless dead."

My problem with the supernatural was that I couldn't prove it existed. No one could, unless you just took their word for it. Of course, neither could I prove that atoms existed, but someone out there could to my satisfaction, without having to drop an atom bomb on my doorstep. Though that would be the ultimate proof.

My problem with dismissing the supernatural was that if in confronting the beauty, harmony, and ultimate *sense* of the universe, I was not seeing the visible hand of God, what more proof did I need? Whether a ghost was an unhappy disembodied spirit or a figment of my imagination, what on the grand scale of life and legend did it matter? Let me believe what I would, but right or wrong, when I died, the debate would still go on without me—and without everyone else alive today.

That's what I had said. But evidently I hadn't said it very well, though all the votes weren't in yet.

"I don't know what I believe," I said. "This afternoon in my office, with the sky all warm and blue, and the sun streaming in my north window, there wasn't a ghost to be found. Tonight, listening to Robby Rumaley talk about Bobby, the Lost Scout, I felt that I could have walked right out into the shadows and shaken his hand. So what *do* I believe, Ruth? You tell me."

Ruth, however, was no longer listening. "Run that by me again, Garth. The part about Bobby, the Lost Scout."

So in brief I told her what Robby had told me. When I finished, she thought a moment, then said, "It's possible."

"Come on, Ruth. It's something Robby made up."

But she wouldn't back off. "You said yourself that you felt Bobby's presence there in the shadows. Well, I've felt his presence, too. Right here. In this house. In this room."

I closed my eyes and put my fist to my forehead. "Don't tell me that. I've got enough to think about the way it is."

"You're the one who brought him up."

"No. Robby's the one who brought him up, then convinced me that he was real."

"So you admit it."

"I admit that he's a real force. I won't admit that he was ever a real person."

"Stop your pacing," she said. "You're making me nervous."

Without realizing it, I had gotten up and started pacing back and forth across the living room. "Besides," I said, "I've got more immediate problems. Larry Sharp and his friends from the cheese plant tried to trash the *Oakalla Reporter* tonight."

"I wondered what all the sirens were about. If you'd have nipped it in the bud, it would never have come to that."

"Well, I didn't, and it has, so I need your help." I told her what I wanted her to do.

"On one condition," she said when I finished.

"What's that?"

"The Lost Scout. I want you to find him."

Damn. Why didn't she just ask for the moon?

CHAPTER 23

I was on my way down the stairs the next morning when the phone rang. Since Ruth had never made it upstairs to bed, she was the one who answered it.

"For you," she said, holding out the receiver.

"An irate customer?"

"Ben Bryan."

"Yes, Ben, what is it?"

"Robby Rumaley. He's missing. He was supposed to put in a new drain for Fritz Gascho at the hardware store first thing this morning. When he didn't show up or answer his phone, Fritz drove out there to find out what was going on. That's when he called me."

"Why did he call you?"

"You'll find out when you get here."

"What's wrong?" Ruth said after I'd hung up the phone.

"Robby Rumaley is missing."

"Why does that not come as a surprise?"

I got in the Impala and drove out to Robby Rumaley's. Another soft new day, perhaps a couple of degrees warmer than yesterday, was in store for us. It would be a great day to fish for bluegill in Grandmother's pond. If I found Robby, he and I might just do that, and to hell with everything else.

One look at his front porch said that probably wasn't going to happen. The empty Old Style can sat undisturbed on the top step where I had last seen it. A large pool of blood had collected on the porch, then spilled over onto the step, running downhill onto the sidewalk where it finally gave out.

"Well?" Ben Bryan said after I had seen my fill.

"I don't know what to think, Ben."

Ben put on some latex gloves, then opened the plastic bag that he had been holding at his side. It contained a bloody fillet knife with a thin, curved, eight-inch blade.

"Does this look like something Robby would own?" he said, showing the knife to me.

"Yes. It's a fillet knife."

"I know what it is, Garth. Did Robby ever go fishing?"

"He used to. I don't know about lately."

Though I tried, I couldn't get my mind to work. Too much was happening all at once. I didn't want to think anymore.

"Where did you find the knife?" I said.

"In the bushes beside the porch. Whoever put it there didn't take a lot of time hiding it."

"Maybe he didn't have much time," I said.

"That thought occurred to me, too."

"Robby was alive and well at nine," I said. "Because I was here with him."

Ben looked around at the knot of people that had already started to gather behind us. "I wouldn't say that too loudly, Garth. Not until we get a handle on what is going on."

"You have any opinions?"

"Not right off hand. There's no sign of a struggle either inside or outside the house. Had he been attacked, surely Robby would have put up some kind of a fight."

"I'm not so sure about that, Ben. Robby was pretty far down when I talked to him."

"About what?"

"Life in general, I think."

We watched as more cars pulled into Robby's yard, as word of his disappearance spread. Despite his battle with the bottle, Robby was one of Oakalla's most beloved citizens. Even his four ex-wives agreed on that point, which is why each had let him keep the house.

"Speaking of which, my life was a whole lot easier, when your friend, Abby, was here," Ben said.

I avoided the blood on my way down the steps. "What a coincidence. So was mine."

I drove to the Corner Bar and Grill to eat breakfast. I wasn't hungry, but knowing me, I knew that I'd better eat something before Mr. Hyde reared his ugly head. As I came to the Y, where School Street split off from Madison Road, I saw Robby Rumsley's white panel truck parked behind the Corner Bar and Grill. Had it been parked there when I drove by earlier? I couldn't remember.

It seemed that I couldn't get out of the Impala fast enough, but when I went inside the Corner Bar and Grill, it was like a tomb in there, and Robby Rumaley was nowhere in sight.

"Is there something that I can help you with, Garth?"

Bernice said.

"I saw Robby's truck outside and was hoping . . ."

She gently shook her head, killing all hope. "No. It's been there all week, Garth."

I sat down at the counter that ran the length of the dining room and quietly ordered breakfast.

The quiet followed me to the cheese plant, which itself seemed subdued. Nobody went out of his way to help me, but nobody got in my way either. I stood a moment, taking in the spilt-milk smell that always reminded me of our dairy back in Godfrey, Indiana. Those were the days, I thought. Those were the days.

Larry Sharp came out of his office as far as the steel railing that surrounded it, took a long look down at me, and went back inside. "Ned Cleaver around?" I said to the first person I came to.

"No. He didn't show up for work this morning."

"You have a sledgehammer handy? I need to straighten out my car." Which, in Jessie's case, would take more than a sledgehammer.

He motioned to the back of the cheese plant. "There's one in the storeroom, I think."

I thanked him and went back to the storeroom where there wasn't a sledgehammer to be found among all the wooden cheese boxes and assorted cardboard boxes stored there. It occurred to me, only after Dennis Hall and a few of his buddies had made their way in there, that perhaps I'd made a tactical error.

"What are you doing snooping around in here?" Dennis said.

"I'm looking for your sledgehammer. You haven't by chance seen it, have you? The state police seem to be very much interested in it."

Dennis looked around at his buddies for support, but they suddenly found other places they needed to be. I was starting to think that the cheese plant's was a fair-weather militia, which was just as well from where I stood.

"We don't own a sledgehammer," he said.

"That's not what the guy on the forklift said."

"Well, he's wrong."

"How about a fillet knife, say with a curved blade about eight inches long? Any of you guys in the militia own one?"

Dennis Hall was one of those not so subtle people whose faces betray their every thought. He wanted to cut and run, but his pride wouldn't let him.

"I don't know anything about any militia," he said. "Fillet knife either."

"You do know that Robby Rumaley was killed with one."

"The way I hear it, he's only missing, not dead."

Dennis wore jeans, work boots, and a black T-shirt. His jeans and shirt, like his voice, were drum tight.

"Believe what you want, Dennis," I said. "You sure there's not a sledgehammer around here somewhere?"

"I told you there wasn't."

"Then, I guess I'll be on my way."

As I started past him, Dennis spun me around grabbing both my biceps. His grip was more powerful than even Ned Cleaver's. Already I could feel my hands start to tingle.

"How was Sandy?" he asked, face to face.

"I don't know. We didn't do anything."

He kept the pressure on. I tried not to let him know how much it hurt.

"That's not what she said."

"Well, it's possible that she doesn't remember last night as well as I do."

"Yeah, I guess that's possible," he said, relaxing his grip a little.

"I'm glad you agree." I shook free and hit him with a left hook in the solar plexus. "Because it's the truth."

The last I saw of him, Dennis Hall was bent low to the cheese plant floor, apparently counting his toes.

I drove to the north end of Home Street where Ned Cleaver lived. His was a neat two-story brown brick house with a big concrete front porch with a high wide brick railing around it, two tall wide front windows standing side by side with the space of a single brick between them, and a badly weathered, down-to-bare-wood front porch swing, whose chains had started to rust from disuse.

Though now in his mid-fifties, Ned Cleaver had never married; had never even dated anyone in the fifteen years that I'd been working the fish fries and the homemade ice cream socials with him. There was a story, probably true, about a Vietnamese woman that he had left behind in Vietnam, who was later executed as a spy by the Viet Cong. Ned didn't talk about Vietnam much, and when he did, it was to politely, but firmly, redirect your questions to something else. And while technically he lived on Home Street, he listed his address as Diamond Street, which used to continue as part of his driveway back to the old softball diamond, which was used until 1961, when they built the new one in the park. One of the reasons, perhaps the main one, that Ned had bought that particular house was because of all of the fond memories that he had made on that old softball diamond as a kid. In some ways, he hung on to the past even tighter than I.

Ned was out back, trimming the hedge that ran between his yard and Rolf Peterson's to the south. Ned's back yard had a fruit tree growing every few feet, all of which were now in bloom, and ended in a plowed field that used to be a vacant lot. When I was a kid, the field was the place where Oakalla used to hold its free shows, and upon our blanket with a bushel of popcorn between us, Grandmother and I used to sit and watch nearly every show—at least until the popcorn ran out.

I walked over to where Ned was clacking away with his trimmer, paring down the hedge so that it would be waist-high all along the yard. He had changed clothes from when I'd seen him last to another pair of jeans and a different T-shirt, this one yellow and faded, but he had yet to shave for two days now.

"Morning, Ned," I said. "As always, you do good work."

"What is it, Garth?" He continued with his trimming, making it clear that he wasn't going to stop to talk to me.

"You enjoy your walk last night?" I said.

"What walk was that?"

"The one down Gas Line Road. At least I think that was you I saw in the company of Dennis Hall and his sledgehammer."

He stopped trimming long enough to kill the deerfly on his neck, then started up again. "I'm afraid you have the wrong person."

"Maybe. Maybe not. But I did think you were above that sort of thing."

"You're saying this to a combat veteran of Vietnam? Believe me, Garth, given the right circumstances, there's nothing I'm *above*."

"Does that include murder?"

"It includes whatever you want it to. But I haven't killed anybody lately, if that's what you're asking."

"That's what I was asking. You heard about Robby Rumaley?"

"I heard he's missing. When Larry called to ask me why I wasn't at work, he told me about it."

"Why aren't you at work?"

He closed the trimmers, locked them, then held them down against his right leg. "Ask what you came to ask,

Garth, so I can get done what I need to do."

"The Lost Scout. Robby Rumaley said last night that he knew him."

"Bobby, right?"

"Yes," I said, surprised that he would admit it.

"Did Robby tell you that he was the only one of us Scouts who ever saw him?"

"No. Though I wondered if that was the case."

"That's the case."

"Then you and Bobby weren't rivals? He and Robby didn't win the two-man canoe race?"

Ned was looking out over the plowed field, which was being planted even as we spoke. "Is that what Robby told you, that Bobby and I were rivals?"

"Among other things. He also said Bobby was a natural at everything he did."

Ned's smile took me by surprise. It was not something that he did often, or well.

He said, "God, it was great, wasn't it, being a kid. You could be anybody you wanted to be and nobody could tell you different."

"That's your answer?" I said.

"I owe Robby that much."

He unlocked his trimmers and went back to work. I stood watching him, wondering what I'd just learned. When it became obvious that I wouldn't learn any more, I left.

At home I called Ben Bryan and told him that perhaps we had better impound Robby's truck until we could find out what was going on.

He said he already had, then added, "Garth, that wasn't chicken blood there on Robby's front steps."

"Somehow I knew that."

"But there was none in Robby's house. I checked it again after you left."

"What about his truck. Did you check that?"

"Nothing there either."

"Maybe we had better let the state police know what's going on just in case."

"As soon as you're off the phone."

I let Daisy out of the basement, put her on her leash, and we headed for Camp Collier. Daisy sat right beside me in the front seat whenever we drove anywhere, leaving some of those in Oakalla to speculate to Ruth about the "hot young babe" I had in the car with me. I figured Daisy needed room to run with no male dogs about, and I needed some time to think. If she pointed a grouse in the meantime, so much the better. We hadn't been hunting together for a long time—not even the pretend hunts that Doc and I would take her on with our unloaded shotguns. She had to miss it as much as I did.

Along with Daisy, I had brought Grandfather Ryland's Model 97 twelve-gauge shotgun. For years it had stood behind Grandmother's pantry door collecting dust, and in the years since, it had stood in my bedroom closet collecting dust—since it had a full-choke barrel and was not even a good pretend grouse gun, loaded or not. Today it was loaded, however, with some three-inch magnums, #2 shot goose loads, which I'd picked up at a garage sale somewhere, thinking that someday I'd have a use for them. I wasn't expecting trouble, but then I wasn't expecting Preston Kurtz to pull his Colt .45 on me the last time I was there. Be prepared. That was the Scout motto.

We parked next to the mess hall and went up the hill toward Cabin 10. Still on her leash, Daisy led with her tail wagging double time and her nose to the ground. "Slow down," I said, as she dragged me through our umpteenth low-hanging branch. "I'll let you go in a minute."

I had kept her on lead because I didn't want her to surprise anyone at Cabin 10 and get herself shot. But I need not have worried. A close examination of the cabin and the garbage pit told me that no one had been there since I had, and no one was there now—not even the ghost, who failed to chill me as it had before when I went up into the loft. In her eagerness to get at a red squirrel, Daisy tripped the trip wire, pulling the can out of the bush, so I had to reset it again before we started back down the hill.

After slamming into a juniper tree, I unsnapped her leash and let Daisy go on her merry way because I could no longer keep up with her. Besides, I had come here to think, and I couldn't think while being dragged down the hill, dodging everything in sight.

Who was Preston Kurtz and what was his agenda? And who had been staying at Cabin 10? It could have been Preston Kurtz who had been staying there, but why two sleeping bags and why go to all of that trouble when he had a truck and camper handy? So if not Preston Kurtz, then who? Had he been the one, as I believed possible, to put the punji sticks where Albert Vice was sure to fall on them? Was Albert Vice his target all along, or just a victim of circumstance?

And as long as I was thinking about such matters, where had Robby Rumaley gone and why? Had Bobby really come for him at last? If so, I either had to rethink my opinion of Bobby, or Robby Rumaley himself.

Since I no longer heard Daisy thrashing around through the underbrush, I assumed that she was on point. The trouble was that I couldn't see her anywhere. In her lemon-and-white coat, she blended in perfectly with the new leaves, and there wasn't any use calling for her. Once she went on point, she stayed there until either I found her and flushed the bird, or the bird got nervous and flushed on its own.

So I tried to make as much noise as possible in order

for the grouse, if that's what she had pointed, to hear me and take off. Except it's a lot harder, short of beating a stick against a tree, to make noise in the woods in May than in October. Wet, snow-flattened spring leaves don't crunch nearly as well underfoot as do frosty, freshly fallen autumn leaves.

So that failing, I fired the shotgun, which left my ears ringing, but the woods strangely quiet; and still no Daisy. I fired again, this time bruising my shoulder. At least I knew the shells worked.

Worried now, since the Lost 1600 is pocked with sinkholes and sunken caves, I began to call out to Daisy for fear that she might have fallen into one of them. When the answering woof was weak and seemingly distant, though I knew she couldn't be that far away, it confirmed my fear. She was underground somewhere.

"Daisy?" I yelled again.

She woofed again. It sounded like she was just below the crest of the small knoll that I was on and not where I would expect either a cave or a sinkhole to be. I took short gingerly steps because I didn't want to fall in there with her. At that, I nearly did, stopping inches short of almost certain death.

Someone had taken hardwood saplings, sharpened and fired them, then dug a hole and buried them points up two feet below the forest floor, leaving at least the top foot of each of them exposed. He had then covered them over with branches and leaves to hide his handiwork, and to insure a hard, likely fatal fall for whoever was unlucky enough to drop in. In this case it happened to be Daisy, who luckily fell between the first row of sharpened sticks and the edge of the hole and was pinned there with the sticks at her back, but none sticking in her.

"Hang on, girl, I'll get you out of there in a minute."

"Woof!" Such trust could move mountains.

Lying on my stomach, I could reach down far enough to grasp Daisy's front legs, but not get my hands all the way behind her shoulders without risking toppling into the hole myself. As I started to pull her up, she started to pull backwards, afraid to let her back feet leave the ground.

"Damn it, Daisy, it's for your own good."

"Woof." Bullshit, loosely translated.

I hated to let go of her for fear that she would avoid me from then on, which would leave me no choice but to leave her there while I went in search of a shovel. But in the end that was what I had to do. The tug of war wasn't doing either one of us any good.

"Woof?" Daisy said as I left.

"Hang in there. I won't be long."

I remembered that there was a shovel at the garbage pit behind Cabin 10. Although it wasn't all that far back up the hill, it seemed like an eternity as I imagined all the pitfalls that might be in my way. No one who has never been to war can imagine what war is like. But I was starting to get an inkling.

Sweating now, deerflies feasting on my wet back, I went even slower on my way down the hill than I had going up. Daisy meanwhile had given up on me. She lay curled in a tight ball at the bottom of the hole.

"Oh ye of little faith," I said.

"Woof" you.

It took over an hour to dig her out. Neither did she in any way help matters. The closer I got to her, the harder she tried to get out on her own, making it almost impossible to shovel around her flailing legs. Then, in her eagerness to thank me once I broke through, she bowled me over on her way out of the hole, using my chest as her springboard to freedom. But that's why we call them man's best friend.

I could have gotten her out with a lot less work by digging a sloping shallow trench to her, but I wanted in the hole myself so that I could get at the sharpened sticks with the shovel. When I had chopped them all off to ground level, I put Daisy on her leash, and we very slowly made our way the rest of the way down the hill to the car.

CHAPTER 24

I knew what I should do. All the way back to Oakalla I told myself that as soon as I got there, I would call the state police, who in turn would call the governor, who likely would call out the National Guard, who would search every square foot of the Lost 1600 for booby traps, like the one Daisy had found. What a media circus that would be. Though on a much different level, it would be Waco and Oklahoma City all over again, and added to the lives already lost, there would be more.

Ned Cleaver, Dennis Hall, Larry Sharp, and their cronies would take a hard fall, probably deservingly so, but in the end would truth, justice, and perhaps more importantly, Oakalla be served? Did we want to be known as the fruitcake capital of the world, and did I want to wash my hands of this without first trying to get to the

bottom of it? I didn't think so, but neither did I want anyone else to get hurt. From now on, if I didn't make the
call, whatever blood was spilled at the Lost 1600 would be
on my hands.

Ruth, who had been sitting in her chair dozing,
watched me pass through the living room with my shotgun in hand and Daisy at my heels. "Should I even ask?"
she said.

"After I put Daisy in the basement."

Daisy voiced not a whimper of complaint when I
opened the basement door, but instead made a beeline
down the basement steps for her food bowl. Before I went
upstairs to put my shotgun away, I checked on supper
and was disappointed not to smell anything cooking in
the oven or to see anything cooking on the stove.
Grumbling to myself the whole way up the stairs, I
decided that my phone call to the state police could wait
at least another day.

"You been here long?" I said to Ruth, as I took a seat
on the couch.

"I just got here."

"That explains about supper, then."

"Sorry, Garth," she said, not really meaning it.
"You're on your own tonight."

"The shelter?"

"Where else," she said with a sigh. "We're making
progress, but it's slow. Abby can't afford to underwrite the
whole thing, and the money we have coming in from other
sources is just a dab here and a dab there. Though that old
doctor's bag you advertised should help us out some."

"I thought it was all smooth sailing from here on."

"You thought wrong. But if it falls through, at least
one of us will be happy."

I let that pass. The damage had already been done as
far as I was concerned, so there was no use arguing about

it, and for Abby's and Ruth's sake, I really did want the shelter to succeed.

"Ned Cleaver says he never saw Bobby, the one Robby Rumaley claims is the Lost Scout," I said.

"Do you believe him?"

"He was there at the time. He has no reason to lie."

"Then what was that shotgun business all about? And why was Daisy so anxious to get to the basement?"

I told her, then finished with the admonition, "So . . . It goes without saying. We stay out of the Lost 1600 from now on."

Her eyes opened wide. "Then how do we find the Lost Scout?"

"Forget the Lost Scout! There is no *Lost Scout!*" I exploded. "He's only a figment of Robby Rumaley's imagination."

"I beg to differ," she said calmly. "Now, I have to leave in a few minutes. Do you want to hear what I learned or not?"

"Is it important?"

"You'll have to decide that for yourself."

"Yes. Then I want to hear it. But I'm telling you, Ruth, the Lost 1600 is a death trap. I came that close . . ." I held my thumb a fraction of an inch away from my forefinger. "That close to calling the state police a minute ago and having a quarantine put on that place until it's safe to go in there again."

"Why didn't you?"

"There are a lot of reasons. The integrity of Oakalla included."

"Your real reason."

I sat back against the couch and raised my hands in surrender. I knew she had me. So did she.

"I want to know the truth of the matter."

"And?"

"And I want to find the Lost Scout."

"Thank you. Now, if you were to look behind the shelter house in the park, say, before daylight tomorrow morning, you might find out something that's been going on for quite some time now. Or so Aunt Emma claims, and she's seldom wrong in these matters."

Ruth's aunt Emma was a retired Army nurse and a storehouse of knowledge about Oakalla—second only to Ruth, according to Ruth, second only to God, according to Aunt Emma. Aunt Emma was also an alcoholic, who yearly confounded her doctor by ignoring his advice and living to tell about it. Though in truth, she rarely drank more than a couple of shots of Scotch a day anymore. She said that when you got to be ninety, why tempt fate.

Ruth said, "I also heard from another source that come the weekend, if you were to wait at the west end of Diamond Street from dark on, you might learn something, too."

"Is Friday considered the weekend?"

"Friday night is."

"Thanks, Ruth. I appreciate it."

She rose wearily from her chair, then used its arm to steady herself. "I'm not sure you should thank me. Now, neither one of us are going to get any sleep."

After Ruth left, I got in Cecil's patrol car and drove to the hospital to see him. He was about to eat supper, so I went down to the cafeteria, filled up my tray, and joined him.

"Where's Helen?" I said between bites of my turkey Manhattan, which, except for the boxed mashed potatoes, wasn't bad for hospital food.

"She's been here all day. I told her to go home and get some rest. Advice that I might pass on to you."

"As someone once said, Cecil, I can sleep all I want when I'm dead." Though, if truth be told, once I started to

fill my belly with turkey Manhattan, I could hardly keep
my eyes open.

"You about to bag the bad guys?" Cecil was eating
soup, which because of his swollen lips, he kept dribbling
down his chin.

"About. A lot depends on what happens tonight."

"I'm not pressing charges," he said matter of factly,
"no matter what happens."

This was news to me. "You mind telling me why?"

"Because, if they were all to go to jail, it would cut
the heart right out of this town."

"True, but they all deserve to go to jail for what they
did to you."

Unable to find his napkin, Cecil used his sheet to
wipe the soup from his chin. A country boy will survive.

"And what will be served by that?" Cecil said.

"Justice, for one thing."

"I didn't take this job to serve out justice. I took it to
keep the peace. So far I've done a piss-poor job of that.
But I aim to get better at it, and I aim for Ned Cleaver,
Dennis Hall, Larry Sharp, and even Kristina Vice, if she
has a mind to, to help me. They can't help me much from
prison."

"They can't hurt you there either."

He laid down his spoon and crossed his arms. With
his brace and bruises, his puffed face and blackened skin,
all that I could recognize of him was the milk-water blue
of his eyes.

"My mind's made up, Garth."

"Well, you'll just have to unmake it, if it turns out
that one or all of them are involved in either Albert Vice's
death or Robby Rumaley's disappearance. Then it won't
be up to you anymore. Me either."

"Do you think that's likely, Garth?"

"I think it's possible until I learn otherwise."

"You're a harder man than I thought," he said with a note of disapproval in his voice.

"I didn't start out that way, Cecil."

"Is that a warning?"

"An observation. Under duress, a lot of so-called good people can do some incredibly bad things—to themselves and those they love. Whether they had reason or not, or would do it again, is beside the point."

"One strike and you're out, is that it?"

"If the strike is a high hard one, yes. Otherwise, there might be room to negotiate."

Cecil tried to smile, but his swollen lips wouldn't let him. "That's all I wanted to hear."

"Good. Because my supper's getting cold."

"There is one other thing, Garth," he said, seemingly hesitant to broach the subject. "They plan on releasing me Sunday. On Monday I plan on being back in my patrol car."

"I'll have it sitting in your driveway first thing Monday morning."

"You don't mind giving it up? I hear from more than one source you've been making good use of it."

I minded, but not for the reason he thought, which was that I wanted his job. "No, Cecil, I don't mind. In fact, I'll be delighted to have you back on the street."

He made a happy exaggerated dip into his soup bowl. "Go ahead, eat up before it gets cold."

So I ate up. It was only after I'd left that I remembered the question that I'd come to ask him.

At dusk I parked the Impala in our garage and started walking north along the alley that ran behind our house, intending at the first opportunity to cut over to Home Street. Although the day had been warm, the evening was cool, and night would grow even cooler as the hours passed.

I had observed that once darkness fell on a still clear night, the temperature dropped about a degree an hour until sunrise. If there was a deep layer of snow on the ground, it would drop even faster. If there was a wind or the clouds rolled in, all bets were off, since either could influence the temperature, usually holding it up.

It was a useless thing to know, among all the other useless things I knew and by definition, would never use. Still, there were those days in spring and fall when Ruth would ask whether she should bring in her hanging plants or not, and relying on my past observations, I would tell her. Not that she listened. But at least I had an informed opinion to offer her. Which was why I went on gathering useless facts and making useless observations. With the many faces of man, the infinite appeals to God, how could I have an informed opinion about them if I didn't stop, look, and listen every once in a while?

Ned Cleaver's front porch light was on, which might or might not mean anything, but what it did was to make me wary of crossing Home Street there. So rather than arouse anyone's suspicions, I went on past Ned's house and turned right on Diamond Street, as if I were taking the same walk that I had hundreds of times before. But as soon as I put a house between Ned's porch light and me, I turned north into a vacant lot, then circled west around behind Ned's garage.

I was at a disadvantage because I didn't yet know what I was looking for, or where I should wait. But Ruth had said to wait at the west end of Diamond Street and Ned's garage sat directly on top of it. Years ago, I could have had my choice of dugouts, backstop, or concession stand. Or that big lonesome burr oak that had lost its top to lightning and thus wore its leaves like a skirt—one that shaded the home team's bleachers and played hell with pop flies along the third base line.

Standing there in the dark with only the moon and stars for company, I could almost feel the dew fall, as everything around me, including my sweatshirt and tennis shoes, was soon soaked. It didn't help my comfort either to not know how long I might be there. With no guarantees, I could stand there all night and still not learn anything. But then, if I had wanted guarantees, I would have taken up accounting.

I heard Ned's garage door start to open before I ever saw the car lights spray the garage. That meant that Ned had been standing somewhere inside watching the street, and that made me glad that I had gone the long way around to get there.

I barely had time to run around to the north side of the garage before Sandy Hall drove her Chevy S-10 inside and the garage door started to close. My next move was instinctive and not very smart, but I ducked into the garage with her and hid snugged against the passenger side of her pickup, as she got out and hurried inside the house.

Ned Cleaver was waiting for her at the door. Either he picked her up or she jumped into his arms, and that's where she stayed, as they waltzed through the kitchen into another part of the house. As the saying goes, you could have knocked me over with a feather.

CHAPTER 25

I sat in Dennis Hall's Dodge Ram pickup behind the shelter house in Oakalla's Centennial Park. I had been there for over an hour, waiting for him to leave Kristina Vice's house. As Alice had said, things were getting "curiouser and curiouser."

From Ned Cleaver's garage, I had gone home to lie down on the couch, while I awaited Ruth's return from the shelter. She dragged in some time after midnight and avoided me by heading straight upstairs to bed. I slept fitfully for the next couple of hours, then headed for the park on foot.

Though I was not totally surprised to find Dennis Hall's pickup parked there behind the shelter house, I did feel that my earlier left hook to his solar plexus now made us even. If anyone were "bonking" Kristina Vice tonight, it should have been me. Could have been me. Instead, I was sitting in a coffin-cold pickup freezing my butt off. Regrets? I bet old Blue Eyes had a lot more of them than he let on.

I heard Dennis Hall's heavy footfalls coming up the gravel drive behind me. At least he wasn't whistling. Then the driver's side door of the pickup opened and he jumped in. He was in such a hurry to leave that he didn't see me at first. When he did see me, his first instinct was to run, until he saw who it was.

"You," he said. "I might have known."

He was flexing the fingers on his right hand, making a fist and breaking it again. He had a large hand. It made a big fist.

"Do you want to tell me what's going on," I said, "or do you want me to guess?"

"I want you to get out of my truck before I spread you all over this park."

I started to get out of the pickup. "Have it your way, Dennis. But don't go too far. The state police will be coming for you soon."

He put his hand on my arm to stop me. But unlike yesterday, there was no force in his grip.

"On what charge?" Dennis said, releasing his grip when he saw me take my hand off the door handle.

"Assaulting a police officer for starters. The rest depends on what happened last Saturday night."

"With Albert you mean?"

"What else would I mean?"

He shook his head, looking relieved. "You've got the wrong man, Garth. I wasn't anywhere around Oakalla last Saturday night."

"Where were you? And don't lie to me, Dennis," I said, seeing that he was about to. "If I can find you here, I can find where you really were Saturday night."

He started to protest, saw the futility of it, and slumped down in his seat with his eyes straight ahead. "Kristina and I were in a motel in Madison. You can check it out if you want to. It's a Holiday Inn. We registered in my name."

"How did you manage that?"

"I told the guys that I was going to my cousin's wedding in Chicago. Kristina told Albert that she was meeting an old friend from college in Rockford. Her friend was supposedly on her way across the country, so there was no way that Albert could check up on her."

I watched as the trees in front of us began to take shape. It would be daylight soon.

"Did Albert have reason to check up on her?" I said.

"It wasn't our first time, if that's what you mean. We had been seeing each other a couple months or so before that. It was our first time to get a motel together, though."

"There's a first time for everything, I guess."

Dennis turned to look at me. Pain and confusion were spread across his broad face. "But it's not been the same since Albert died—for either of us. I think Kristina misses him a lot more than she lets on, and as for me . . . I don't know what's wrong. Last night, all she wanted was to be held, which was fine with me. . . . If you know what I mean."

"Maybe you need to talk to somebody about it, Dennis."

"I am talking to somebody about it. I'm talking to you."

"I mean somebody who can help you. You're carrying a load of guilt it seems to me, and probably not all of it is from screwing your best friend's wife."

"What's the rest of it, then?"

I glanced out to the west and saw grey mare's tails in the pastel blue sky. Much to my regret a change in the weather seemed on its way.

"My guess is that you feel you should have been with Albert last Saturday night. If you had been, maybe he wouldn't have died."

"There's no maybe about it," he said, looking away. "If I would have been there Saturday night, none of this would have happened. I would have been on point, instead of Albert."

"You also might be the one dead."

"I've thought of that, too," he said. "I don't know which would be worse."

"If we could ask Albert, I bet he could tell us."

"Yeah, I'll bet he could." He didn't see the irony, but then Dennis Hall was not a subtle man.

"If you weren't involved in Albert's death, then why did you get involved in the cover-up?" I said.

Dennis came to life, as he put a hard two-handed grip on his steering wheel. "If you're talking about throwing his body into Hidden Quarry, you'll have to talk to Larry Sharp about that. I had nothing to do with that operation. Neither, I don't think, did Ned Cleaver."

"He wasn't at Camp Collier either?"

"Not according to the other guys in our outfit."

"What were any of you doing out there at Camp Collier after dark?"

"It's where we train, usually with a bunch of guys from Ortago. You know. Their outfit against ours, trying to capture the other's flag. Except that they couldn't be there Saturday night, so Larry decided that we'd go out on our own." He shot me an angry glance. "If you'd have answered your phone Monday evening, I would have told you all this then. Seeing Albert all white and bloated the way he was . . . I wanted nothing more to do with that business."

What was I doing Monday evening when I heard the

phone ring? Oh yes, I was coming up from the basement after chasing Daisy around the yard.

"Why did you change your mind about calling me?"

"Kristina changed it for me. She said what would people think about us when the truth came out."

"So instead you all go out and beat up on Cecil Hardwick. Whose idea what that?"

"That was Larry's idea. He said we could all lose our jobs, maybe even go to jail, if word ever got out about the militia and they tied it to Albert's death. We never intended to hurt Cecil as bad as we did, just to warn him off."

"And Thursday night, whose idea was it to trash the *Oakalla Reporter*?"

Dennis didn't look nearly as crestfallen as I might have hoped. "That was more the booze than anything else. We all agreed that you were a general pain in the ass and needed to be taught a lesson. I think it was Kristina's idea to go after the *Oakalla Reporter* instead of you." His smile spoke volumes. "So if you're still after her, she's all yours. I don't think I'll be seeing her again."

"You going back to Sandy?"

"Why? You after her, too?"

"Just asking."

He shook his head, looking sad. "No. I think she's got somebody else lined up, though she says not. You know, it's funny, Garth. I know what she is, and yet I still love her. How sick is that?"

"Maybe it's not sick at all."

"That's what Kristina said. I used to go to her and talk about Sandy. You know, what was I doing wrong and how could I make it right? One thing led to another . . . Well, you know the rest."

The red oak leaves above us had begun to show their points. It was nearing full daylight now.

"Time for me to go, Dennis," I said as I opened my door. "Or people might talk."

"Tell Cecil I'm sorry about what happened to him. I used to haul his milk when I was just starting out, before he went automated on me."

"Why don't you tell him yourself."

"I tried already. That first morning at the hospital. When you were there."

He wanted me to believe that his had been a social call that morning, but I wasn't sure I did. I doubted that Dennis had come to the hospital to put a pillow over Cecil's face, but had the opportunity presented itself, I wasn't sure what he would have done. Neither, I didn't think, was he.

"Try again. This time during visiting hours."

"I might just do that," he said. Neither of us believed him.

"One last question, Dennis. You live above the post office, right. Did you notice anything strange going on next door late Sunday night?"

"Which direction?"

"East, across the alley."

"I noticed a strange pickup there behind the post office when I came back for a change of clothes."

"What time was that?"

"After midnight. I didn't leave Kristina's until then."

"Can you describe the pickup for me?"

He gave it some thought. "Black, with a white camper shell. I might be wrong about the color of the pickup itself, since it was dark, but that camper reminded me of a big white puffball."

"Have you seen it around town since?"

When he hesitated before answering, I thought perhaps that he had. "No. But now that you mention it, I did hear something funny going on down there night before last." He gave me a sheepish look. "You know, after we left your place and scattered for home, I thought maybe somebody was trying to steal my truck, had stolen my truck, until I realized that it was still up at the Corner Bar and Grill and Hiram still had my keys."

"What made you think that?"

"I kept hearing doors banging, then an engine start up. I wondered what the hell was going on until I saw Dale Phillips drive away in his truck."

"What was so unusual about that? Maybe he just wanted to get an early start on the weekend."

"On a Thursday night?"

I didn't know what to make of that, if anything, so I said, "Why didn't you just go home with Kristina, since you were already in the neighborhood?"

"Because when we scattered, I had the bad luck to end up with Ned, who insisted he walk me home."

"Sounds like he was just looking out for you."

"Or himself," said Dennis, who was not always as simple as he appeared.

"Thanks, Dennis," I said as I closed the door.

He started the Dodge Ram, put it in gear, and threw gravel all the way out the drive.

CHAPTER **26**

I waited for his dust to settle before I moved on. It was peaceful there behind the shelter house—birds singing, dawn breaking through the trees. It reminded me of the hymn that Cat Stevens sang to fame. "Morning has broken, like the first morning. Blackbird has spoken, like the first bird."

I didn't see Kristina Vice there waiting for me until I went around the southeast corner of the shelter house. It was almost as if she knew where I was headed next.

"Morning, Garth," she said.

Kristina wore the same white terry robe that she had on Thursday morning, some furry red houseslippers, and a strand of sunlight in her hair. Some women will always be beautiful to look at, no matter what you might think of them. Kristina Vice was like that for me.

"Morning, Kristina," I said, without stopping.

She put her hands in the pockets of her robe and began to walk with me. I didn't want her there beside me, but yet I did want her there. To figure it all out would have taken me more time than I had, so I stopped to see what she wanted.

"Yes, Kristina, what is it?"

She reached up and picked something out of my hair. A twig it looked like.

"I came to apologize for the other night. After you turned me down, all I wanted was my pound of flesh."

"Is that all I am to you, a pound of flesh?"

"Does it matter?"

"No. Not now."

She shrugged. "Then why ask?"

"What about Dennis Hall? What was he to you?" If she noticed that I used the past tense, she didn't correct me.

"One of those things . . . That shouldn't happen. But do."

"Kristina . . ." I stopped. I didn't know how to say it.

"Yes, Garth?"

"God damn you."

I walked on. She didn't go with me.

Larry Sharp was backing his extended cab Chevrolet pickup out of his garage when I arrived at his house. For a moment, it was touch and go as to whether he was going to stop for me or not, even as I tapped on his window, but in the end, he did. I went around the truck and opened the passenger door. If he changed his mind about talking to me, at least I'd have a ride back into town.

Before us was his two-story colonial brick house with the white pillars, standing just east of town along Gas Line Road in one of the fields that Dick Davis and I used to roam. Larry had built the house for his late wife, Becky, who, ever since visiting Georgia as a child, had dreamed of living in such a home. And there they had lived, happily from all reports, for a few years. And there he had lived, by himself, for the past two years.

"What's on your mind, Garth?" Larry said.

"I was wondering where you were off to so early in the day? Is it time for work already?"

"You have a watch. You tell me."

I looked at my watch. It wasn't yet six A.M. "I don't think so, Larry."

"I called a special meeting," he said.

"To do what?"

"Resign."

"Why don't you just quit the militia instead?"

He looked over at me without hope, like someone who either didn't know, or didn't care that he'd just been thrown a lifeline. "I didn't know I had a choice."

"You might not have. But it couldn't hurt your cause any."

We were wasting gas, sitting there with the motor running. I reached over and turned off the ignition.

"But it's *my* militia. I'm the one who organized it."

"Then disband it."

"What will the guys think?"

"Dennis Hall will probably be relieved. I don't know about Ned Cleaver, but I think he might be, too."

Larry nodded his agreement. "Ned already told me he was quitting. Busting up a man for no reason was bad enough, but busting up a printing press was somehow worse, he said."

I didn't know if I agreed, but since it was my printing press we were talking about, I didn't argue.

"So there's your out," I said. "You can't have any kind of militia without Ned anyway. If you have any doubts—"

which he was about to voice—"go back to last Saturday night."

"I don't know what you're talking about, Garth."

"I'm talking about Albert Vice—how you put him on point, a place he had no right to be, and how it got him killed. That's what I'm talking about."

It was getting hot in there with the sun streaming in on us. Larry turned the ignition back on just long enough to roll down our windows.

"How do you know what went on there?" he said, thinking that someone had ratted him out.

"Because I was there along Owl Creek when it happened."

"You saw it?" He was doubtful.

"I heard it, then saw Albert's body later. So cut the crap, Larry. I can make a case against you if need be. Even if I have to arrest the whole cheese plant to do it."

"You wouldn't do that," he said. "It would cost Oakalla too much."

"This time, I'll make that exception."

He shook his head. He knew me too well. "I don't think so, Garth. But to clear the record, it was Albert's idea that he be on point, not mine. I didn't even want to go out there without Ned and Larry, or the guys from Ortaga, but Albert convinced me that we needed the practice. I think with Kristina gone for the night, he just needed something to do to take his mind off of it."

"Were he and Kristina having problems?" I said, not knowing how much he knew.

"He thought that she might be seeing someone else. From day one he'd been worried about her, convinced that she had too much on the ball to stay with somebody like him. So he smothered her, I think, just trying to prove how much he loved her. As if love matters," he said bitterly.

"You had a good marriage," I said, not understanding his bitterness.

"Yes. But it didn't keep her from dying on me."

I leaned back in my seat to let that wash over me. Then I said, "Whose idea was it to throw Albert into Hidden Quarry?"

But Larry's thoughts were still on Becky. "What was that, Garth?"

"I said whose idea was it to throw Albert into Hidden Quarry?"

"Mine, I'm afraid. He was dead long before we ever got him out of Camp Collier. I knew if we took him to the hospital, there would be a lot of questions to answer, so I panicked and tried to hide his body where nobody would find it, while I figured out what to do next. It was a gutless stupid thing to do, but it just wasn't me I was thinking about it."

"You're right, Larry. It *was* a gutless stupid thing to do. But what followed was worse."

"You mean Cecil Hardwick."

"That's exactly what I mean."

"I know," he said. "But things started to snowball after that. It was like I wasn't even in control anymore. Life had me by the balls, instead of the other way around."

Larry had gotten something on his hand from the steering wheel. He was trying hard to wipe it off on his slacks.

"You could have said stop at any point along the line. You still can."

He began to wipe harder against his slacks. From my vantage point, he didn't seem to be making much progress.

"I said I was on my way there to quit."

"The cheese plant, not the militia."

"It's the same as."

"No, it's not, Larry."

"I'll think about it," he said.

"Think hard. Because if in the future I learn it's still operating, I'm going to point fingers and name names, regardless of what it does to Oakalla."

"It's my constitutional right, damn it."

"Just as it is mine to blow the whistle on it."

"I said I'd think about it."

"While you're thinking, tell me this. Who set the trap that Albert fell into?"

"I wish I knew, Garth." He seemed to be telling the truth.

"Then who burned those sticks that Albert fell on?"

"I didn't know anyone had."

"You're sure *you* didn't?"

"Positive, Garth. We were in too much of a hurry to get Albert out of there to waste time on a fire."

That left only one person who could have built the fire and burned the punji sticks, the same one who had hit me over the head.

I opened the passenger side door. I'd learned about all I could here.

"Where are you headed now?" Larry said.

"Back to town."

"I can give you a ride. I'm headed that way."

"Thanks, but no thanks."

"Garth, you have to understand about the militia. After Becky died, there was this great big hole in my life. It just didn't seem to have any meaning anymore. Now, it does."

"You're back on the team again," I said, understanding more than he thought I did.

"That's right," he said, unable to hide his excitement. "But this season is all year round."

"Remember what I said, Larry. I'm giving you a week to disband."

"And if we don't?" he said, calling my bluff.

What would I do? What could I do? I didn't know, but I'd think of something. I closed the door and started walking back to town along Gas Line Road.

"It wasn't our fault that Albert got killed," Larry said as he pulled alongside me. "So why are you blaming us?"

I stopped, wanting him to understand. "Larry, I don't care if you want to play soldier. And I don't care if you use real guns and live ammunition and even shoot each other every once in a while, as long as you keep it in house and no innocent party gets hurt. But what happened the first time somebody did get hurt? You beat up Cecil Hardwick and then came after me—Oakalla's peace officer and its fourth estate. That's anarchy, Larry, any way you want to slice it. So if what you're doing naturally leads to anarchy, then I'm against it. Any civilized person should be."

"But we're not the real enemy, Garth. The guy that built that death trap is."

"No. But you'll do until he reveals himself."

He drove on. I walked slowly on in to town, knowing sadly, way down deep in my heart, that I probably hadn't seen the last of Larry Sharp, or his militia.

CHAPTER

Barefoot, clean shaven, wearing jeans and a T-shirt, his wide flat feet bone white, Ned Cleaver sat calmly on his front porch swing, as if he were waiting for me. I sat down on the swing beside him; he pushed off and we began to swing, back and forth between shadow and sunshine, the rusty chains creaking with every pass. The effect was hypnotic, reminding me of just how relaxing a front porch swing could be.

"You don't seem surprised to see me," I said.

"I'm not."

We swung some more while I waited for his explanation.

"Sandy swore she saw someone outside when she pulled into the garage last night. Then Dennis called a short while ago. It wasn't hard to figure where you'd come next."

"Actually I went to see Larry Sharp after I spoke to Dennis."

"And?"

"He hates to give up the militia, I think."

We both waved at a passing car that had tooted its horn at us. "Maybe I'll have a talk with him," Ned said.

"It wouldn't hurt. I gave him a week."

"More than I would have given him."

As we swung, I noticed that the early clouds had evaporated in the sunshine. But the sky didn't seem as warm as yesterday, or the blue as bright.

"I bet you're wondering, why Sandy?" Ned said.

"Among other things."

"Why not Sandy?" he said, putting me on the spot.

I didn't have an answer for him, though Kristina Vice seemed more his type.

He said, "She's bright, she's fun. She has terrible judgment, men in particular, but a great big heart. And if she's here with me, it keeps her off the streets."

"Then you really care for her?"

"As much as I've ever cared for anyone." But don't call it love, his eyes seemed to say.

"And she for you?"

"Enough to lie for me if I asked her to," he said, beating me to the punch.

"So there's no point in asking her if she was here with you last Saturday night."

"No point at all."

"Was she?"

"You'll have to ask her."

"Is she here?"

"No. I don't know where she is. In Madison shopping, I think."

We continued to swing, Ned providing most of the impetus with his big ham-like feet. "Someone might think you have cause to want Dennis Hall dead," I said.

"They might. Except he's not."

"He might be if he'd been on point last Saturday night."

"True, but he wasn't."

"You do know what a punji stick is?"

"I've made their acquaintance, yes. Except, according to the report I got, Albert wasn't killed with a punji stick, at least not the ones Charlie made. Charlie's were single simple affairs, designed to put maybe one man out of action. The thing that got Albert was built for a water buffalo."

"You saw it, then?"

He shook his head no. "Just heard reports, that's all."

"But you'd agree that it would probably take a Vietnam veteran to come up with the idea?"

"Not necessarily. A man could read how to do it just as easily."

"Is that your best guess?" I said.

"I have no best guess. But I will tell you one thing. Civilian or vet, only a madman would build something like that, not knowing who might fall into it."

"Maybe Bobby did it."

"Bobby?"

"The Lost Scout." I waited for him to deny it, hoped in fact that he would. When he didn't, I said, "Give me some help here, Ned. You're the one who said there was no Lost Scout. Or have you changed your mind?"

"I haven't changed my mind."

"What then?"

Because something had changed in him this week. The old Ned Cleaver was no longer there. In his place was someone I no longer knew, or wanted to know.

"I've just had some time to think, that's all, about what Robby told you. There *was* a guy he brought into our cabin the last night we were there."

"Cabin 10?"

"Yes. Cabin 10. Why is that important?"

We had stopped swinging. He had done it so smoothly I barely noticed.

"Never mind," I said, not wanting to ask if he, too, had felt a chill there for fear of his answer. "What do you remember about the guy that Robby brought in?"

"Not much. He seemed kind of a disappointment to me, but that was only because Robby had bragged so much about him all week, even Jesus Christ would have been hard put to follow that build up."

"You think he was a ringer from one of the other cabins?"

"I thought so then. I'm not so sure now."

"Why the change of heart?"

"You had a lot to do with it. You seemed to believe Robby, and despite what else I might think about you, you're nobody's fool. That got me to thinking about that week there at Camp Collier, and how Robby was hardly ever around with the rest of us. So either he could have been hanging out with the guys from another cabin, or . . ." He left it up to me to fill in the blanks.

"Funny," I said. "You had me convinced that he was all in Robby's mind."

"He might have been for all I know. He was only there for part of that one night, and then he disappeared."

"While on a snipe hunt?"

"No. That's Robby's story, but it's not true. He just slipped off in the middle of the night to who knows where."

"And you never heard him scream for help?"

Ned had become very still. All of his being seemed locked in concentration, so when he finally did speak, only his mouth seemed to move. "The funny thing is, I

might have. Something woke up all of us there in Cabin
10. We thought at first it was the ghost, until Robby sat up
and said, 'Where's Bobby?'"

"What did he sound like?"

"It. He sounded more like an it. Half human, half animal, I never heard anything like it, not even in Nam."

"Somebody in extreme pain?" I said, remembering
Albert Vice's screams in the night.

"Pain and anger both. I can't describe it. It was too
savage to be human, and too . . . *outraged* not to be.
Which was why I told the guys it was a wildcat and for
them to go back to sleep."

We started swinging again. I was glad when we swung
back out into the sunlight.

"Not a wildcat?" I said.

"No. I don't think so."

"Not a ghost either?"

"I'm not sure about that, Garth, having never heard
one."

"That you know of."

"That goes without saying."

"So did any of you go looking for Bobby the next
day?"

Robby did. He came back empty-handed.

"Did you check to see if any of the other troops were
one Scout short?"

"I asked at breakfast. No one was."

"Thanks for your time, Ned." This time I stopped the
swing myself. Then at the bottom of the steps, I said,
"Was that you who drove Cecil to my office Wednesday
night?"

"Yes. I didn't think he could make it on his own.
Then when I saw his car outside the Corner Bar and Grill
not two hours later, I thought maybe it was following me.
Like in that Stephen King movie."

"*Christine*?" I said.

"Yes. I think that's the one."

As he spoke, I saw Sandy Hall framed in Ned's front window, sticking her tongue out at me. Maybe they *were* meant for each other. Who was I to say?

"There's one last question, Ned. Why did you get involved in the militia in the first place? You've been to war. You had to know where it would lead."

He shook his head as if at the folly of life. "As strange as it may seem, I joined it to keep the other guys out of trouble."

"Then why didn't you?"

"If you're talking about Albert, he was dead and in Hidden Quarry before I knew anything about it. If you're talking about Cecil Hardwick, he was going to get busted up whether I went along or not, so I did what I could to see he survived. If you're talking about your printing press, well, that was personal."

"I didn't sleep with Sandy, Ned."

"I know. She told me. And Garth, if it *was* me who set the trap for Dennis that Albert fell into, I wouldn't have gone after your printing press with a sledgehammer. I'd have gone after you. You might remember that for future reference."

I assured him that I would.

Much later that day I sat in the morgue of the *Oakalla Reporter* with my eyes closed and my head resting on the back of my chair. I had been there all evening. After leaving Ned Cleaver, I had eaten lunch at home, then taken Daisy on a drive out to Grandmother Ryland's farm. It was my very favorite place to walk and think, and this was one of my favorite times of year to be there, when the May apples were up, the wildflowers were in bloom, and before the weeds got too high or the bugs got too numerous to be a nuisance.

I would have liked to have taken a couple turns around the pond in Grandmother's rowboat just to see how the resident coot and muskrats were doing, but Daisy needed to romp more than I needed to row, so we walked out to the far end of the farm where the white pines grew. But whatever insights that I thought might come to me there apparently had other plans. Daisy came home tail-wagging happy. I came home sullen and frustrated.

My stint in the morgue hadn't improved my mood any, except to add eye-weary to the above. Nowhere in all of the back issues of *Freedom's Voice* that I searched could I find anyone who could be Bobby, the Lost Scout; except for perhaps Robert Anderson, who along with Tony Jenkins, had robbed the Linberg State Bank of nearly $100,000 and was captured in California two weeks later. It was possible that Robert Anderson alias Bobby had wandered as far west as Camp Collier and posed as a Boy Scout for a week, while deciding what to do next. That would explain why he seemed more shadow than substance to everyone but Robby, whom no one believed anyway.

Except Robert Anderson was serving life in prison, so he couldn't have fallen into a ravine somewhere and died, no matter what Robby, Ned and the rest of Cabin 10 heard the night he disappeared. He also couldn't be the one that Ruth was seeing in her dreams; nor was he Preston Kurtz, even if he was out of prison by now.

So who *was* Preston Kurtz and what was his part in all of this? He wasn't Robert Anderson because Robert Anderson was eighteen in 1959, and Preston Kurtz was older than Robert Anderson would be now. Neither was he Tony Jenkins, Robert Anderson's partner in crime. Tony Jenkins' beetle-browed piggy face just didn't fit Preston Kurtz, or anyone else around Oakalla that I knew.

Which left me grasping at straws, or in this case, panning for ghosts.

I had worked my way back to the June 25, 1943 issue of *Freedom's Voice* before I found them—photographs of two recruits who had died while on night maneuvers at Camp Collier. They had died on the night of Saturday, *June 19*. If I read my 1959 Boy Scout calendar correctly, *Friday, June 19* was the date that Bobby went over the hill, so to speak, and the Scouts in Cabin 10 had heard the screams in the night. A coincidence, true, but enough of one to make me take a hard look at the two recruits' photographs to see if perhaps I saw Bobby there. I didn't, much to my relief. Both recruits who died seemed clean-cut, boy-next-door types, and their brief obituaries bore that out. Not a "presence" between them, as Robby Rumaley had said about Bobby.

With nothing more to learn there in the morgue and my back door unlockable because of the damage to it, I went to my office to pick up Fran's antique doctor bag in case someone, after reading about it in yesterday's paper, decided to help himself to it. I wasn't encouraged when I found my office door open and the black bag nowhere in sight. After a futile five minute search, I gave up and went home.

CHAPTER

Ruth and I had finished Sunday breakfast and were sitting across the table from each other, not saying much. She had a glazed, zombie-like look about her from lack of sleep, and the black smudges under her eyes had widened and deepened in color. For the first time since I had known her, she looked gaunt, as if even her old comfortable clothes no longer fit her.

"I'm sorry, Ruth. I wish I could be more optimistic," I said. "But I'm at a dead end. If Robby Rumaley ever turns up, then maybe I'll have someplace to start again."

"You haven't had any luck finding him?"

"I haven't tried, but Ben Bryan and the state police have. So with any luck, it will be only a matter of time."

"Which I haven't got." Even her voice sounded weary.

"Hang in there, Ruth. That's all I can say."

She rubbed her face, then her eyes, as if to get the sleep out. "What about Bobby?"

"He could be the Lost Scout, but I don't think so." I told her why.

She agreed. "No. Not if he turned up in California later. The bones I'm seeing are still there in the Lost 1600."

"With a couple of suitcases beside them."

"Satchels is more like it."

"Like the military might use?"

"I don't know, Garth. They're not as clear as the bones."

"You couldn't be picking up a signal from somewhere else?"

"I could be, but I'm not." She got up and refilled her cup with coffee for the fourth time.

"That's not going to solve your problem," I said.

"No, but it'll keep me from falling on my face."

"Why don't you forget the shelter for a day and try to get some sleep. I'll find somewhere to go if you need the house to yourself."

"No. I promised Liddy Bennett we'd paint walls this afternoon."

"I'll paint with Liddy. You can beg off."

"You'd do that for me—after all you've said about the place?" There was the tiniest note of tenderness in her voice.

"Not just for you. But for Abby, too. I know it means a lot to both of you, so I might as well get on board."

"Thanks just the same, Garth, but I'll do better if I keep busy."

"Then I'll go with you and help."

"No. Liddy said that she had something she needed to talk about, and she'll clam up if you're there." She made a stab at our last pancake, but then lost interest when it slipped off her fork. "But I will take a rain check."

I speared the pancake, and cut it in two, and scraped the larger of the two pieces onto her plate. She needed it more than I did.

"How are you handling Abby's fall off the wagon?" she said.

"How did you know about it?" Because I hadn't told her.

"She called the shelter one night this week. Don't ask me which night because they all run together."

"Why did she feel the need to talk to you about it?" I said.

"Because she knew you'd be hurting and wanted my advice."

"What did you tell her?"

"These things happen."

"Easy for you to say."

Her brows rose in question. I noticed that she had made no move toward her half of the pancake, but then neither had I.

"So you're not taking it well?"

"I do okay as long as I don't think about it. *Really* think about it, in living color. Then I start to get a little crazy."

She got up and dumped her pancake in the waste basket, then put her plate in the sink. "That's what you get for thinking."

"Yeah. Pop used to tell me that when I'd get bent out of shape over something. No words of advice?" I said when I saw that she was headed for the door.

"You're not married, Garth. You've got to cut each other some slack."

"I was just there two weeks ago."

"So? That has nothing to do with it, Garth, believe

me. You're not really a part of her life right now, and she's not really a part of yours. That you're doing as well as you are is a testimony to both of you."

"I'm sorry, Ruth, but that doesn't help."

"I didn't say it would."

"There is something you might do for me, Ruth, though I don't see how it will help our cause anyway."

"What's that?"

"Check with Aunt Emma to see what she meant by 'quite some time.' The way he told it to me, Dennis Hall has only been seeing Kristina Vice for a couple months now. And while you're at it, ask your other source how long Ned Cleaver has been entertaining late night visitors."

"If I have time." Which meant that she probably wouldn't.

She left. I cleared the table, washed the dishes, and was about to make a call when the phone rang.

"Garth, it's Clarkie. I'm back."

It was a testimony to the week I'd had that I'd forgotten he was even gone. "How was your trip?"

"Great! The guys in Rochester want me back as soon as they're up and running for a while to check out any glitches. And my sister and her kids loved having me there in Saint Paul, especially after they showed me their computer."

It was strange to hear Clarkie, the quintessential Eeyore, sound so happy. It gave me hope for the rest of us.

"But that's not why I called," he said. "I think I got a fix on that guy you asked me about."

"Preston Kurtz?"

"Right. But his name is not Kurtz. It's Ronald Preston Curtis. You must've gotten his name wrong when he introduced himself."

"I might have. I'd just had one of the worst nights of my life, so I wasn't tracking too well by then. What did you say his name was again?"

"Ronald Preston Curtis."

R. P. Curtis? Somehow that name was familiar. "Tell me about him, Clarkie."

"Starting when?"

"His military background, if he has one."

"He does. He served as a military adviser in Vietnam 1961-1965, joined the Secret Service in 1966, where he specialized in terrorist activities, took a desk job in Washington in 1985, retired in 1996. Hobbies include stamp collecting and fly fishing. There's a lot more, and a lot more that's classified, but that's it in a nutshell."

"Was he ever a political science professor at the University of Wisconsin–Whitewater?"

"No."

"At least I got that right."

"But he did lecture there for a semester while on leave from Washington."

"Why there, I wonder?" I mused aloud.

"I was hoping you could tell me."

"And the physical data all fits?"

"He's five-ten, one-sixty, short brown hair. What else do you want to know about him?"

"Age?"

"He was sixty on January 31."

About what I thought. "What did Preston Curtis do before he joined the military?" I said.

"I was wondering when you'd get around to that. He was a deputy sheriff in Green Lake County."

"Green Lake County?" I was starting to get excited. "Isn't Linberg in Green Lake County?" Which was where the Linberg State Bank was held up in 1959.

"It might be. I'd have to check on the map."

"Are you going to be home for a while, Clarkie?"

"All morning. Why?"

"I might need to call you back."

I hung up, put on my shoes, and drove the Impala to the *Oakalla Reporter*. It pained me not a little that I would have to give the car and keys back to Cecil Hardwick the first thing tomorrow morning. Sad to say, I hadn't missed Jessie in the least.

Deputy Sheriff R. P. Curtis *was* the one that had arrested Robert Anderson at his home in Barstow, California. To believe that was merely a coincidence was asking too much of me.

I called Clarkie and told him what I wanted. Meanwhile I searched my office, again in vain, for Fran's antique doctor bag. Was it what Preston Curtis was looking for when he broke into the back of The Last Dance, and if so, why? He had to have followed me there. Otherwise, he wouldn't have had any reason for being there. Even more of a puzzle, however, was why had he followed *me*?

The phone rang. In my eagerness to answer it, I kicked my waste can and sent it rolling into the wall.

"Yes, Clarkie?"

"It's not Clarkie. It's Liddy Bennett. Where's that housekeeper of yours? She was supposed to meet me here at the shelter a half hour ago."

"And she's not there yet?"

"Would I be calling if she were?"

"Hold the fort, Liddy. I'll get back to you."

"You know the number here?"

"Yes."

Did I know the number there? It was tattooed on my heart.

"Well, give me a call as soon as you learn something," she said. "I'm not waiting another half hour."

The moment she hung up, Clarkie called. "Here's the information on Robert Anderson. He served his time in

Marion Federal Prison in Marion, Illinois, and was released June 7, 1992. He would have been released several years earlier, but he put a fellow prisoner's eye out with a spoon for spilling soup on him."

"Anything else on his record?"

"Burning homemade candles after lights out, so he could read. Things like that. Nothing serious."

"Is there any chance that he and Preston Curtis have since made connections somewhere?"

"It's not likely, Garth. There's an addendum from Preston Curtis, who as you know by now was Robert Anderson's arresting officer. He says that Robert Anderson is a dangerous sociopath, who is capable of fooling the most astute observer of human nature. Twice he testified against him at parole hearings."

"To no avail, it seems."

"I don't know, Garth. He helped keep him there in prison for over thirty years."

"Thanks, Clarkie. As always, you've been a big help."

"Just give me a call if you need anything else."

He had no more than hung up when Liddy Bennett called me back. "Garth, it's Liddy again. You ever find Ruth?"

"I haven't had a chance to look, Liddy."

"Well, I'm going home. If she wants my help, she can always give me a call."

"I thought it was the other way around," I said. "I mean, wasn't it your idea to get together there at the shelter today?"

"What on earth for? Or do you think my idea of fun is painting a ten-foot ceiling on a beautiful Sunday afternoon in May?"

"You didn't need to talk?"

"About what? We said everything worth saying to each other years ago."

"Thanks, Liddy. When I see her, I'll deliver your message."

"You can also tell her this for me. It'd do both of us a whole lot more good if she'd forget that shelter for a day and get some sleep. She's about to run us both ragged."

She banged down her receiver. I held on to mine for a moment as I tried to figure out what Ruth's game was.

"Shit!" I said, as I slammed down the receiver and headed for the door.

CHAPTER

Ruth's yellow Volkswagen beetle was parked there at Camp Collier where Preston Curtis's black GMC pickup had been parked the week before. I pulled up beside the Volkswagen and jumped out of the Impala. But when I opened the trunk to take out my shotgun, I saw that it wasn't there. It should have been, I thought, until I realized that I had removed it to my upstairs closet.

I started down the hill toward Owl Creek, then stopped when the hairs on my nape started to tingle. Though a strong southwest wind shook the tops of the trees and scattered puffs of yellow pollen like exploding fireworks, down among the trunks where I was, it was hot, close, and strangely still. Maybe that was what had spooked me—that and all the clouds streaming by overhead, bunched and herded by the wind like fat sheep. Something ill was in the air that day, and I felt, as I had eight days ago, that I was walking right into trouble.

I came to Owl Creek, crossed it at the now familiar rapids, and went on. But not before I felt its icy water tug at my legs, reminding me just how cold it was.

Passing the spot where my camp had been, I began to look for footprints there in the mud along the base of the bluff. Presently I found some that I took for Ruth's, since they were narrower and considerably shorter than mine. For a big woman, Ruth had small high arched feet, which for some reason was a source of pride for her.

The footprints led along the shelf as far as it went, then began to climb with the terrain when the shelf gave out. Owl Creek soon became a thin black ribbon at least a hundred yards below me, and the wind, blocked until then, swooped down over the top of the bluff with surprising strength and fury, making my already tenuous footholds seem even more slippery.

Climbing on all fours now, I crossed over the top of the bluff and soon found myself in an old-growth forest of beech, maple, and poplar. Interspersed within them, without apparent rhyme or reason, was an occasional thick, dark-walled stand of spruce or pine, as if an envious tight-fisted Norse god had scooped it up roots and all and stuck it there just to please himself. There within the big trees the wind found the going tougher and was forced upward once again to ride among their tops. The footprints followed a deer path. I followed the footprints. It was my fondest hope that they would keep going south in a straight line and lead both Ruth and me safely out the other side of the Lost 1600. But that was not to be. When they came to a shallow ravine, they dropped down into it and began to bend back north toward Owl Creek.

The ravine widened and deepened into a canyon, and

the air grew noticeably cooler even before the sun disappeared behind its rim. Now immersed in deep shade thousands of years old, I felt that I was entering a netherworld, where only white snakes and blind fish would feel at home. A great horned owl silently cruised a few feet above the canyon floor, looking for a late lunch.

Pushing deeper into the canyon, I found it hard to walk without walking in water. Springs seeped through the rock in rust-red swatches and dripped down upon me, and every dip in the path, every crack in the sandstone, seemed to breed its own pool, create its own fountainhead, until the water beneath my feet began to flow. The narrow mud-slick ledges along the stream were not much better for walking, but they did reveal a footprint every few feet to tell me that I was on the right track.

When I saw the owl veer upward and turn back my way, I wondered what might be ahead. I saw sunlight again for the first time in what seemed like hours, as the canyon was intersected by a ravine running east and west. A sunlit cross marked the intersection. Ruth stood in the middle of it with her back to me, as if confused about which direction she should now go.

"You lost?" I said from behind her.

Her knees buckled. She almost went down. "Garth Ryland, that better be you."

"This is your lucky day."

She slowly turned around, wearing a look of relief.

It was an awkward moment for both of us. She really was glad to see me, but hated to let it show. For my part, I didn't know whether to hug her, or to yell at her for taking the chance she had—not to mention, scaring the crap out of me.

"You had no business coming here by yourself," I said.

"Maybe not. But here I am."

"So where to now?"

"There, I think." She pointed to the west. "That's where my feet seem to be leading me."

"I hope they're in consultation with your head."

Her answer surprised me. "No, Garth. The less I try to think about it, the better off I am."

"You know, it's supposed to storm," I said as we started west up the ravine.

"Not until tonight. With any luck, we'll be out of here by then."

I had to laugh at that. With any luck, neither one of us would have been there in the first place.

Since it was Ruth's show, she led and I followed. The ravine quickly narrowed and began to climb, and we were soon back in shadows again. But at least we weren't walking in water anymore.

"How much farther?" I said.

"I won't know until I get there."

"How are you holding up?"

"Fine, as long as I don't have to waste my breath answering questions."

I got the message.

About a hundred yards farther on, the ravine seemed to end against the face of a sheer rock wall about thirty feet high. It was too steep to climb, even on our best day.

"End of the line," I said.

"Maybe not."

"We can't go any farther, Ruth."

"I'm not talking about going any farther."

She began to dig at the talus that had gathered there at the base of the wall. I had no choice but to help her. Fortunately, there were no rocks so large that we couldn't move them, so we made headway in spite of the fact that there were two chiefs, and no Indians, and that each had a different idea about what rock should be moved next.

"If we move that one, the rest are going to come tumbling down," I said about a red chunk of granite about two feet across.

"That's the idea." She dug under the rock, then held out her hand to show me that it was wet. "That water has to be coming from somewhere."

Try as I might, I could find no argument for that.

"On three," I said, as we each grabbed hold of the rock.

The cave that we finally uncovered went back only a few yards and stopped. The water that Ruth had discovered was not coming from the cave, but a cracked-quartz seam in the rock just below it, and the cave itself was dry. Ruth was the first one into it. I followed when she had cleared the entrance. We were both stopped short by what we found.

"The Lost Scout," I said in reference to the skeleton with the bullet hole in the back of his skull.

"The lost somebody, anyway," she said.

On the floor of the cave beside the skeleton was a rusted handgun that appeared to be a .38. On beyond it were two canvas bags filled with money, which Ruth had mistaken in her dreams for satchels. With the name, Linberg State Bank, on the outside of each bag, I had a pretty good idea of where they came from.

"Are you all right?" I said to Ruth.

Visibly shaken, she had taken a seat on the floor of the cave, her right hand resting on the leg of the skeleton. "I will be soon."

"You and your dreams did one hell of a job."

She shook her head. Praise was the last thing she wanted to hear. "You have any idea who it is?" she said.

"Yes. But I'd like to wait until we get home." The sooner we put the Lost 1600 behind us, the better.

"What about the money?" she said, as I helped her to her feet.

"We'll have to leave it here."

"Why?"

I picked up one of the canvas bags to hand to her. Even I was surprised at how heavy it was.

"Because it's too heavy to carry out of here."

She took the sack from me and threw it over her shoulder. "We can do it, Garth."

"Then you plan on keeping the money?"

"No. But I know where my share is going."

Adrenalin took us out of the cave and part way down the ravine before reality set in. Neither one of us had had much experience as a pack horse, and that was what we really needed to get the sacks of money out of there.

"Where's Dennis Hall when you need him?" I said as we stopped to rest.

"I'll tell you one thing," Ruth said, as she used her sleeve to wipe the sweat from her eyes. "I'm not going back out the way we came in. I'm going to follow that canyon south as far as it goes."

"That's uncharted territory, Ruth. It might not be wise."

She shouldered her load again. "Wise or not, that's the way I'm going."

"I was thinking specifically of punji sticks."

"Then we're safe. There's no way in the world anyone could ever dig a hole in this rock."

Ahead, the bright cross on the canyon floor had become a T, for as the sun had moved farther to the north and west, it had draped a shadow across our ravine. Welcome though the sunlight was, I wasn't looking forward to walking in it.

"It's shadier to the north," I said, as we stepped into the sunlight.

"It's also about two miles farther."

Then Ruth stopped suddenly, and I had to pull up

short to keep from overrunning her. "What's wrong?" I said.

"Open your eyes."

I then saw what she saw. Preston Curtis had stepped out from behind a fallen tree and was pointing his Colt .45 at us. He was back to wearing his khaki shirt, his forest green pants and tie. He could easily have passed for a forest ranger, which perhaps was what he had in mind.

"So we meet again," he said to me.

"It appears so."

"Thanks for saving me a lot of work."

"I wish I could say you were welcome."

Both Ruth and I dropped our money bags at our feet. No sense in carrying them any farther.

"What now?" I said.

"You and your large lady-friend can pick up those bags again and carry them out the same way you came in. From there, I'll tell you where to go."

"And if we refuse?"

"I'll shoot you where you stand."

"You'll shoot us anyway, so what's the difference?"

"Not so," he said, sounding offended.

"You're not the one who littered this place with death traps, who's been living here off and on the past few months?"

"No. I just arrived here last Sunday. You were there. You should remember."

"I also remember that you told me that you were a professor of political science at Wisconsin–Whitewater."

Preston Curtis smiled, but just barely. "A small untruth. All part of the game. Which you play very well, by the way."

Tired of standing, Ruth took a seat on her money bag. If Preston Curtis minded, he didn't say so.

"It's not a game to me," I said.

"Pity you, then. You miss out on all the fun."

I was beginning to think that Preston Curtis had slipped a cog somewhere along the line. Or perhaps he was born that way and had spent his whole life covering it up.

"Speaking of fun, why did you follow me into Oakalla and break into Fran's building last Sunday?" I said. "Or was that just part of the game, too?"

"Who is Fran?"

"The one who used to own the things you ransacked."

"A mistake," he said. "Blame it on poor judgment. I saw you here, ran you through my computer, and decided to find out what you were up to. When I saw you take a great deal of interest in those things there in the building, I was curious as to why."

"You thought the money was there?"

"Or something that might lead me to it."

The owl, who had been hunting the canyon all afternoon, sailed lazily our way as if curious about what was going on. But when he caught a glint of Preston Curtis's Colt.45, he veered abruptly and headed back up the canyon as fast as he could fly.

"How did you know the money was here?" I said.

"A process of elimination. I knew Robert Anderson was travelling light because the trucker that picked him up on U.S. 51 and gave him a ride to Memphis told me he was. I also knew he'd wrecked his car between Linberg and where he was picked up along 51. There were several places along the two points where he could have hidden the money, but not so many where he could hole up for a week without anybody knowing where he was. Or where he could have killed and hidden Tony Jenkins for all time."

"What makes you think Tony Jenkins is dead?" I said.

"I know Robert Anderson."

For some reason, that ran a chill up my spine.

"Cooner?" he said, noticing my shiver.

"Something like that."

"He *is* dead, isn't he? Weren't there bones in that cave?"

I admitted that there were.

"So there you have it. Robert Anderson was smart enough to know dead weight when he saw it and figure out a way to cut himself free of it."

"You think he expected to be caught?"

"Once they wrecked the car, it was inevitable."

I glanced at Ruth, who appeared to be drowsing atop her bag of money. She looked bone-weary, but not defeated. I took heart in that.

A flock of noisy crows approached from the west, saw us standing there, and abruptly wheeled south, the same way that the owl had gone. I had never wished for wings before, but this might be the day.

"Where is Robert Anderson now, do you know?" I said.

"Florida, the last I heard."

"You haven't been keeping tabs on him?"

He paused before answering. It made me wonder why.

Preston Curtis said, "I tried, but he's a hard man to keep track of when he wants to be."

"Then I think I might be worried about his showing up someday."

Preston Curtis smiled. It seemed as cold and calculated as he was. "I don't think I have to worry about that. Right, Big Tree," he said to Ruth, as he motioned with his Colt.45 for her to stand up.

Ruth gave him a stony look as she rose and shouldered the money bag. I too hoisted my bag and followed her out into the canyon. I barely heard the shot that felled Preston Curtis. He was dead before he ever hit the ground.

CHAPTER 30

In that same instant, Ruth and I dropped our bags of money and ran back into the shadows of the ravine to our west. She took the south side of the ravine, and I followed her, as we flattened out behind a boulder. All the while we were running, I had expected to have the shooter fire again and have one or both of us go down, and was surprised when it didn't happen.

"Why do you figure he didn't try for either one of us?" Ruth said from behind the boulder when she had caught her breath again.

"Maybe he's planning on us carrying the money out for him."

"Fat chance of that."

"Well, it's a cinch that Preston Curtis won't be much

help to him."

"I couldn't care less. Big Tree, indeed," she said, still steamed by what he had called her. "I'm glad somebody shot him or I might have had to."

"There is another possibility," I said.

"About what?" Her thoughts were still on Preston Curtis.

"About why he didn't shoot us. He might be using a single shot. A lot of sniper guns are."

"Is that supposed to cheer me up?"

"No. It's meant to keep your head down."

"There's no danger in me doing otherwise, I assure you." She raised her head ever so slightly to try to see over the boulder. "You have any idea who that is up there?"

By up there, she meant the top rim of the canyon, where the shot had likely come from. "No. No idea whatsoever, or whether he's friend or foe."

"We keep saying he. It could be a she."

I thought back to Albert Vice's closet and the .30-30 that I saw in there. Maybe it really belonged to Kristina Vice and not Albert. Maybe the whole arsenal did.

"You're right, Ruth. It could be a she."

"You have anyone particular in mind?"

"Kristina Vice."

"You think she's capable of it?"

"I'm not sure what she's capable of, Ruth. I'm not sure I even want to know."

"That didn't stop you from dancing cheek to cheek with her. Or entertaining other thoughts of her, from what Abby said."

"I've never claimed to be a great judge of women."

"Amen to that." She turned to look west up the ravine. "You think we can get out that way?" she said.

"Not a chance."

"I don't think so either. So what do we do, then?"

"Wait until it's just dark."

She scowled. I would have to do some fast talking to sell her that idea. "What's to stop him from coming down here after us in the meantime?" she said.

"Nothing. Except he'll have to move to do so. If he moves, he loses his vantage point, also sight of us. If he does either, we could pick up Preston Curtis's Colt.45 and be waiting for him."

"But hidden here behind this boulder, we can't know that he's moved."

I was afraid she was going to say that. "I'm just trying to think like him."

"Hard to do when you don't know who he or she is. Is that what you would do, try to wait us out?"

"No. I've never been much good at waiting."

"Then why wait now?"

"Because we can't afford to be wrong."

"In either case, it seems likely to me."

I said. "True. But there is one more argument for staying put. If he thinks we might by chance carry the money out for him, then he might let us, so that he doesn't have to, or is unable to."

"Or she."

"That would be doubly true in the case of a woman, since we both know how heavy those bags are."

"Not for Big Tree," she said with venom. "Am I really all that big, Garth?"

"You're bigger than Preston Curtis. Or just as big." I saw no point in lying to her.

"But none of it's fat."

"I don't think he was saying that."

"What was he saying, then?"

"Ask him, next chance you get."

"You're saying let it go, is that it?"

"In so many words. Also, as you're fond of telling me, you always have to consider the source."

"Who is . . ."

"Dead."

She thought a moment, then said, "Point well taken."

Dark came early there in the bottom of the canyon. High on the eastern rim, the sun still glittered in the wind-tossed leaves, but down where we were, at eye-level with the ground, it was hard to see more than a few yards ahead.

"I think it's time," I said to Ruth.

"If you ask me, it's past time."

"Let me go first."

"So you'll be the first one shot?"

"If it comes to that. I'm hoping it won't."

On our way out of the ravine, I stopped only long enough to take Preston Curtis's Colt .45 from his hand. He had been shot through the heart, or so I guessed by the location of the blood on his shirt. He hadn't bled much, not nearly as much as Albert Vice or Robby Rumaley, but he certainly was dead.

It was a guess as to which way to go from there. The way we came in was probably the safer route, but it would be full night by the time we reached the bluff above Owl Creek, and tonight, especially in the wind, I didn't want to try to descend it in the dark. But neither did I want to walk headlong into an ambush or to find myself impaled in a pit of punji sticks. In the end, it was Ruth who made the decision for us. When she got to the canyon, she turned right and started walking north. I, who had been kneeling beside Preston Curtis, had to run to catch up with her.

"Don't be in too big of a hurry," I said. "We don't know where he is."

"All the more reason to put some distance between

us," she said, not slowing down.

"Unless he's coming our way."

She slowed down to let me pass her. She did it grudg-ingly—not because she thought I was right, but because she would hate to be wrong.

"Okay, you set the pace," she said.

Not trusting the footing on the muddy ledges, I stayed in the stream bed, whose water, like Owl Creek, ran ice cold. Soon my feet began to cramp, making it hard to walk.

"What's wrong, Garth?" Ruth said, after I'd stopped for the third time to stretch my toes out.

I told her.

"Would taking your shoes off help?"

"I doubt it."

"Then you'll just have to grin and bear it."

"That's what I'm trying to do."

The sun had now set, and the blue-black sky above us was still filled with fat white clouds drifting to the northeast. Now and again, when the clouds parted, I could see the yellow first quarter moon high above the west rim of the canyon. It gave a ghostly foxfire glow to the seep-water eyes along the canyon walls, as if they were alive and burning.

Then from out of nowhere I felt an icy draft burn my cheek. I stopped dead in my tracks.

"What's wrong now?" a disgruntled Ruth said.

"Don't you feel it?"

"Feel what?"

"Never mind. You will when you get here."

I moved on. But when Ruth got to the place where I had felt the draft, she kept right on going.

"Are you losing it, Garth?" she said after I'd stopped again.

"Didn't you feel it?"

"I repeat, feel what?"

"An icy draft of air came out of nowhere and landed on my cheek. The same thing happened to me in Cabin 10 earlier this week."

"Is that the cabin that's supposedly haunted?" She was taking me more seriously now.

"Yes."

"Is the draft still there?" she said.

"No. It left when I moved."

"Maybe it was trying to tell you something."

"Like what?"

I hadn't thought too much about it, assuming that Ruth would feel the draft and we'd go on. But with her now on the alert, so was I.

"Like we'd better slow down," she said.

"I don't know how we could go much slower."

"Just remember what I said."

A couple steps later I heard, rather than saw, an owl fly over as fast as its short stubby wings would carry it. When a second owl followed closely behind it, I had to wonder if we were alone in there.

Feeling my way, I climbed up onto a shelf that was as smooth and slippery as marble. As I reached down to offer Ruth my hand, I heard the splash of someone's footfalls coming up the canyon toward us.

"Be quick," I said, as I pulled her onto the shelf. "We don't have much time."

Ahead was an overhang that with its black mouth and closed walls was almost tunnel-like in its appearance. I hated tunnels. Even railroad whistles, when I could clearly see the other side, nearly squeezed the life out of me before I could make my way through them.

""What now?" Ruth said when I stopped in front of her.

"I can't go in there."

She eased around me and took my hand. "Close your eyes," she said.

I did, then kept them closed, as she led me under the overhang.

Whoever it was, was splashing ever closer, but I didn't dare open my eyes for fear of what might happen. Ruth had a tight grip on my hand, and I was thankful for that. It gave me something to hang on to when I very much needed it.

Splash! Scrape. Splash! Scrape. He was moving very slowly and dragging something behind him. It couldn't be his rifle. It would be no use to him that way. What then? A shovel? With a start, I remembered that after using it to break off the punji sticks, I had let his shovel lie. Maybe he had found it there and was now coming after me to exact his revenge.

His footfalls, reverberating against the walls of the overhang, became unbearably loud—until he stopped. Then they became unbearably still. Ruth's fingers tightened on mine, as she, too, felt the pressure build to call out and get it over with. Only my earlier years as a hunter saved us. The game that flushed was almost always dead meat. The game that didn't flush usually lived to enjoy another day.

Then he moved on. I could feel Ruth's hand crumble in relief.

We waited until the last echo from the last footfall had died before we crawled out from under the overhang. The sky had never looked so good to me. The moon had never seemed brighter.

"Thank you," I said to Ruth.

"Now, we're even."

What she meant was that she had gotten me into this, and now had gotten me out of it. It was a relief to both of us not to have any owed favors hanging over our heads.

We had walked for what seemed miles when the canyon suddenly began to narrow, until we were passing between two vertical walls of rock barely the width of my arms apart. "End of the line, I'm thinking," I said.

I was right. The canyon ended in Owl Creek about two hundred yards west of where I had crossed Owl Creek earlier that day. Had I chosen to go west instead of east, it would have proved a much shorter trip.

"What now?" Ruth said, looking down at Owl Creek as it swept along the bluff just below us.

"We swim. You do, don't you?"

"Not in this half century."

"They say it's like riding a bicycle. Once you learn, you never forget how."

"Easy for you to say."

She held her nose and jumped in. When I saw her bobbing on the surface, I followed her into the water.

Ruth and I were cruising the borders of the Lost 1600 in the Impala, looking for the vehicle of whoever it was that had been in there with us, and was in there now. So far we hadn't found it, and Ruth was getting anxious to pick up her Volkswagen and go home.

"One more try," I said, as I turned onto a gravel road so narrow, rutted, and out of the way that it had never been named.

"Why don't you just call for help?" she said. "That's what the police radio is for, isn't it?"

"Because there's nearly $100,000 down there in that canyon, Ruth. Would you rather wrestle the state for it, or accept it as an anonymous gift to the shelter?"

"You would do that?" She sounded surprised.

"Yes. I would do that."

"What do you get out of it?"

"If I'm lucky, the $10,000 reward for finding Tony Jenkins. That failing, there's always the truth."

"You don't believe Preston Curtis's story?"

"Not all of it."

"Why would he lie to us when he was the one holding the gun?"

"Men like Preston Curtis lie on general principles. It's a habit they form early in life and never break."

"Like you."

"Sometimes it takes one to know one."

Unlike the day, the night was still, and had been for a while. There was only the slightest rustle of wind in the trees that crowded the road, as we drove slowly down a steep hill, gravel crunching under the tires, crickets and tree frogs screaming at us through our open windows.

"And how do you plan to come by that money?" Ruth said.

"You'll have to leave that up to me."

I saw the glitter of chrome through the trees, then the white outline of someone's vehicle. But when we pulled into the brush behind it, I was disappointed to see Preston Curtis's pickup and camper.

"Where are you going?" Ruth said, as I grabbed a flashlight and got out of the Impala.

"He has something of mine that I want back."

I turned on the flashlight and was surprised by its bright wide beam. Everything in that car worked. And I bet Cecil took it all for granted.

The cab of the pickup was locked, but I could see inside well enough to know that what I was looking for wasn't there. He'd left the camper unlocked, but it was no help either. Even after opening every drawer, looking in the stove, cabinets, refrigerator, and under the bed, I couldn't find it.

But I did admire his set up, complete with computer and printer. Too bad he didn't retire gracefully and fly fish by day, while working on his stamp collection at night. What, after all, was another $100,000 in the larger scheme of things? Especially to someone like Preston Curtis, who after thirty years of government service obviously wasn't hurting for money. There had to be more to it than that. My guess was it was the thrill of the hunt and ultimately, the chance to go one up on Robert Anderson and stay there.

"Any luck?" Ruth said when I got back in the car.

"No."

"What were you looking for anyway?"

"Fran's antique doctor bag. Somebody took it from my office at the *Oakalla Reporter*. I thought maybe he had."

"What would he want with it?"

I started the Impala and headed back to Camp Collier. "It's a neat thing to have, and it was among Fran's things when Preston Curtis went through them last Sunday. I thought he might have decided to come back for it."

"I think you give him too much credit," Ruth said. "He can't be everywhere at once."

"Then who did take the black bag and why?"

"It could have been anyone in Oakalla. You surely advertised it loudly enough."

I turned on the brights. There on the fringe of the Lost 1600 it was hard to see for all of the trees.

"You might be right about Preston Curtis, Ruth. I don't buy his explanation for breaking into Fran's building the way he did. He didn't seem the kind of man to jump to conclusions."

"You *do* have a reputation, Garth, for getting to the

bottom of things."

"But he wouldn't have known that, and neither would his computer. I think he followed me from the moment I left Camp Collier, and only later decided I was up to something."

"Which was?"

I dimmed the brights. With them on, I couldn't see for all of the bugs. "That's what I don't know yet. But it must have something to do with Fran's things."

"Or his building?"

I glanced at her to see what she meant by that, but apparently it was nothing. "That's a possibility, too."

"Anything else about Preston Curtis's story you don't buy?" she said.

"The part about not knowing where Robert Anderson is. If I had to guess, he's gator bait somewhere."

"Then who booby trapped Camp Collier?"

"I don't know for certain, but I do have some ideas on that."

"You think Preston Curtis might have had a partner—either somebody he sent on ahead, or better yet, somebody here who knew the territory?"

"As unlikely as that seems, yes. That's why I'm going to have one last look through Fran's building when I get back to town."

"And let whoever's after our money get away scot-free?"

I noted it was now *our* money instead of *the* money. How soon the worm can turn, especially when the money's already spent.

"I didn't say that," I said. "As slow as he seems to be moving, I'll have time to do both."

"I have my doubts about that. But I know you well enough not to argue."

If so, it was a first.

When we returned to the hill at Camp Collier where we had left Ruth's Volkswagen, I could see the flicker of lightning far to the west. But strangely, the sky overhead was clear.

"Storm's coming," I said.

She yawned. "Let it come. The way I feel, I could sleep through a tornado."

"You might get your chance."

"Not tonight, Garth. Tornado or not, it will just have to wait for some other time."

She opened the door to the Impala, sat there for a moment gathering strength, then forced herself to get out of the car.

"Ruth, did you get a good look at whoever it was in the canyon with us tonight?"

"No. I didn't look at him for fear he'd see my face."

"You have any ideas about what he was dragging?"

She glanced to the west where the storm seemed growing. "As strange as it sounds, Garth, I think he might have been dragging a leg."

"Yeah. That's what I think, too."

She started to close the door, then changed her mind. "What are you getting at, Garth?"

"Think about it, Ruth, in light of all that's happened."

She thought about it for quite a while, long enough for the storm in the west to stretch its quivering gold tentacles both north and south along the horizon.

"Oh." At last she understood. "No wonder you're in no hurry."

CHAPTER

I followed Ruth home, where
I traded Preston Curtis's Colt .45 for Grandfather's Model
97 Winchester. I couldn't hit a bull in the butt at twenty
paces with a handgun, but I could do a whole lot of damage from that distance with a full-choke twelve-gauge
shotgun.

"You ever check back with your sources?" I said to
Ruth before I left.

"No. I didn't have time."

"Do. If you would, please?"

"What's the point?"

"It's a loose end. I'd like to tie it up."

"Anything else while I'm at it?" Her sarcasm always
wore a thin veil.

"As a matter of fact."

I drove to the post office and parked alongside Dennis

Hall's Dodge Ram pickup. Evidently he meant it when he said that he and Kristina wouldn't be seeing each other any more. Too bad for him. Too bad for me. It would have been a great ride while it lasted.

The key to Fran's back door was hanging on a nail between the doors, where Dale Phillips said that he would leave it. I went inside, taking the Model 97 with me and locking the door behind me. Normally I didn't like to carry a shell in the chamber because the Model 97 was hammer fired and could go off if my thumb slipped either while cocking or uncocking it. But tonight I felt the need to have a shell in there.

Maybe it was the silent storm, growing in the west, cinching the night with tension, until it seemed ready to blow inside out. Maybe it was the week I'd had—two people dead, one missing, too many narrow escapes to count. Whatever it was, I would make no apologies for being a little reckless.

Dale Phillips was right. There were several books there in Fran's bookcase that I not only wanted, but would have: *Bob Son of Battle*, *Boru The Story of an Irish Wolfhound*, *Kazan the Wolf Dog*, and *Silver Chief Dog of the North*. Like *Big Red*, which was standing on my desk at work among my other treasured books, they all had Fran Baldwin written on the inside cover. It had turned out that we were even more alike than I knew. But then hadn't we both deeply loved and lost the same woman? With a last lingering touch, I reluctantly left the bookcase behind and started moving boxes.

Minutes later I had uncovered the door that led into The Last Dance. With a rush I went through it on my way to Dale Phillips' upstairs apartment, which was easier in the dark than in daylight. All I had to do was to follow my flashlight's beam and close my eyes to everything else that was there.

Dale Phillips did not keep a tidy apartment, but I hadn't expected him to. Dried and shriveled apple cores, withered black banana peels, and brownish stains of unknown origin littered his floor, while his clothes and books were piled wherever he could make room for them. He had no closets, or didn't use the ones he had, and his unmade butter-blond bed and matching chest of drawers looked disposable, as if they belonged downstairs with the rest of his junk. He had a brass pole lamp with three ruffled orange globes to read by, but two of the globes were cracked, and when I turned the lamp on, only one of the lights worked.

I leafed through several of his books and was disappointed by what I found. I had expected Dale Phillips to read only nonfiction of the most basic sort: how to build a pipe bomb, how to redecorate your neighborhood with flying body parts, how to conduct jungle warfare, or how to make punji sticks and other toys for the outdoor playground. Instead, most of his books were paperback westerns, and most of those by either Zane Grey or Louis L'Amour.

I heard a tapping sound. For a moment, I didn't know where it was coming from, then realized that someone was knocking on Dale Phillips' front door. I debated about whether to answer it or not. But if I didn't and someone called 911, I might have some hard explaining to do.

"I'm coming," I said.

The man who had knocked had salt-and-pepper muttonchops, a flattop gone to seed, and a broad acne-scarred face that registered no surprise in seeing me there with a shotgun in one hand, a flashlight in the other, and a darkened room behind me.

"I'm sorry," he said. "I thought Dale Phillips lived here."

"He does. I'm watching the place for him while he's away."

"You don't know where he might be, do you?"

"Not for sure. He told me he was going to LaCrosse this weekend."

The man shook his head. "He told me that same thing. But he's not there. If truth be known, he's missed a lot of our meets lately."

"And your name is?" I said.

"Frank Swackhammer." He started to offer his right hand, then withdrew it when he saw that mine still held the Model 97.

"And you're on your way where?"

"Shipshewanna. Dale said to stop by if I was ever in the neighborhood. Well, I'm in the neighborhood."

Swackhammer? Where had I heard that name before? "Are you and Dale recent acquaintances?"

He smiled. Both of his eyeteeth were missing, which seemed to go with the rest of him.

"No. We go way back," he said.

"To where?"

"Why do you want to know?" He didn't seem suspicious, just curious, which in itself made me wonder.

"Because your name's familiar." Then I remembered why. "Frankie Swackhammer. You're Dale's partner in crime."

He laughed. "Is Bobby still telling that old wives' tale? I'll bet he told you he hurt his leg in a motorcycle accident, too. The truth is, he fell down a ravine back here in Wisconsin, and that was after knocking off a bank, not a filling station."

I stood there tongue-tied, not believing my ears. "Did you just call him *Bobby* a moment ago?"

"A slip of the tongue. Tell him it won't happen again."

"As in Bobby Anderson?"

He took new note of the shotgun, and I saw suspicion on his face for the first time. "What's he done now?"

I nearly collided with him on my way out the door. What hadn't he done?

I didn't have time to circle all of the Lost 1600 in search of Bobby Anderson's battered green F-150. As soon as he had both bags of money in hand, he would leave for parts unknown, something that Dale Phillips, as I knew him, never would have done. My best hope, and on it I hung my hat, was that he couldn't carry both bags of money out at once, and thus would have to make another trip back into the canyon. If I could find where he was parked, I might intercept him before he could accomplish that mission. But time, I knew, had to be drawing short.

Not just for me either. Bobby Anderson had to be having a few anxious moments of his own about now.

The storm, though taking its own sweet time about it, was slowly advancing from west to east, erasing ever more of the sky as it came. There was no pause in the lightning, not even for me to look away, as bolt after bolt lashed out, branched, caught fire, then spread to a neighboring cloud. Orange, then yellow, then veins of purest gold, the storm had at last found its voice—a long low steady grumble that never paused for breath.

Most of us knew that a storm was not a living, breathing thing with a heart, mind, or soul, but a few, those who claimed to know storms well, begged to differ. Not heart, mind, or soul perhaps, but like a fire, a live thing, nevertheless, with a personality all its own. Some storms were all sound and no fury, scattering chickens, leaves, and a few large rain drops, but little else. Others started to shrink the instant they were born, or died from stage fright the moment they went on radar. But this storm seemed different. This storm, like the night that gave it birth, seemed ready to burst and if I were Bobby Anderson, alone in the Lost 1600, I would fear it. Almost as much as I did him.

Then I found his F-150 pickup on the north side of
Camp Collier, two hills and a hollow away from Cabin 10.
It was hidden behind some cedars back on an old logging
road that had grown over just enough to be hidden from
the county road, unless you were looking for it. Pulling
back onto the county road, I drove a couple hundred
yards north and parked the Impala behind some brush.
Bobby Anderson would be coming up the hill from the
south. He wouldn't see it there.

My plan was to wait in ambush for him, then take it
from there. But first I had to be sure that I was right.

Inside his camper was a canvas bag full of money, the
same one with the star tear in the canvas that I had been
carrying earlier. Along with it was a bolt-action.30-06
Springfield with a military sniper scope mounted on it.
The Springfield was a single shot, so it wasn't either love
or mercy that had kept him from killing Ruth and me.
The third thing that I found was Fran's antique doctor
bag. The fourth was Robby Rumaley, wrapped and tied in
a sheet of clear plastic. I didn't need to open up the plastic to see how Robby had died. There was a deep dark
crease that ran under his chin from ear to ear. But
swollen as he was, Robby didn't look much like himself.
He looked like a Kewpie doll—the little lead-bottomed
savages that used to line the carnival racks, and dare me
to knock them over.

Robby was right after all. Bobby had come for him, as
Robby said he would. But whether Bobby had killed him,
or Robby had died by his own hand, leaving Bobby no
choice, if Robby was to share in their last great adventure
but to take him along, I didn't know. I doubted that it
would ever be in my power to know. Better to let it remain
a mystery, one of those things that, for our own sake, we
are better off not knowing.

I took Fran's doctor bag with me from the camper

and hid it in the cedars where no one but me could find it. It was a childish thing to do, but if I died out here, I wanted to deny Bobby Anderson that one small pleasure.

He was, I was now certain, the one who had been living in Cabin 10—on weekends, as he alternately searched for the money, and booby trapped the Lost 1600 to keep others away. Maybe he knew Preston Curtis was hot on his trail and would soon be at Camp Collier. Maybe not. Maybe he had built the booby traps only after Larry Sharp and his militia began playing their war games there. And again, maybe not.

It was hard to read a Bobby Anderson, who played by no rules but his own. An innocent bystander? I didn't think that concept crossed Bobby Anderson's mind the whole time he was cutting, sharpening, firing, and planting those punji sticks. I didn't think that it was a concept he held. In his world, there were no innocent bystanders, only survivors.

Why then had he spared my life after he had cold-cocked me along Owl Creek? Maybe he liked me well enough not to kill me unless he had to. Maybe my death would serve him no good purpose. Was I grateful? You bet. But not enough to give him a second chance.

As for the ghost of Cabin 10, had he followed me today, warned me off there tonight in the canyon as Bobby Anderson approached? What really had led Ruth to those bones there in that cave? And if a storm had no mind's eye, why was this one now taking dead aim on the Lost 1600?

The wind, rising to a shriek, would have made it hard to hear without the thunder. Together they cut me off completely from everything but my fear of Bobby Anderson, and left me at the mercy of the lightning, which seemed everywhere at once—staccato, strobe-like bursts that did more to smear the landscape than reveal it.

There. Something ancient and troll-like came limping

CHAPTER

The storm had passed. It was raining gently—just enough to feel when I held my hand out the window. I sat in the Impala with Fran's black bag on the seat beside me and a $100,000 in stolen bank money in the trunk. I felt like a thief. Worse, I felt like a fool. But that was to be expected, I guessed, since I was one.

A Wisconsin state police car pulled up behind me, and my young cop friend and a shorter, rounder, older man that I didn't recognize got out and put their hats on. Both were in uniform. Neither looked happy to be there. Still, they'd made good time, considering our location. It hadn't been more than two hours since I'd called them. I got out of the Impala and went to stand in the glare of their headlights, while they waited for me. Bobby Anderson, alias Dale Phillips, lay where he had fallen after I'd shot him. He was the second man that I had killed. I hoped that there would never be a third.

"You called the coroner yet?" the shorter, rounder, older cop said to me.

"He's probably lost, but he's on his way."

"Garth Ryland, this is Lieutenant Frazier, my boss," the young cop said.

The Lieutenant nodded at me but didn't offer to shake my hand. "You mind telling me what went down here?" he said.

I watched the rain bead on the plastic covering of the Lieutenant's hat, saw the "don't shit me" look in his eyes. This wasn't going to be easy, even for a natural liar like me.

"Have you ever heard of the Linberg bank robbery?"

The Lieutenant and my young cop friend exchanged glances. Evidently they had.

"My father died in that robbery," the Lieutenant said. "Sheriff Milton Frazier."

"And the man who killed him?" I said, saving us both time.

"Bobby Anderson. The man you claimed to have killed tonight."

"Which explains why you're here."

"In part. I would have come in any case," he said. "Just to meet you."

Flattered though I was, I doubted that he'd meant it as a compliment. His perpetual scowl said as much.

"You know the players and the particulars, then," I said. "R. P. Curtis came here looking for Tony Jenkins. Bobby Anderson came here looking for R P. Curtis. Now all three of them are dead."

"Why did you come here?" the Lieutenant said.

"I came here looking for my housekeeper."

"And why did she come here?"

"She was looking for the Lost Scout."

The Lieutenant turned to the young cop for help. "Is it always like this?" he said.

"About."

"Should I believe him?"

"Mostly."

I smiled. My confidence in my young cop friend had never been higher.

"Take it a little further," the Lieutenant said to me.

So I told them as best I could about how Ruth's dreams had led me to the Lost 1600, Bobby Anderson, and finally today, to Tony Jenkins.

"What about the money?" the Lieutenant said.

"What money?"

"The $100,000 that Bobby Anderson and Tony Jenkins stole in the bank robbery."

I shrugged, trying not to give myself away. "I was all throughout Bobby's camper. It's not there."

He spent the better part of the next ten seconds studying me before he said, "I suppose I shouldn't ask."

"It would be in my best interest if you didn't."

"Just don't embarrass us on this."

"My lips are sealed."

"And I don't want it turning up in a tax audit somewhere down the road."

"Rumor has it that it's going to a good cause."

"See that it does, then." He took off his hat to wipe his forehead with a white handkerchief, exposing his round nearly bald crown to the rain. "Don't get any ideas, Ryland, about future events. This is to thank you for taking Bobby Anderson off the street. I'll sleep a little better from now on. My whole family will."

"At least one of us will," I said.

"Come again?"

But I shook my head, It was not something that I

need bother him with yet.

"You mind answering a question for me?" I said. "You knew R. P. Curtis. What kind of man was he?"

"A good man . . . Once." The Lieutenant said with what seemed like regret. "Up until Dad got killed. He never stopped blaming himself for that. I think it ate away at him until there wasn't much of the old R. P. left."

"He and your father were close?"

"Like father and son. Mom and Dad took him in after his own parents died. He was still rooming at our house when Dad got killed."

"Why did he blame himself for that? He wasn't there at the bank, was he?"

Lieutenant Frazier put his hat back on and snugged it down over his bald head. "No. But he should have been. He and I had sneaked off to go fishing that morning."

"So it was personal between Bobby and him," I said.

"You might say that."

That explained a lot, but not everything. "After Bobby got out of prison, why didn't R. P. just shoot him and leave him in a swamp somewhere?"

The Lieutenant nodded at his young charge to tell him that he was ready for them to get on with it. "That wasn't R. P.'s way. If he couldn't take you fair and square, he wouldn't take you at all."

"That didn't stop him from pulling his gun on me twice," I said.

He shrugged. "You're still alive, aren't you? That's more than I can say for him." He had reached up to put his hand on the young cop's shoulder. "Let's go, Michael. We've still got a lot of work to do here."

"Watch your step," I warned. "This whole place is booby-trapped."

"More of Bobby's doings?" the Lieutenant said.

"I used to think so."

CHAPTER 34

Ruth and I sat at the kitchen table drinking a cup of coffee. It wasn't yet daylight, though it seemed like it should have been long ago. She said that it had blown a little and rained a little in Oakalla, but that was all. I told her that she should have been where I was. Then I told her what had been going through my mind as I sat in the Impala waiting for the state police to arrive. She nodded. Already she knew.

"So when you called Albert Vice's sister, what did you find out?" I said.

"Not much from her. She's not what I'd call a friendly woman. But I found out from Wilmer Wiemer that Albert and she own a two-hundred acre lake within a two hour's drive of both Chicago and Milwaukee."

"Which Albert was about to sell to her?"

"They were supposed to close this past week. Albert died on a Saturday night."

"Poor timing on his part, I'd say."

Ruth sat back in her chair, looking relaxed for the first time in weeks. "Not according to Wilmer, whose advice Albert didn't take. He said Albert was giving the lake away at the price he was asking. He said Albert should hold out for at least a million."

"A mistake Kristina Vice is not likely to make," I said, blowing on my coffee to cool it.

"Not likely."

"How did Albert and his sister come to own the lake?"

"It was one of their father's developments. It's been tied up in court until recently, until all of his creditors were paid off. I guess he had an ace in the hole after all." Much to Ruth's dismay, if I read her right.

"Some ace," I said.

"Some hole."

"Speaking of which, there's $100,000 in the trunk of the Impala. I have to get it out of there before I turn the Impala back over to Cecil Hardwick in a couple hours."

Ruth's look was all-assuring. "I'll find a place for it," she said.

"So does this mean that you'll be spending less time at the shelter?"

"Are you trying to bribe me?"

"If necessary."

She thought about it, then said, "To be honest, Garth, I'm ready to come back home for a while."

I didn't say anything more on the subject for fear that she might change her mind.

"One other thing, Garth, though this should come as no surprise. I checked back with my sources as you said. Aunt Emma swears that Kristina Vice has been keeping somebody's company for over a year now. Carrie Henderson swears the same is true of Ned Cleaver. Which would lead one to believe the obvious."

"I figured that might be the case," I said as I rose from the table.

"Just when did you figure that?"

"Right after I killed Bobby Anderson. When I sat there in the Impala with his blood on my hands, watching the storm blow itself out. What, I had to wonder, was Bobby, who had a bum leg anyway, doing in the Lost 1600 the night Albert Vice was killed? Not looking for the money, I didn't think, which would be his only reason for being there. And why build a death trap, unless he were crazy, that in the end would only attract more people to the Lost 1600, if someone was so unfortunate as to fall in it? While Bobby Anderson, or Dale Phillips as I knew him, wasn't the last of the late great thinkers, he wasn't stupid either. And probably not the monster I made him out to be."

"Then who did build those death traps?"

"For now, I'm reserving judgment on that."

"So you shot the wrong man?"

"No. He would have killed me had I not killed him. But had I known the truth, I might have gone about things a little differently."

"What is the truth? Do you know?"

I reached down for one last drink of coffee. "Not for certain. But I'm about to go looking for it."

The storm had washed away all the tension and left the air cool, clean, and still. So very still in its aftermath.

As I walked up Home Street toward the north end of town, I thought about Cecil's bad bull, which had reached out to gore us all. I had wanted to believe that it was a rogue bull, who, by chance, had blindly wandered into

town to wreak his havoc. There would be some comfort in
that, if no satisfaction. But, as usual, our bull was home-
grown. We had raised him from a calf—fed him, watered
him, answered his every need, so felt safe to turn our
back on him.

Would we ever learn, I wondered? And if we did,
would the gain be worth the loss? Knowing what I did
about the fragile pinions of humanity, I doubted it.

Ned Cleaver sat at his kitchen table, wearing jeans, a
red crew-neck T-shirt with a small pocket on the left side,
white athletic socks, and no shoes. He was smoking a cigarette, drinking a cup of coffee. A red pack of Marlboros
lay on the table in front of him.

"You mind if I come in?" I said on entering through
the garage-side door.

"It looks like you already are."

I took a seat across from him at the kitchen table.
Unlike mine, which was linoleum, Ned's kitchen had an
oak parquet floor with a brown brick border, and a brown
brick fireplace on the west side. I sat facing the fireplace.
In winter, with its close confines and thick brick walls, a
fire going and supper on the stove, it would be downright
cozy in here. Today it was cool, though—almost cold.

"Tell me you did it for love," I said.

"Did what for love?"

"Killed Albert Vice."

"I wasn't aware that I had killed Albert Vice."

"Then tell me that you didn't."

He finished smoking his cigarette, then stubbed it out
in a small brass ashtray already overflowing with spent
butts. Either he had been sitting there for a long time or
he didn't often empty his ashtray.

"Coffee?" he said.

I shook my head no. "Was it for love?" I repeated.
"Or the money?"

"What money is that?"

"The money that Kristina's going to get when she sells the lake that Albert owned."

"Oh, that money," he said in a voice as flat as a funeral drum.

"You don't deny it, then?" I said.

"What's to deny? A beautiful woman, a million bucks. A lot of men have killed for less. I should know. I was one of them."

"You were at war."

His cold blue eyes were never more intense, or remote. "I still am."

While I waited for his explanation, Kristina Vice padded into the kitchen to sit beside us at the table. She was barefoot, wearing an old yellow-and-blue Oriental silk robe that must have belonged to Ned. I noticed that the red polish on her toenails had started to chip.

"You didn't waste any time," I said to Kristina.

She shook out a cigarette from the pack on the table, lighted it, and handed it to Ned. As she lighted one for herself, she and Ned exchanged a glance. Sadness, it seemed, was the rule of the day.

"We didn't know how much time we had left," she said.

"That will be up to the state police. And Cecil Hardwick, if he's so inclined. After this morning, I'm out of it. In fact, as soon as I leave here."

"But they know what you know?" Kristina said.

"They will. Unless you can convince me otherwise. Or kill me, like you did Albert and Robby."

"I never killed Robby," Ned said. "If he's dead, he died by his own hand."

"Are you saying that you weren't there in the shadows the night he died?"

"Yes, Garth. That's what I'm saying."

"I don't believe you."

"You're welcome to believe whatever you want."

"And Albert? You weren't there the night he died either? You didn't build that trap he fell into?"

"I think you already know I didn't."

"I want to hear you say it."

"I didn't build the trap he fell into."

"Then who did? I'm almost sure now that it wasn't Bobby Anderson."

"Who's Bobby Anderson?"

"You knew him as the Lost Scout."

Ned nodded to himself, as if the last tumbler had just clicked in his mind. Then I knew what he knew.

"It was Robby, wasn't it? He was building those traps, while Bobby was out looking for the money. They weren't intended for R.P. Curtis or the general public. They were intended for you and the militia," I said.

Ned raised his brows, then lowered them again. His tight-lipped smile said that I had guessed the truth.

Ned said, "Because he was small, and a drunk, and a good man in spite of himself, people forget that Robby pulled two tours of duty in Vietnam, the same as me. People forget that he was a killing machine, the same as me, that he came back with the same baggage. He hated the militia with a passion, Garth. He called us toy soldiers, and the Baby Patrol. He said he'd stop us any way he could."

I waited for him to continue. When he didn't, I said, "When did you learn what he was up to?"

"Almost from the beginning, when he first started on the Bobby business. Everybody thought he was just blowing smoke. I knew Robby well enough to know that he wasn't."

"You think he recruited Bobby instead of the other way around?"

"I think they recruited each other. Neither was as good as when the other was with him."

"So they really were a team all those years ago?"

Ned's look was one of envy. "As tight a team as I've ever seen. Two misfits at that."

"So you decided to follow them one day to see what they were up to. When you learned, why didn't you stop them?"

Ned's gaze had held rock steady until then. When it faltered, I knew why.

"Of course," I said. "With Dennis in Madison with Kristina, you could set Albert up for the big fall and no one would be the wiser. But *you* would need to be there to keep someone else from taking it for him and thus ruining everything. You were the one who cold-cocked me and carried me to that sand beach. For a while I thought it was Bobby."

"I won't deny it."

"And you did your best thereafter to muddy the waters."

"In what way muddy the waters?"

"Having Larry Sharp and friends dump Albert's body into Hidden Quarry . . ."

"They didn't need any help doing that," he interrupted. "And what would I have to gain by giving it to them, since we needed Albert's body to prove that he was dead."

"And sicking Larry and Dennis on Cecil Hardwick, and Kristina on me," I said, not to be denied.

"Larry and Dennis didn't need any encouragement." His cheeks, white up until then, had a faint pink glow. "As for Kristina, I don't tell her what to do."

She smiled at me as if to say, "Nice try."

"But you could have stopped Dennis and Larry at any point along the line," I said. "Did you know that Dennis went to Cecil's hospital room early Thursday morning? I don't think it was to wish him a speedy recovery."

"Dennis is Dennis. Larry is Larry. I'm not their keeper, Garth. Don't expect me to be."

"But damn it, you have it in you . . ." I stopped, seeing the futility of it.

"Once upon a time, Garth. No longer."

Meanwhile Kristina had put her bare foot on top of mine and was stroking my ankle. She did it so casually it almost seemed natural.

"Why?" I finally said to Ned when I could think of nothing else to say. "Why did you really do what you did to Albert?"

"I did nothing to Albert. He did it all himself."

"You know what I mean."

I waited for what seemed like minutes for his answer. When it seemed that he wasn't going to answer, Kristina jumped in.

"Why not?" she said, removing her foot from mine, leaving an ache in its absence. "Dennis had been coming on to me for a long time, the same with Sandy to Ned. And Albert had been balling Sandy behind my back for years, long before I ever started up with Ned. So there was no trust to break. No innocent party . . ."

"Kristina," Ned said, cutting her off.

"In all of this." She took a drag on her cigarette and started up on my ankle again.

"You asked why," Ned said to me. "I owe you an answer, but I can't give you one. Except to say that with Albert and me, it was personal."

"How personal?"

"Very personal. He was always itching for some *real* combat. I thought I'd give him his chance—the same chance thousands of us had, when you can't see the enemy or even know what lies one step ahead."

"Plus, there's Kristina and a million bucks to consider."

"That there is."

I turned to Kristina. "And you? Or should I ask?"

"Don't ask."

"And all of those tears for Albert? What am I to make of them?"

"Don't try to make anything of them. But they were real, in case you're wondering. You can love the person and still hate what he is." Her foot had stopped atop my ankle. "The flip side is likewise true."

I was fighting to keep the upper hand, but in vain it seemed. "And Sandy? What's going to happen when she finds out the truth about you two?"

I followed Kristina's glace to the doorway on my left where Sandy Hall stood wearing Ned's faded yellow T-shirt that almost reached the dimples on her knees. Sandy smiled and waved at me before she went about her business. I had never seen her look happier.

"You see, Garth," Kristina said. "Nothing is ever as simple as it seems."

I felt myself stand. But I didn't trust myself to walk until Kristina took me by the arm, snugged it up against her breast, and led me to the front door.

"And also, in case you were wondering, Garth, and I know you are . . . Where you and I are concerned, it wasn't an act. And though I know you'll never darken it again, my door is always open." Her smile was as radiant as the sunrise. "Do have a nice day."

An hour later I rowed to the center of Grandmother's pond, all the while taking in great drafts of the freshly washed country air. Cecil would have to wait on his Impala. So would my sources and advertisers—so would the *Oakalla Reporter* have to wait on me.

I had come to two conclusions in the past hour. Three actually—the third being that I wasn't going to drown myself in the pond, no matter how much I might feel like it.

My first conclusion was that Ned Cleaver was telling the truth about Robby Rumaley. Robby knew that Dale Phillips was Bobby Anderson, had known all along, and likely, with Bobby's help, had cut the sticks and dug the pit where Albert Vice died. That would explain why Robby had made himself so scarce after Albert's death, why he would commit suicide rather than return to the scene of the crime. It would also explain why, when he arrived at Robby's house to find him dead, Bobby simply wrapped up Robby, his best and only true friend, and took him along on their last great adventure together.

What it didn't explain was who was out in the shadows while I was talking to Robby—if anyone. It wasn't Ned Cleaver, or he would have told me so. It wasn't Bobby Anderson. He had no reason to be there—or the legs to carry him had he reason to be. So whom did that leave? And in the final analysis, did it really matter?

My second conclusion was that Bobby Anderson was not the Lost Scout. Neither was Robby Rumaley, or Ned Cleaver, though I could make a good argument for each. No, the Lost Scout ran a newspaper, lived on Home Street with a seventy-something housekeeper and a lemon spotted English setter, and drove an old brown Chevy sedan named Jessie. He had never been to war like Ned Cleaver, had never found himself at the bottom of a bottle like Robby Rumaley, but he, too, once had his dreams. And he had once believed, as they had, that if you did the right thing, or tried to, all would be right in the end.

Now, he wasn't so sure, even if this day, all dewy bright with promise, would, despite the clouds sure to come, persevere to a golden sunset. What he did know, however, was that he would persevere to the end—until he either ran out of worms, or daylight.